Watching Me

TETHERED TO YOU, BOOK 1

KRYSTAL KAE

DARK ORCHID PRESS

BEFORE YOU READ

This book contains sexual themes, language, discussion of weight loss, violence including violence against women and brief mention of rape, discussion of past suicide attempt, and references to and depictions of death.

SPECIAL THANKS

To my husband for designing the book cover and providing endless amounts of support when I was completely and utterly lost in this process, thank you. You were my rock from start to finish and you've helped make my dream become a reality. I love you.

To my editor, Rebecca, thank you for all of your work in this. I wouldn't have arrived at this point without you. Your time, effort, and skill are truly appreciated.

To the readers that found this book, thank you for giving it a chance.

CHAPTER 1

Violet

1:21 a.m.

My phone had illuminated the time with a quick double tap of my finger. I kicked off the blankets rather abruptly, furious about the tangled heap that had been confining my legs.

I was too hot.

I threw an arm over my forehead, aggravated that I had to be up at six to start getting ready for work. I stared up at my ceiling, barely visible in my dark studio apartment due to the blackout curtains hiding the blinds behind them.

Usually, all I needed was darkness to sleep and even a sliver of light would keep me awake. Some people needed noise or a television to doze off but not me. I normally found comfort in the dark.

So why the hell couldn't I succumb to sleep tonight?

Perhaps it was because I was sexually frustrated. Brett had left after he'd found his release, before I was able to claim mine. He'd been too spent to even help get me off.

Okay, well, maybe he hadn't exactly left of his own accord. I was pretty pissed that anytime we had sex it was all about Brett and his body's needs. I'd thought that maybe sex with him would get better as time went on, especially if I was honest and open with him about what I wanted and needed in the bedroom. But, after eight months, I didn't see any light at the end of the tunnel.

When we were out and about, he was the perfect gentleman and boyfriend—paying for dinner even though I insisted, holding doors open for me or perfect strangers, even surprising me at work with flowers or food on occasion. But apparently, he left his chivalry at the bedroom door. He was greedy and maybe even naïve when it came to sex. He didn't even like to talk about it, which is why I'd gotten angry and thrown his ass out of my apartment tonight.

Sometimes I felt like I was talking to a wall. I kept him around in hopes that he would change for the better in that department, but maybe the joke was on me.

Maybe I was the naïve one.

My hand fumbled around the nightstand in search of my water bottle. I swore I had set it there earlier before my first attempt at going to sleep. I let out an aggravated sigh, realizing I would have to get up and get another from the fridge.

Sitting up, I swung my legs around to the side of the bed and let them dangle off the edge. My toes grazed the cool wooden floor beneath them, sending a shiver up my spine. I normally kept my apartment cool, as I would rather be chilly and cover up than hot and not able to cool down. But tonight, my body couldn't figure out what it wanted. The thought crossed my mind that an area rug might not be such a bad idea in here. Or slippers. Those would also help to shield my skin from the frigid cold air that the register pumped out at the head of my bed.

Reluctantly, I stood and turned in the direction I needed to go. Not two steps later I rammed my foot into the corner of my dresser. Pain shot through the side of my foot and I crouched down to grab at the site of impact.

"Fuck!" Tears sprang to my eyes as the pain quickly began to radiate up through the entirety of my foot. My hand slid over my skin and I was hit with the realization that it was wet.

"Are you kidding me?" I was bleeding? Seriously?

I stood and reached for something to balance my unsteadiness; the closest thing was my standing mirror. Thankfully, it was locked in place, but it still wobbled at my touch.

Limping to the bathroom, I turned on the light to check the damage. I squinted at its brightness, but sure enough, there was blood. The pain felt as if I had torn off a part of my foot.

Anger bubbled through me at the memory of how the corner of the dresser came to be so rough and jagged in the first place. Brett and one of his buddies had damaged it when moving me into my apartment by dropping the corner onto the concrete steps out front. I fisted my hands, wanting to place every inch of blame on Brett for everything that was going wrong tonight.

I was sexually frustrated, wide awake, and bleeding because of him.

I decided right then and there that I needed to break it off for good with Brett. This was the last straw. I had been making up excuses long enough, and I was over it and over him. I wasn't happy in our relationship and I was trying too hard to think of a time when I'd felt that I was.

I made quick work of cleaning up my mess and luckily had enough supplies in my first aid kit to bandage up my foot. It wasn't a pretty sight to see, but it would have to do for now.

Thank you, Grandma, I thought to myself. I had rolled my eyes when she'd given me this dated kit upon moving into this very apartment, but it had come in handy.

I was probably due to give her a call and check in. Hell, the woman had raised me after I'd lost my family in a car accident when I was five. And as much as I'd wanted to get the heck out of her house when I got my first big girl job, I had to appreciate all that she'd done for me—raising and feeding me, allowing me to make my own mistakes. I knew I couldn't have been easy to live with, but the woman had stuck by my side anyhow.

I made a mental note to call her on my lunch break tomorrow. I was sure she would be thrilled to hear my plan to break up with Brett. She had always thought he was too cookie-cutter clean and that something had to lie beneath the surface.

Nobody is that perfect, Violet. I could hear her speak it so clearly in my head.

She didn't need to know that he was lacking in the bedroom, but I was sure she would appreciate the good news regardless.

Though awkward, I wobbled on the heel of my right foot. Limping to the kitchen, I retrieved the stupid bottle of water and some pills for pain relief, and headed back toward my bed. I planned my route back with the light of the fridge, trying to memorize my path before shutting the door. I should have known my damn way around this apartment by now as it was crazy small. But still, I didn't want to reinjure my foot or cause harm to any other parts of my body before crawling back into bed and trying once again to get a little rest before work.

I tapped my phone again once under the comfort of my covers.

1:42 a.m.

Oh my god. Was this night ever going to end?

A cool finger drew a line along my arm. Back and forth, over and again, coaxing me to stir. It sent tingles through me as I tried to murmur a "go away" and pulled the blankets up, over my head and all. I felt like I had finally fallen asleep and now I was becoming groggy. Everyone that was important in my life knew better than to mess with me and my sleep. I needed all the rest I could get, otherwise I would be a zombie at work in the morning and no amount of coffee would be able to help me.

A hand found its way beneath my blanket, skimming over my side and diving under my loose-fitting tank. The hand lay flat across my belly and I squirmed under its touch.

"Cold." My voice cracked as I noted the icy hand's presence. As much as I wanted to be left alone to the serenity of sleep, I liked the thought of being held, of a body behind me as the bed caved behind my back. Brett was never much of the cuddling type. Wait a second, had he come back? He did have a key, after all. Was he trying to make up for his poor attempt at sex earlier?

The body behind me inched closer, the mattress dipping more as he closed the space between us. I lifted the blanket and granted him access to the covers and me. I didn't understand why he was so chilly. It was as if he had just walked out of a freezer. I shivered as his cold skin made contact with mine.

5

"Where have you been?" I mumbled, unsure if I could even be heard as my face was halfway in my pillow. I didn't really care about his answer. I was still planning on dumping his ass later today. Maybe even tonight if he caused anymore problems.

"Waiting for you."

His voice didn't match Brett's and I wondered if I was hearing him correctly as his body curled up against me. His erection pressed against my behind, exciting and annoying me at the same time. His foot brushed up against my injured one and I tensed.

"Ouch." I clenched my teeth together and pushed my face further into my pillow, trying to quell the ache.

"I'm sorry," the voice apologized. It was deeper than Brett's but still somehow had a light tone to it. I came to the realization that I must be dreaming.

"May I fix it for you?" the voice questioned.

I turned my head away from my fluffy pillow and, with my curiosity piqued, I answered him. "My foot? Sure, knock yourself out."

I rolled my eyes. Gee, for a second there I'd thought I was going to have a sexy dream about a stranger. The erection had seemed promising.

He sat up, taking the covers with him, and moved toward the foot of the bed. I rolled onto my back, waiting to see the man who would appear.

However, it was cloudy around him. Was that right? I couldn't make out a face, just a figure. A bare-chested figure of a man?

Taking my foot in his hands, he lifted it up off the bed and began to unwrap my poor attempt at wound-dressing. His large hands encompassed my foot and I felt pressure and a searing heat. As a reflex, I attempted to jerk my foot out of his grasp but was unable to. A sharp pain shot through me that resembled the impact against the dresser. I held my breath to stifle a scream that wanted to erupt. Alarm bells were ringing in my head; I couldn't recall ever feeling pain before in a dream, nightmare, or whatever the hell this was.

And then it vanished.

The impairment was nothing but a memory as I gaped at what little I could see. Gently, he set my foot down and away from my other leg, parting them. I was still reeling over the fact that the pain was completely gone and there was no throbbing whatsoever in its wake. It was nonexistent, as if it had never happened. Disbelief settled over me as I lay there, stunned into silence.

My heart began to race as he bent down, inching toward me. It felt as if time had stopped as he approached me in slow motion.

I was eager to try to make out his face, wishing that my apartment wasn't so damn dark for once. Never had I ever had a dream so realistic, minus the whole hazy room bit. Perhaps I was just too damn tired to make anything out.

Frozen in place, I let him close the gap between us once more, and I could barely make out his features. One thing was for sure—with his build, this was certainly not Brett. And in this moment, I was thankful for that fact.

"May I pleasure you? I have waited a long time to do so."

His request and phrasing had me mentally scratching my head. Even though this might be the hottest dream my crazy brain had ever conjured up, the fact that this mysterious man was asking for permission to "pleasure me" had me all hot and bothered in a fraction of a second.

I nodded my head and tried not to sound too needy when

I responded. "Yes." My agreement to his request didn't even sound like me with its airiness.

Fingertips hooked into my panties and he slid them down my legs. I lifted my tank off, arching my back to remove it as well, and tossed it onto the floor. Everything around me seemed like it was in a cloud of smoke, hazy and distorted. Right now, I didn't care who was about to fuck me, I just didn't want to wake up. I would ride this out as long as I could.

Descending upon me, his head lowered to the bareness between my breasts and he kissed me, his lips soft and cold just like every other piece of him that made contact with my skin.

I squirmed beneath him. My body was ready and waiting, hoping, better yet *wishing* that this would last. That this was really happening.

My breath quickened right along with my rising pulse. His lips began to leave a trail of kisses, exploring my body with his mouth. He would drag his lips ever so lightly as he moved in another direction to plant another one on me—on my chest, stomach, sides, and up toward my neck.

Eager to taste the lips that had been tasting me, and wanting to see his face, I reached for him. His smooth jawline felt like stone beneath my touch; I brought him to my lips and I kissed him deeply. He smelled of citrus and yet he tasted of a hard liquor that I couldn't place. One that made me think it would burn on its descent down my throat. Together with the citrus, it was a heady concoction.

Perhaps a bit too eager to feel him inside of me, I lifted my legs, grazing his bare sides as I granted him entrance. Had he slipped into my bed without any clothes on? I had no idea why I was wasting my time or my thoughts on his lack of attire or his overall appearance. I would probably forget all about this shortly after waking anyway. It was rare for me to remember any kind of dream in the mornings that followed, just bits and pieces.

As I let one hand get tangled up in his soft hair, the other pulled at his muscular back, drawing him in closer. I ached for him, my southern regions throbbing and awaiting his arrival.

He broke away from my lips only enough to let his words escape. "Do you accept me as I am?"

I really didn't feel like talking. And as strange as his question was, I wished he would just shut up already and screw me.

"Ask me again after you fuck me."

I wasn't used to foreplay—that skill was something Brett definitely lacked—and it made me all the more hot and bothered. I wasn't used to feeling so worked up. I might explode the second he entered me at this point.

The man on top of me almost seemed otherworldly. The way he talked and the cloudiness that surrounded us transported me to a place I had never been. If I didn't know any better, I would say that I was drunk beyond belief and perhaps high on some shit. I hadn't thought my mind could make up something so realistic that it took hold of every fiber of my being.

He entered me with ease and I gasped at his fullness. His member was just as icy as the rest of his body but it began to warm inside of me. My chest rose and fell, hitting him each time my breasts peaked. My hands found their way to his back and I hugged him in close, wanting to feel every inch I could get my fingers on. I wished for lights and a mirrored ceiling so I could watch his taut muscles as he moved. I couldn't keep still. I writhed beneath him, reveling in his back and forth movements. For once in my life, I was speechless. He filled me in a way I'd never thought possible. The way his body molded to mine—it just felt right.

The rustling of the sheets beneath us with every thrust, mixed with our panting, had me in a frenzy. Gone was his frigid body temperature as he seemed to acclimate to our heated exchange. We climbed together, picking up speed, and he began hitting a wall within me that I hadn't even known existed until now.

Slowing to almost a pause, he bent his head and his mouth covered my nipple. I thought he might plant another kiss, but instead his teeth bit down in a playful nip. My breath hitched in surprise at the action. It must have amused him, as I could feel him grinning against me. He proceeded to lick my high point, and blew cool air over the surface. I hadn't thought my nipple could get any harder.

I left one hand on his shoulder, while the other played with the back of his hair as he moved over toward my other breast. I anticipated the bite, but I guess he was one for teasing. He sucked on it, kneading my flesh with a free hand as he worked it over in his mouth. And when I least expected it, his teeth came down on it too.

I winced as I let out a slight moan of pleasure. I clenched around his shaft, still aware of his presence and eager to feel him move against me again.

"Please," I begged as I tilted my hips toward him. I feared that I would be left unsatisfied, which was what normally happened when it came to sex. I wanted to feel release. I wanted to explode around him. I honestly craved to know what it was like to reach climax during sex, not after and not before.

His arms came up under my shoulder blades, almost cradling me beneath him as he placed his hands over my shoulders to cup them, locking me in his hold. It was then that I had the chance to make out his facial features; he was mere inches away now. He had a narrow face that harbored bangs, brushed to the side, and a perfectly shaped nose that led to his parted lips. But the thing that stuck out the most was his eyes. They seemed…pitch-black. Black as the background of my apartment behind him.

Before I could really focus and try to commit the sight of him to memory, he began to move. I was locked in place beneath him, his fingers digging into my shoulders. He moved quickly, pounding into me, and I quickly climbed. The friction he created against my nipples added to the swirl of sensations in which I was reveling. My legs rocked against him wildly and my toes began to curl as I could feel myself building—building toward a climax that I so desperately craved. Maybe it was selfish, but hell, I didn't care.

Another thrust and I came undone.

I cried out, locking him against me as my nails dug into his back. His head bowed down into my neck as he found his release, and he stiffened as his cock emptied inside of me, although I wasn't sure how there would be enough room for it.

Reaching for his face, I pulled it out of the crevice of my neck and kissed him. Hard. It felt weird to thank him for helping me finally achieve a climax during intercourse, so I tried to express my gratitude with my mouth. Closing my legs around his hips, I hugged him tight, not wanting him to leave, not wanting this dream to end.

We kissed for what seemed like an eternity, and sleep started to creep in. I was beyond exhausted yet satisfied at the same time. And I was happy, to say the least.

When my grip on him faltered, he removed himself and pulled me in toward him, to cradle me like he had before when we were beneath the blankets. I shivered, my body temperature dropping with our lack of motion, and he drew up the blankets around us. He held me against him, curling his legs up under mine, and kissed the top of my head.

A perfect fit, I thought to myself as I let out a yawn that didn't hold back.

I was beginning to drift, my breath becoming slow and steady. How could I *feel* so much in a dream? Pain, pleasure, happiness. Confusion set in as I wanted to check my phone for the time but didn't have it in me to raise my arm to do so.

"Do you accept me as I am?" His voice was a whisper in my ear.

I grinned to myself. He had followed through with his question after he screwed me, just like I'd asked him to.

I managed a small reply of amusement before drifting off. "I do."

CHAPTER 2

Violet

A familiar band tune came to life on my phone and I groaned at the realization of my alarm going off. I slid the little icon to the side to snooze it for ten minutes. *I just need ten more minutes, please?*

I started to doze off again but caught myself when a flood of memories came rushing back.

Kicking Brett out.

My foot.

The sexy man with black eyes who had appeared in my bed and consumed me.

My eyes popped open and I reached for the lamp on the bedside table. The light blinded me and I muttered a curse. My underwear and tank top lay on the floor beside the bed, next to the dresser where I had rammed my foot. Confused, I looked down at my body. Yep, I was naked.

Fumbling through the sheets, I felt something sticky between my legs and froze. Had I really had sex last night? I had cleaned up and showered after Brett left, so what else could explain this aftermath? Panicked, I pulled out my foot and examined it. No gauze, no wound, nothing. *What the actual fuck?*

I leapt from the bed and over to the door, examining the three locks on it, but everything was sealed tight. Brett couldn't have got in even if he had wanted to. The chain, deadbolt, and doorknob were all secure, just the way I'd left them after kicking him out last night.

I needed some coffee and another damn shower. That dream must have had me pretty worked up to put me in this position.

My phone began singing again and I groaned. Ugh, another day of work.

Wincing as I sat down in my office chair, I placed my hand over my lower abdomen at the slight discomfort. I had experienced it when I fell into my car this morning, and again just now in this awfully hard and worn-out swivel chair. I knew nothing of the woman who had occupied this office before me, but the chair had obviously been here longer than I had.

I'd never encountered aftereffects like this after screwing around with Brett, or anyone before him for that matter. There was no evidence of anyone else having come into my apartment, and my foot injury had just vanished as if it had never happened. So why was there this lingering sensation that someone had pummeled into me?

None of this made any sense.

Closing my eyes, I tried to recall the dreamlike encounter. Unrushed, the stranger with black eyes who had taken his time to explore my body. The hair I had tangled my fingers into, his muscled back that moved and stretched as he kissed and tasted me. All I'd needed to do was plead for him to seal the deal and fuck me, and he had obliged without hesitation.

I'd be the first to admit that this had to be too good to be true, but something still didn't sit right with me.

Whipping out my phone, I typed a quick text to Brett: *Available tonight? Need to talk.*

Maybe he was behind it after all. I mean, he did have a key of his own. But that still didn't explain how the chain was in place.

I laughed at myself for even thinking of the possibility. We'd had sex numerous times. I knew what his body felt like, knew how far his shaft could penetrate me.

He had nothing on this mystery man with the dark eyes.

As the morning went on, I answered phone calls and emails as if I were on autopilot. Luckily, nobody stopped into my office with account questions or to talk about a possible loan, and for that I was extremely grateful.

At times, I could barely concentrate on anything work related for more than a couple of minutes. Others, I was charging ahead and detail oriented on my tasks. Reports, delinquency letters, travel notifications, and balancing ledgers kept me busy every moment I wasn't worried about losing my marbles.

Honestly, I was nowhere near alright, and the remnants of my so-called sex fantasy of a dream still felt so real. I even occasionally tilted my pelvis forward in my chair to feel the sensation that caused that little twinge of pain. Each time I did,

I thought about him. I was obsessing over it all no matter how much I tried not to.

A knock on my door caused me to jump, and I turned my attention to the presence that had snuck up on me. My boss, Damian, approached. He was clad in his usual work apparel that he never strayed from. I swore he had almost every color imaginable when it came to polo shirts with our company's logo embroidered on them.

His brown eyes were hot on me and I tried not to shrink as if I were in trouble. How long had he been standing there?

"Everything alright? You've been kind of quiet this morning." Every word he ever spoke was so crystal clear that I'd always wondered if he moonlighted as a public speaker or something. He definitely had the voice and clarity to do so.

"Um…" I took a moment to mull over my words before answering. "I guess my mind is elsewhere. We've been pretty dead today and I had problems sleeping last night. I'm on my third cup of coffee and I still don't feel like myself."

I wanted to lean back and relax into my chair but feared that it might cause a facial reaction if I did. Damian was good at reading people; that was part of the reason he did so well at his job. I had little doubt in my mind that he could probably calm a storm if necessary with that baby face of his. I'd witnessed him with irate members of our financial institution more times than I could count, and his wins overpowered his losses.

He nodded slightly, studying me. "Do you need to take the rest of the day off?"

I perked up at the thought but attempted to smother it so I didn't seem too overzealous. "Would you be okay with that?"

He scoffed, rubbing his hand along the perfectly sculpted facial hair of his jawline. "Violet, you never take a vacation or use your sick time. I usually have to tell you to, anyhow. And besides, I think the heat outside is keeping people away. So go home, get some rest."

A genuine smile crossed my lips. How on earth did I get so lucky to have a boss like him? And why was he still single? That thought had plagued me many times in the year and a half I'd been working here.

Damian had hired me before I even graduated college, and to this day I still wasn't sure what he had seen in me. Lord knew my resume was a piece of work in itself—no two jobs alike, and none prior to this had any kind of experience with finances like the work I was doing now. Whatever it was he saw, I was grateful for the opportunity it gave me to build my savings and move out of my grandma's to start a life on my own.

"Thank you. I think I will then."

"Good, see you tomorrow." He gave me a lazy salute and left, returning to his office just down the hall. I noted how odd it seemed for him to offer a farewell in that manner, but shrugged it off and turned my attention back to my desk.

I turned on my "out of office" messages for my work phone and email, and began to turn things off. I was eager to get out of here and head home. I nodded goodbyes as I bumped into a few coworkers on my way out the door, but nobody questioned my leaving.

As I stepped out and into the parking lot, the late morning heat hit me like a wall. There wasn't a cloud in the sky, but the sun was on its way to making the day a miserable one and I slipped my sunglasses from the top of my head and into place to shield my eyes from the brightness of the outdoors.

Once in the confines of my car, I cranked up the air to full blast. My blouse was already sticking to my skin and I threw my purse into the passenger seat. I dialed my grandma, and on the third ring she answered, her aging voice filling the speakers of my small car.

"Hello?"

A tension I hadn't realized I was holding on to left my body as soon as she picked up. The cool air began to fill the space around me and I was grateful for it.

"Hey Grandma, it's me." I pulled my hair up and into a hair clip that I kept stashed in my car along with several hair ties and bands. One cup holder was filled to the brim with the assortment of them.

"Hello Vi, aren't you at work, dear? Is everything okay?"

"Just crazy tired. I didn't sleep well last night and my boss suggested I use some personal time to go home and get some rest. How are things there?" I put my car into gear and began to exit the parking lot.

"Fine. Fine. Well, that was nice of him. You know, your boss is a rather fine gentleman."

I rolled my eyes. Grandma might have been a widow who was pushing seventy, but she never passed up an opportunity to appreciate a good-looking man. I'd been mortified when she had tried to play matchmaker when we ran into Damian at the grocery store shortly after I'd started working for him. The level of embarrassment I'd felt in that moment was an all-time high, which made it difficult to return to work after the fact. Fortunately, we'd both acted like it had never happened, and neither of us had brought up the incident since.

He was only a few years older than me, which didn't seem like much after leaving the world of high school. Grandma always stated that age was just a number, but then my grandpa had been ten years her senior. Damian was good-looking, don't get me wrong, but I would never put myself in that position with someone who worked above me. I didn't want or need the drama that could come from something like that.

"Speaking of men…" I toyed around with how I wanted to break the news to her and decided to just blurt it out. "I'm breaking up with Brett today. I thought you would like to hear that."

The car went quiet and I bit my lip, waiting for her response. I had expected her to be ecstatic and go back to inserting Damian's name back in the conversation, but the silence stretched longer than I had anticipated.

"Are you still there? I thought this was what you were hoping for? You don't like him."

My brows pinched together and I could feel my sunglasses beginning to slide down my nose. I began to think that maybe I should have had this conversation in person instead of over the phone.

"Well…he called here earlier." The hesitation in her voice had me on edge.

I blinked in surprise. Why on earth would Brett call her? "What? Why?"

"If you're going to break up with him, do it quickly." She seemed perturbed.

"What did he call you about, Grandma?" I came to a stop at a red light and I impatiently waited for both her answer and the light to change.

She sighed, gruffly. "Well hell, I never liked him anyway," she mumbled, almost as if it hadn't been meant for my ears. It was obvious she was a bit worked up by the tone in her voice. "He tried asking for permission to marry you and I flat out told him no."

My eyes widened as I froze in place. What. The. Fuck.

"No," was all I could utter in reply.

"That's precisely what I said, Violet. I told him that I didn't appreciate the fact that he would even request such a thing over the phone when he never bothers to come around here in the first place. You know I never thought much of him from the start, and I've never been able to put my finger on why. I don't like that boy and I'm not going to beat around the bush about it anymore. I don't want you to marry him."

I burst out into a fit of laughter. Seriously? Marriage? After last night, did he really think that proposing to me was going to fix everything? Why on earth would I want to commit to a lifetime with him when I couldn't find satisfaction in the relationship I had with him now?

Absolutely not. He was beyond delusional.

A rather large truck that filled my rearview mirror lay on his horn and I jumped. Apparently, I had missed the signal change to green; I stepped on my gas pedal, sending my car forward fast enough to press my back into my seat.

"Well, Grandma, you don't have to worry. I don't want that. And I can't believe the one time he puts forth the effort to talk to you, it's to ask about marriage. Absolutely not."

I could picture my grandma in her brown and worn rocking chair, placed perfectly center in front of the television stand in her living room, needle and thread in hand. The woman loved to embroider while watching her drama-filled television shows that were playing during this time of the day, which I was no doubt interrupting right now.

She had tried to teach me once upon a time but I didn't have a knack for it. She loved embroidering so much because it was something she and her mother had done together when she was growing up.

I wished I had fond memories such as that with my mom, but sadly I'd been robbed of that chance.

"I'm so glad to hear you say that, darling. You're a smart

girl. Mr. Right is out there somewhere for you. But it's not Brett."

"I know. It's not Brett."

It was a rare occurrence for us to agree on something, especially while on the topic of men. There had been one guy I brought home shortly after graduating high school who she didn't totally show disdain for, and that was only because she knew his grandmother from a book club she used to be a part of. But he wasn't exactly a motivated individual when it came to a relationship, so I'd cut him loose maybe a month into dating.

The rest of the drive was uneventful as we created small talk. When I arrived at my apartment building, I said my goodbye and told her that I would visit soon. I cut the engine and as soon as the air from the vents came to a halt, I all but bolted from the car. My cheeks thawed quickly as I crossed the road in a small sprint, toward the brick apartment building that towered above me.

I opted for the stairs, hoping that the three flights would do me in so that when my head hit my pillow it would be lights out for a while. I fanned myself as I made my way up, instantly regretting my decision due to the humidity that overtook the stairwell. When I came to the second floor, I took the easy way out. I exited into the hallway and made a left turn toward the elevators. The smell of spices filled my nostrils as I passed a few apartments and it made my stomach growl. Along with my coffee this morning I had managed to choke down half a granola bar, but that obviously hadn't lasted long. The smell lingered as the doors closed and took me up to my floor.

I strolled down the hall and to my door at the end of it. As I stepped into my apartment, I paused. Last night's imagery returned, burned into my mind, and I still couldn't believe that something that had felt so real could be nothing but a dream.

Locking each mechanism on my door with careful precision, I threw my purse onto the small table a few feet away. Kicking my shoes off, I padded over to my bed and stared at it. I hadn't even had the chance to make it earlier since I'd been in such a rush to get out of here.

Stupid as it may seem, I decided to retrace my fuzzy steps from last night. I pointed in each direction as I did just that.

Bed. Needed water.

Hit my foot on the dresser. The pain had felt so real. The throbbing sensation and the wetness on my hand from the blood. I rubbed my thumb and forefinger together as if I could recall the texture.

I remembered trying to steady myself with the mirror, and my eyes fell on a mark where my hand must have made contact with it. There was a stain on the wood and a spot on the glass that had never been there before last night. My heart sped up as I reached for it, fingers grazing, not trusting the image that was smack dab in front of me.

The first aid kit. The bathroom.

I ran the short distance there, examined my surroundings, and sure enough, in the trash was a pile of bloodied paper towels along with gauze and bandages from wrapping my foot.

"What the…" I couldn't even finish my sentence. What was happening? I couldn't comprehend how this could be.

I ripped off my ankle sock and found no trace of injury, no scar and no bruise. Absolutely nothing. Ripping off my other sock for good measure I found the other foot unmarked, just the same. Nothing out of the ordinary could be seen.

I was going out of my mind.

Hands on my head, I exited the bathroom, my breath quick and erratic. It was as if I had just finished running a race.

My mind was reeling—nothing made sense. If this was real, then who the hell had been in my apartment last night?

A hand came to lie on my shoulder and before I could let out a scream, everything went black.

CHAPTER 3

Violet

Cozy. I felt as comfortable as I could in my bed, still clad in my work clothes. I was curled up perfectly against a man who made me feel complete and whole. I didn't need anything else but this. I felt secure. *Safe* even, dare I say it. But how could I be with a total stranger? It made no sense.

None of it made sense.

My eyes popped open to reveal that I was indeed on my bed, facing my nightstand. A small sliver of sunlight escaped the window in front of me; by the coloring and angle of it, it was most likely sunset. To my surprise, a familiar arm was wrapped around me, a body pressed against me. I tried not to panic. I knew full well I had locked my door, all three mechanisms to be exact.

Relax, I told myself. I couldn't hear any breathing behind me to tell if he was awake or asleep. If I were to make a run for it, would I make it to the door in time? For living on my own, I had nothing to protect myself with. Maybe I could make it to the kitchen? The studio apartment wasn't that large after all. I probably had a better chance to make it there to arm myself than I did to make it out the door with the locks still fastened.

But then again, how the hell did he get in here in the first place?

"You're awake."

The familiar voice didn't ask, it was more of a statement. I drew in a shaky breath before I could respond. I wanted to keep my tone level, but how could I? I was in fight-or-flight mode.

"And you're...real." My throat went dry. There was a stranger in my bed. One who had fucked me gloriously last night while I thought it was nothing more than a dream. Because of my stupidity, I had let him.

A small chuckle sounded from his chest and I felt it vibrate through me at my back. "I am very much real." He hugged me tighter across my stomach, securing me in place. Running didn't feel like much of an option anymore.

"I thought you were...a dream."

He was clearly amused, as he laughed once more, but the sound he made wasn't unpleasant or malevolent. "Do you normally have dreams that realistic?"

No, definitely not.

I wanted—no, I *needed*—to know where I stood with this man and what he wanted from me. I tried to swallow but failed, afraid to ask one of the many questions that were burning in my mind, but also scared of what answer he might give. "Are you going to hurt me?"

There was a long pause that made me even more uncomfortable beneath his grasp. Every breath felt heavy and I hated how much my body moved when I was willing it to stay still.

This was it. This had to be it. This was how my life was going to end.

"Why would you think that?" he questioned as he released me. A gush of air left me now that I was free from his hold. From the bounce of the bed, he had left me there; I slowly crept toward the edge of the opposite side. "I would never hurt you, Violet. I love you."

What?

I scurried up from the bed and scrambled to get my bearings as I stood on shaky legs. I finally came face-to-face with the man who I'd thought my mind had conjured up last night, and a sense of ease, not fear, settled over me. No longer was I frightened by him, but some sort of unexplainable calm settled over me at the sight of him and I was at a loss for words.

He was bare chested, sculpted but not chiseled to the point that it might look unnatural. With his physique, he would look damn good on a calendar with his dark denim that hung low on his hips. His brown hair had some length and was tousled about; it could have used a trim, but the messy look suited him. His facial features were what I had for the most part gathered last night—with the exception of one thing.

I did recognize him, that I knew for sure. He was without a doubt the stranger in my bed, but I could have sworn his eyes were pure black from corner to corner. Even in the darkened apartment, I clung to the image in my head. But the ones that were studying me now, just the same as I was studying him, were blue.

"Your eyes." I finally spoke, unable to move. "I swore they were…" The words sounded just as crazy as they did inside of my head.

"I was afraid I might startle you if they were normal. Well, *my* normal that is." A sheepish grin formed.

"What do you mean, *your* normal?" My curiosity was taking over my initial instinct to flee and get the hell out of here. My eyes narrowed, studying him.

The man closed his eyes for a beat, and when he opened them, the air in my lungs seemed to vanish. Even though we had been shrouded in darkness, I had been right.

His eyes were black from corner to corner—no white, no irises, and no pupils. They were nothing but black pits of darkness. I found little comfort knowing that I wasn't crazy after all and I had really seen it. I wished I could explain it away as some sort of parlor trick, but I came up blank in my search for any sort of explanation. He hadn't needed to touch his eyes in order to make them change, and yet they transformed with no more than a blink.

"Who are you?" I asked. "What…are you?" My voice grew louder as I took another step back, the width of the bed not enough distance between us. "How did you even get in here?"

"My name is Kadriel, and I will admit I am not from your world as you know of it. More so another plane of existence, or realm so to speak. And you released me."

I shot him a disbelieving look. This had to be some sort of prank. I began scanning my surroundings in the chance that I might catch some sort of camera that didn't belong here.

His face remained poised as his muscled arm pointed not at me, but to my right, and I turned slightly to follow its direction. It seemed as if he was referring to the standing floor mirror at my side. I shook my head, not understanding.

"How?" I approached it, examining. This mirror had belonged to my mother and my grandmother before her. It was one of the few things I still had left from my life with my parents. I looked behind it and tilted it every which way, trying to figure it out.

Why was I even entertaining the idea that this mirror could be a part of the equation?

My gaze paused on the dried blood, remembering my injured foot once more. The smallest amounts tainted the glass and the oak.

"That's it," Kadriel confirmed.

I glanced back at him, scrutinizing, but his face remained expressionless.

"Your blood on the mirror set me free."

Laughter bubbled up through me and I lost it. "Are you supposed to grant me three wishes or something? How the hell can you come through a mirror? That's absurd!" Tears sprang to my eyes as I tried to calm myself down. "Who put you up to this?"

Kadriel crossed his arms, waiting for my hysteria to settle down. His demeanor shifted as his chin dipped down.

"Wait, you're serious." My amusement faded and I faltered. For a split second, I believed the words that were coming out of his mouth.

He nodded, eyes seemingly fixed on mine, if they could be. How could I really tell he was looking at me and not at something else entirely? He was taller than me, but the angle of his head made it seem like I was his focal point.

"Wait, what did you mean last night when you said you had waited a long time to…to…" I gestured to the bed between us, unwilling to accept the fact that I had slept with a complete stranger. My eyes bulged at the realization.

"It's like I said before. I love you, Violet. I have for some time. And I probably even know you better than anyone else does."

I placed a hand on top of my head and began pacing back

and forth. "God, how fucked up am I?" I spoke out loud, more to myself than him. How could this imagination of mine possibly conjure up a story this elaborate, a scenario that felt so real? I was going to end up in the loony bin.

"You're not."

"Some guy with black eyes comes through some sort of mirror portal thing and claims that he loves me? Can heal an injured foot? Give me the best sex I've ever had? This isn't real! This *can't* be real."

"It's very much real." Kadriel tried to take a step forward, but I held up my hands in defense and it stopped him right in his tracks. "I will take that as a compliment though. Thank you."

I attempted to shoot daggers with my eyes. "Are you some sort of stalker? We've never met, so how could you know me? I think I would *remember* you."

I exaggerated that last statement as I knew it to be true. I had no logical explanation for the eye color change, or how he could have entered or left the apartment without a trace. The mirror bit was ludicrous in itself, but I was certain that if our paths had ever crossed before, even for a fraction of a second, I would remember him.

He had a voice that could make me melt and a body that would make me bend to his every whim. Attractive features that would draw my attention no matter how brief of an interaction we had, and cause me to stir up some sort of fantasy. Although I was sure it wouldn't be anything close to the likes of what I was experiencing right now.

"As someone who has had a brush with death twice, I thought you might be more understanding of the impossible."

If my blood could run cold, it would have. Slowly, I pivoted away from him and the mirror, cornering myself off and away from everything. "I don't know what you're talking about."

"I know you do." His voice was soft, but I refused to believe that we were on the same page regarding what he had just said.

A knock sounded on my door and I jumped, grabbing my chest at the pounding sensation of my heart about to leap from its cage. I grabbed my phone and saw a text from Brett from about three minutes ago, stating that he was here. My phone had still been silenced from work, no wonder I'd missed it.

"Shit. You have to hide. Or...something," I whispered, panicked. The last thing I needed was for Brett to find another man here, especially when I was about to break things off.

"Violet? You here?" Brett's voice sounded from the other side of my one and only entrance and exit.

I groaned, not looking forward to this meeting. I hadn't even had a chance to figure out what I was going to say exactly. Which brought me to another thought—how had I even managed to sleep the rest of the day away? I didn't even remember crawling into bed.

"Just touch the mirror when you're ready for me to return. I'll be watching."

"Seriously?" I scoffed as I shook my head, peeved that Kadriel seemed unbothered and unmoving at my request for him to leave. "Just a second!"

"Okay fine, click your heels together three times," he answered.

"What the hell?" My eyes bulged once more in disbelief as I passed him on my way to the door. I half expected him to go hide out in the bathroom, but when he didn't move, I pressed on. "Please, just—"

"Violet?" Brett called again, dragging my attention back to the poorly timed visitor that was my soon-to-be ex-boyfriend.

Once at the door, I turned and scanned the apartment, but Kadriel was nowhere to be seen. Yep, I was definitely losing my shit.

"Hang on." I clumsily fumbled with the locks as I tried to make sense of how he was able to disappear so quickly. When I opened the door, Brett was still in his suit attire from work, leaning up against the doorway with a smug look on his face.

"Hi," I muttered as he brushed past me. As much as I didn't want to have this conversation in the hallway for anybody to hear, I didn't want him in my apartment either. Knowing that Kadriel had limited places to hide didn't sit well with me, so I would have to make this quick and rip off the band-aid.

"Miss me already?"

My nose turned up at Brett's remark and I was more than ready to get this over with. I let the door remain open a few inches before I swiveled to meet him.

He was loosening the blue tie at his neck and I observed a square-like outline in his pants pocket; I feared the possibility that it might be a ring box concealed in there. I was thankful that my grandma had spilled the beans on that one so at least I wouldn't be blindsided if he tried to pull it out on me.

"Brett, this isn't working." I crossed my arms as my eyes darted away from him, struggling to stay on subject as my mind was still reeling over how quickly Kadriel had vanished.

His head tipped to the side, eyes slanted, as he bit his tongue to the side in his mouth. I hated when he did that.

"Sex? Again? Baby, you know—"

"Don't call me that," I cut him off. "You know I hate it when you do. I'm not a baby and I'm not your baby. I have a name." *Thanks for adding more fuel to the fire of my desire to end things.* Maybe this would be easier than I'd initially thought it would be.

"Sorry, sorry." He held his hands up as he backpedaled in his words, yet he moved closer, his hips jutting out as he did. "What can I do to make it up to you?"

I took a step back, halting him in his advance. "Nothing. I can't do this anymore." I brought my gaze up to his, trying to remain stern in my posture and not waver in my voice.

I could see the realization set in as it registered in that thick skull of his. "You're breaking up with me?"

Brett's voice and presence were getting on my last nerve. I didn't have time to deal with this. I just wanted us—and this situation—to be over so I could figure out where the hell Kadriel was hiding.

He'll be watching. Bullshit. Surely, he wasn't stupid enough to get caught.

"Yes, just give me back my key please."

"You can't be serious. Is this really because of last night?"

I eyed my mirror suspiciously, wondering if I was being watched at this very moment. I felt like I had a giant spotlight on me that I couldn't see. But this was dumb. Kadriel was just trying to get inside my head, telling me that he knows me and loves me. Absurd wasn't even a strong enough word. I shook my head, agitated with myself for believing the story about the mirror even if only for a fleeting moment, and also irritated that Brett was going to drag this encounter on longer than it needed to be.

I sighed. "It's not just last night. It's—"

"You can't base a relationship on sex alone."

Of course he would believe that. Never mind that moments ago he'd called me by the one pet name that I loathed with my entire being and that I had told him several times prior to today to not call me.

"Oh my god, Brett. You're not hearing me. You never seem

to hear me. It's not just the sex, although yes, it does kind of suck. But it's the communication. You don't listen to me. It goes in one ear and out the other."

"Well, I'm sorry I'm not more exciting in the bedroom."

"It's not just the bedroom!" I was at my wits end with him. "But thank you for proving my point. And while you're hung up on it, sure. Let's talk about it. You're boring, predictable, and there's more to it than missionary and blowjobs. I have to keep a bottle of lube and a toy around because sex is all about you. Who the hell cares about my needs, right?"

"I just don't understand where this is coming from." He shook his head, irritated, his face and neck reddening as he tried to loosen his collar some more.

"Just give me my key, please." I held out my hand as I repeated my one request.

"Is there somebody else?" Brett's voice rose.

His question threw me off guard and I faltered as I glanced at my mirror. Could Kadriel truly be watching me at this very moment from whatever existence he was trying to sell me on?

I shook my head at the realization that I had slept with another man while I was still in a relationship. Granted, it had already been over in my mind, but I hadn't broken things off yet. I was a cheater, and I had cheated on Brett. Why was I having this revelation now while trying to break up with him and usher him out the door?

I must have taken too long to answer, and Brett didn't take kindly to it.

"There is!" His voice boomed and I recoiled.

"My god, get over yourself, Brett!"

I stole another glance at the mirror, although I didn't know what exactly I was expecting to find. I was so distracted by the glass and the bloodstained spot that I hadn't even tried searching anywhere else. At least not as hard as I could have been.

"Just give me the key and get out." I held out my hand again, waiting. The time for trying to be nice was over. "I'm done discussing this."

Brett removed his keys from the pocket opposite the mystery box, huffing and puffing. Good thing I'd decided to do this in the privacy of my apartment, given the scene he was making.

I hadn't thought he would have it in him to be so dramatic. He was always so guarded, calm and collected. Scheduled haircuts every three weeks, shirts and pants ironed and picture-perfect. He always tried to give off this poised and polished image around everyone else but me, and I was tired of it. If he put in as much effort with me as he did with his appearance and how the outside world saw him, perhaps we wouldn't be in this predicament right now.

His lips formed a tight line as he struggled to remove the key from the ring. My eyes widened at how long it was taking him, and I tried to resist the urge to offer my help. When he finally released the key, he threw it to the ground in a childish manner and it slid across the floor and under my bed. I stared after the disappearing act, beyond annoyed.

"Seriously, Brett?" I opened the door the rest of the way, trying to signal him out with my free arm. I didn't want to give him the satisfaction of seeing me pick up the stupid key. Maybe it would just go in the trash. At this point, my grandma and I were the only ones that really needed keys anyway. "Get out."

"You're going to regret this, Violet. You need me." The emphasis he put on the word *need* left a sour taste in my mouth. This was a side of Brett that I had never seen before. It was unsettling, and it only solidified my decision to end things.

There was no turning back now, no matter what.

With a flick of my wrist, I drew attention to the doorway that I wanted him to pass through so I could slam the door behind him. He passed by reluctantly, and my senses tingled uneasily in the quiet that fell upon us. Once he had stepped through the doorframe, I decided I wanted to have the last words.

"And just for the record, I don't *need* anybody." I tried to put the emphasis on the same word that had triggered me, and then slammed the door and locked the deadbolt with a flourish.

Leaning my back up against the door, I waited, hoping I would hear him take his leave. What I hadn't expected was a harsh blow from behind. I sprang away from the door and stifled a yelp, my heart up in my throat and pounding wildly.

For once in my life, and for the first time since knowing Brett, he scared me. And as much as I didn't want to admit it, he frightened me more than Kadriel did right about now. How fucked up was that?

I looked through the peephole and saw Brett storming off down the hallway toward the elevator. I sighed shakily in relief and locked the other two mechanisms on the door for good measure.

Was his attitude just because he was upset that he'd been planning to propose and I had thrown not only a wrench but an entire toolbox into his plans? Even so, I didn't want to give him any more of my time or energy—there were other things that needed my attention.

Now that one chapter of my life had been closed, it was time to delve into another—the mystery of Kadriel.

CHAPTER 4

Violet

I took my time searching through and investigating my apartment. I even checked under my bed, retrieving Brett's key while I was down there. Taking extra time in my closet and shower, I was quick to realize what I already knew.

There really was no place for Kadriel to have hidden. He had somehow managed to vanish without a trace.

I felt my walls as I passed, trying to find any kind of inconsistency in texture or sound in the hopes of uncovering something. When I came up with nothing out of the ordinary, I puffed out an exaggerated sigh. My studio apartment didn't offer many places to hide and I had failed to reveal anything that could explain Kadriel's comings and goings.

Cautiously, I sauntered up to the mirror, watching my reflection coming into view as I did so. I was bright-eyed and alert; no doubt my lengthy nap was to thank for that.

How long had Kadriel been in bed with me?

It was then I realized that I may not have been alone from the moment I got home. I recalled the hand on my shoulder before going blank, before waking up next to him. I placed a hand on my shoulder, remembering the touch I had felt.

But I wasn't asleep this time. I was fully awake and aware.

I pinched my arm for good measure, leaving a red mark on my skin. Whatever happened next would either prove I was crazy or that this whole mirror story was true. I bent slightly to place my hand on the mirror where my blood had stained the oak, and waited.

When nothing happened, I removed my hand. I searched the mirror, waiting some more, not knowing what to expect.

After what seemed like forever had gone by, I took a step back. He couldn't have been serious about the whole tapping the heels together bit. Was he?

"Kadriel?" I called as I examined every nook and cranny of the mirror.

It was worn in color, and the wood could have used some love, but even so it was the one item from my past that I could never part with. Brett had tried to get me to buy a new one when I was moving into this place, and I had vehemently objected.

I was angry with myself for allowing our relationship to drag on for as long as it had. Now that things were officially over between us, there seemed to be red flags popping up that I should have seen long before now. I had told Brett what this mirror had meant to me, and he'd tried to get me to forget about it and move on even after the fact. *Douchebag.*

Still, nothing happened as I continued to stare at the mirror.

I weighed the thought of how ridiculous I would look,

tapping my heels together, and decided to do it quickly and get it over with. Maybe Kadriel was just a figment of my imagination after all. I lifted onto my toes and tapped my heels together three times, just like one of my favorite movies, minus the ruby-red slippers.

As I watched my reflection, on the third tap his face appeared behind me and over my shoulder, grinning like a fool. Although for a fleeting nanosecond it was cute, it didn't stop me from whipping around and slugging him in the bicep without hesitation.

"You think you're funny, don't you?" My knuckles ached instantly and I regretted my spur-of-the-moment decision. If he really did know me as well as he claimed he did, he would have known that the act of clicking my heels three times was from one of my favorite films—a classic that I would always make time for, no matter what else was on the television.

"I'm sorry." He laughed playfully, a sound that seemed to make my tense shoulders sag a bit. His chest caught the light from the setting sun and I had to blink away the lustful thoughts that barged in. "Things were pretty tense and I was hoping to put you at ease a bit."

"By making me look like a fool," I spat. I crossed my arms, hiding my knuckles that still ached from his stone-cold bicep that showed no visible mark from my impact.

"Is the mirror some sort of screen that you just sit in front of and watch for a good laugh? Is my life just a reality show to you?" I could feel the heat creeping into my face at the thought of being watched like that. The stalker aspect of it all did little for my nerves.

"No. Never. I promise." He didn't hesitate to answer.

"How can I trust anything you say? I don't even know you." I didn't understand why I wasn't throwing him out at this point. But then, what good would that do if he could just magically pop in like he had done seconds ago?

"I understand that, I do. I have given you no reason to trust me."

I searched his face, wondering. "Why? Why me?"

Kadriel sat himself at the edge of my bed and rubbed his palms against his legs, almost in a nervous manner. I tried not to get hung up on the fixation I had with his eyes, or his bare chest and back for that matter. He was distracting and pleasing to the eye, but I couldn't afford to get caught up in his appearance.

"I requested to tether myself to you your junior year of high school." He kept his eyes cast down to what seemed to be the floor in front of him. "Ever since then, you have been under my watch. No one else is even allowed to view you."

"You make it sound like I'm some sort of restricted channel." As if that should have made me feel any better.

"You kind of are, in that aspect," he mused. "We—myself and some others like me—use reflections to see into this realm. To find and monitor the wrongdoers who must be punished. Reflections are cast everywhere—from mirrors, to bodies of water, to the surface of a spoon. Mirrors are preferred for a clearer image, but we're not limited to them."

I let that information settle for a moment, trying to sort and comprehend it. Reflections were everywhere, but the thought of somebody always being able to watch me weirded me out to no end. Even if I was meant for his eyes only.

"Junior year?" I questioned, wondering why he would bring that specific year up.

"Your heart stopped for the second time in your life, if only briefly." His facial features softened as if saddened before he brought his gaze up to mine. "You have quite the fight to live."

My eyes started to glaze over. "How did you—" I shook my head. "Nobody knows about that. I never told anyone." My voice quieted and I turned away, clasping a hand over my mouth.

In my junior year of high school, I had tried to end my life with an overdose.

My life had been one train wreck after another and I hadn't seen any other way out. The boy I was with at the time had taken my virginity and blabbed about it to the whole school, then made comments about my weight and tried to joke about how somebody else must have knocked me up because it wasn't him.

I hadn't even been pregnant, by the way, which made the remarks about my weight feel even worse.

This then led to some of his buddies joining in with made-up stories about their nonexistent time spent with me. The fact that my few so-called friends believed the lies they spewed only made it that much worse. That they would think so little of me without hesitation or confirmation on my part, it was like a knife to the chest.

My grandma had grounded me once she found out about my "sexual relations," when in reality, it had only been one time. My first time. She was horrified that I would give away my virginity at that age. I'd been ridiculed by my closest friends and left in isolation.

I was the lonely girl who had survived the tragic accident that took her parents and brother at a young age. The girl who, according to that boy and his buddies, would throw herself at anybody in order to have sex. The girl who had no one left to confide in and felt entirely alone in this world.

I had to have been horrible to live with in my teenage

years—my grandma and I had gone through some rough bouts with each other when I lived at her place, and it had taken us some time to get to the decent spot we were in now. But during junior year, I put her through the wringer and I knew it. That year, it felt like the world would have been better off without me.

So that was what he had meant by my two brushes with death.

Hearing Kadriel say that my heart had stopped, I was mentally transported back to my bathroom at my grandma's house. I had woken up in a pile of vomit that I couldn't even remember expelling. I must have collapsed on the way in there, my body halfway into the small space. I could remember the exact spot, engrained in my memory. Head pounding, a sore and raw throat, and my stomach a mess. I probably should have gone to the hospital, but I'd been too embarrassed and disgusted in my failure to die. My stomach rolled just thinking about it.

"I didn't mean to upset you, Violet. Believe me, it wasn't my intention." Kadriel set a hand on my shoulder and I jumped at his sudden proximity, ducking away. I recalled feeling that same touch shortly after arriving home, and then I'd awoken hours later, wrapped up beside him.

"What did you do to me earlier? I felt your hand and then it was lights out. The whole day is practically gone." I used this as a perfect excuse to move away from the previous subject matter.

"You were visibly shaken, so I put you to sleep. With the state you were in, I was afraid you might do something to harm yourself. Or me, in that moment." The corner of his mouth turned up a bit in a lighthearted smile.

"Well, as if you could." He seemed to pick up on my

annoyance and it wiped his smirk clean from his face. "I just put you to sleep for a little while. We did have quite a night and I know you didn't get much sleep."

"What, are you not tired? Are you immortal or something? Sleeping is beneath you?" I let out a brief snort of a laugh as I joked. I immediately regretted how stupid I sounded in both my questioning and reaction. I couldn't believe I was feeding into this nonsense. I had to be crazy in the head—the words coming out of my mouth were flowing just as fast as the thoughts were coming to mind. I should have been more concerned about the fact that he had the ability to knock me out by just one touch.

"Immortal, yes. And I don't require as much sleep as you do, but it is nice to indulge on occasion I suppose. But, sleeping with you? I would gladly accept that routine."

The urge I had to throw my head back and laugh was unreal. Did he really think I was going to sleep with him again after all of these revelations?

I mean, sure, the thought of rekindling what we had last night… It was an experience I would love to revisit, but damn. I had just broken up with Brett not fifteen minutes ago.

"I literally just got out of a relationship. I'm not ready for another kind of anything right now." I waved my arm at him, not knowing which words to use to refer to us. There was no *us*, really.

"Well, he definitely showed some different colors tonight, didn't he?"

So he *had* been watching. I felt a bit triumphant, knowing I'd been right to be suspicious during that whole scene, but the feeling quickly faded. Kade had told me point-blank he would be watching, I shouldn't have doubted that he would.

"You saw that." I bit my lip, wondering if he had ever

really left.

"To be frank, I'm shocked you put up with him as long as you did. I never liked him. But then, I had my sights set on you anyway."

"You do realize how creepy this is, right? You watching me in your one-way mirror? Mirrors? Does that not sound like the definition of a stalker to you? At all?" I turned at the realization that he had most likely seen too much, more than I had even thought, initially. "Did you ever watch us have sex?"

The guilt-ridden look on his face, and avoidance to respond, said enough. His eyes widened only to reveal bigger black pools.

"Oh my god!" I resisted the urge to hit him again and fought to put some distance between us. My apartment was growing smaller by the minute.

Kadriel held up his arms in defense. "I'm sorry! I don't exactly know what I'm tuning in to sometimes, it just happens. But seriously, you should have dumped his ass after the first time."

Even though he had a point, I was still furious with him. He had seen me naked numerous times, and in countless states of vulnerability. To this day I still had issues with my curvy body and its appearance. I couldn't even begin to say how often I stood in front of the mirror, poking and prodding myself, pinching my unwanted belly between my fingers and wishing I could change the reflection looking back at me.

I knew I was my own worst critic, but now I felt exposed in the worst way possible. In any other situation I would have reported his ass to the police, but this wasn't exactly a normal scenario. If this got out, I would be a laughingstock, just like back in high school.

Although pissed, I still didn't know where I stood with

Kadriel. Sure, I was definitely intrigued by him. Terrified? Not so much, anymore. But I was disturbed by his earlier confession of so-called love for me, as well as how often I'd been the center of his attention from the other side. Whatever the other side was.

"Can I call you Kade?" I requested as I retreated some more. I moved to my makeshift living room that consisted of a small brown sofa and entertainment center. Sitting down on the couch, I pulled a blanket up over my lap. Even though I was fully clothed, I felt like I needed the extra barrier between us.

"If you wish."

It was strange, and I couldn't put my finger on why, but I felt comfortable around him.

A tiny part of me still wanted to flee. Another part thought that maybe I was in a coma or something, unable to wake up from whatever this was. The war going on inside my head to decide which things I should or shouldn't do was boggling.

"Why do you believe that you're in love with me?"

My fingers fidgeted beneath the blanket as I stared out the nearest window. It was the only one out of three on this wall that I bothered opening all the way on the weekdays when I had to worry about work. There were three tall and lengthy windows that let in a crazy amount of light if I let them, but I rarely did.

"Where to begin." He came into view in my periphery. "Your persistence in life, first off. Even after what you've been through—losing your family at a young age, and the incident in high school—you still get up and attack each new day. You're reliable, and sincere when it comes to your work. You can be trusted, but burn that bridge and you'll hold a grudge. I can't say that I blame you either, in some of those cases.

"And even through your self-proclaimed goth phase in high school, you couldn't hide your true beauty that lay underneath. Your kindness always showed, regardless of how you felt."

He paused for a moment, frozen in place. "Then there's your relationship with your grandmother."

My head perked up at the mention of her. Kadriel was now at the other end of the couch.

"What about it?" I urged him to continue.

"It's beautiful." He smiled genuinely, as if something had crossed his mind. "I've gathered that you were extremely close early on, even before your family departed. Then, for quite some time after, you were always at war with one another, especially in high school. You were quite the rebel—sneaking out, trying to get away with alcohol and so on. You could barely stand each other. Then once you moved out, you both began to settle down and find peace with one another again. You two have had quite the journey."

"Well, now we should be better than ever since I ended things with Brett," I admitted, out loud but more to myself than to him, slightly uncomfortable yet oddly flattered at Kade's confessions. I was realizing just how much information he really had on me, even from before my junior year.

"Oh, she loathes him. And with good reason."

It was strange how he spoke of my grandma as if he knew her, without having met her—at least, to my knowledge. The thought warmed me and I could feel my cheeks blush. My grandma really was an amazing woman, in more ways than one.

He rounded the corner of the couch and came to kneel in front of me by my feet. "I also know that this blanket has been with you longer than I have, and that it provides comfort." He tugged at the purple, blue, and black striped blanket my grandma had made for me as a child and set it down on the cushion to my side. "And that you tangle your fingers together when you're concentrating very hard on something, or lost in thought."

Guilty that he had noticed and unearthed one of my frequent impulses, I released my fingers. I felt like I'd been caught with my hand in the cookie jar and was unable to respond.

He knew a heck of a lot about me and it wasn't fair. I knew practically nothing of him, as we had just met not twenty-four hours ago and we had more or less started off on the wrong foot. Well, in bed, to be precise.

How many people could say they met for the first time in bed? The very thought had my head spiraling again.

"Say something, please." His dark eyes and facial features pleaded along with his words. I felt like I could get lost in a trance, gazing at his otherworldly eyes.

"You know so much about me." I shook my head and stared out the window. "Had years to study me, even. I think it's only fair that I should get a mirror or something to keep tabs on you." I picked at a piece of lint on my black dress pants and let it fall to the floor. "And what was the word you used earlier? Why have you been with me since high school? Watching me?"

"Tethered. That is the term we use." He stated it very matter-of-factly, straightening his back.

"And what exactly does that mean?" I tore my gaze away from the window and looked at him again. "Why did you tether yourself to me?"

He swallowed hard, and for a second his face fell. I searched his hardened features, waiting and willing for him to continue.

"Is it a bad thing, this tethering? Because all that comes to my mind is tethering a horse to a post, and I hope you're not planning anything of the sort."

"No, of course not. I personally don't believe it's a bad thing, but I guess it depends on how you look at it." He stood, and within a couple of steps he was staring out of the same window that I kept using to break up our eye contact.

I tried not to drool over the sight of his bare back, reflecting on the thought I'd had in bed with him last night— my wish for a mirrored ceiling so I could see him screwing me.

Although, maybe the mirrors were a bad idea now. Nix the mirrors.

Shit, they were everywhere. I became overly aware of my surroundings and squirmed in my seat, uncomfortable in that knowledge. There was nowhere to hide if I took all reflective surfaces into account. There were too many.

"Well, please tell me because my mind instantly jumps to worst-case scenarios. And, considering we just met, those scenarios are kind of frightening." I stood, wanting to be on equal footing with him.

He turned quickly and was in front of me once again, picking up my hands in his icy grasp. He was just as cold as he had been last night, slipping into my bed. "That's the last thing I want. To frighten you."

"Then just tell me what the hell this tethering thing is." I removed my hands from his hold and crossed my arms.

His lips formed a straight line and I tried hard to not think about how they had roamed my body last night. Soft, plush, delectable lips. I bit my own, trying to tear the imagery from my mind. This was not the time to be thinking of such things.

Did he even own a shirt? Who was he to show up sans shirt

and shoes, as comfortable as if he lived here?

"Understand that I will never lie to you. I will only speak the truth because that's what you deserve."

I nodded. "I'm going out on a very weak limb to trust you and hear you out on this, against my better judgment. So, you'd better not lie. Not that I'm going to know any different, but still."

"You have to know that the choice is all yours. I can't force you to do anything. It has to be of your own free will." The stalling was starting to get on my nerves.

"What choice?" I searched his face, trying to keep my view up and away from his naked skin in front of me.

"Whether or not to accept the tethering proposal and leave with me. Start a new life, with me."

I felt like my jaw had hit the floor. "You're joking." I took a step back, stunned, bumping into the couch enough to cause it to scrape across the floor. I really needed to get an area rug or those furniture pads to protect the wood beneath it.

"I'm not. I chose you long ago just as I choose you now. I want you to be by my side for the rest of my existence." Although I knew nothing about this man, he seemed earnest in his words.

I blinked at him in surprise. "So, like a marriage." It wasn't a question.

"So to speak, yes."

I blew out a shaky exhale and pivoted. What the hell was going on with my life? First, my grandma tells me that Brett was asking her about marriage, and now Kade shows up and expects me to just elope? Or *tether*, as they call it?

"We just met." I stepped to the side and tried to put some distance between us. "Officially, anyway. Why on earth would I agree to something like that? Brett was thinking of marriage and we had been together for eight months. We had never even discussed it."

My nose turned up at the thought. No fucking way. "I'm supposed to just drop everything and run off into a mirror with you the day after we meet?"

"Well, technically you have four nights left to decide. I have five nights to court you."

"Ha!" I began to walk farther away from him, but I had nowhere to go. Stupid, small apartment. "That's why you had to spy on me for all these years. So you can woo me in the hopes that I'll accept the offer? Go tether to somebody else."

My words felt harsher than I had meant them to. But what was said was said, and I couldn't take it back now. Who the hell did he think he was, trying to pull off something like this?

"I can't, nor would I want to if I could."

"What do you mean?" I was back by my bed, scrutinizing him from as far away as I could get.

"I can only request a tether here once. Whether you accept or deny me, that is entirely your choice."

"So what if I deny it? That's it? We're done? Do you leave?"

He remained silent in his approach as he came around the couch, seemingly to respect the boundaries I was trying to set. "Should you decide against tethering, then yes, I'll leave. I'll never bother you again and your monitoring will be transferred to someone else."

Kade leaving, and for good? Why did it feel like I had just been punched in the stomach?

I had gotten so riled up over this tethering thing that my hands were now fisted. But the thought of never seeing him again hit me like a blow out of nowhere.

I didn't understand it. We'd only just met, so why was I feeling this way? The thought of never seeing him again almost…hurt.

"What do you mean my monitoring will be transferred to someone else? Am I some sort of threat? Why am I being monitored at all?" He had mentioned punishing others earlier, and I knew I had done nothing to deserve being put in that type of category.

"You are not a threat, no. While that is the main focal point of my job, it is also to locate and keep tabs on those who have cheated death. And you have—not once, but twice."

His words hit hard. They opened a gaping hole in my chest. The air that tried to expand my lungs failed as I recalled him mentioning that my heart had stopped my junior year of high school. News that I hadn't known until today. It pained me to remember those images, reliving them and seeing them in a new and harsh light.

"I…I need some time. Some space. To myself. Please."

I turned my back to him, feeling my eyes burn and a lump forming in my throat. Tears were threatening to spill and I couldn't do this with him here. Not right now.

His feet padded across the floor and then stopped. I stood in place for a while, frozen as tears streamed down my face. How could I feel this way over somebody I had just met? Someone who harbored harrowing information about my past that deep down I knew to be true. I didn't understand, then or now, how I could have lived through that overdose.

I was afraid to go to the bathroom because of the mirror above the sink. I didn't want to cross the room because of the standing one. The fridge, television screen, and even the side of the fucking toaster would all cast some sort of reflection.

He had seen too much of me already—I didn't want him to see me like this.

My emotions got the best of me and I waited for them to

settle down. My stifled sobs slowly eased, and I swiped away the remnants of my tearstained cheeks.

Once my composure was back in place, I glanced around my empty and darkening apartment.

Kade's footsteps had stopped right about where the mirror stood. He had vanished, once again.

CHAPTER 5

Violet

Maybe it was the fact that I had slept half the day away, but I was now in the same pickle as last night with my inability to sleep. I was finally free of Brett, but that did nothing to help my feeble attempt to rest and get back on some sort of sleep schedule.

I tossed and turned in bed, kicking the sheets completely off the mattress one minute, only to grab them all and bury myself in them the next.

I couldn't stop focusing on last night. I was unable to concentrate on anything else other than the connection that we had.

Even though I knew I couldn't base a possible relationship with Kade off of one night, no matter how amazing it was, I was infatuated with his body and what it was capable of doing to mine. The more I thought about the connection we'd shared right here on this bed, the more I wanted a repeat. I thought it might be impossible to have that again—it had to be too good to be true, right?

And what exactly would a life with him entail? Would I be trapped on some other plane of existence or realm by way of a mirror-type portal? What would I even do there? Would I have a job or something? There wasn't exactly much for me here, except—

My grandma.

I knew I wasn't the only family in her life. She had other children and grandchildren who she cared for and doted upon, but we had lived together for so long. We'd been such an integral part of each other's lives after the loss that had taken so much from us.

What would she do if I left?

Kade had mentioned leaving and starting a new life with him, but would I ever be able to come back? And if so, how often? I couldn't imagine leaving for good and never having the chance to see her smiling face again. Her crafty projects, and the smells of baked goods that often filled her house and made my mouth water—these were just a few of the things that instantly popped into the forefront of my mind when I thought about what I would miss.

And this tethering thing. Supposedly he could only do it once? So he would just be shit out of luck if I denied him?

And what was with the five days of courting? How could I possibly get to know someone in five days? Or nights, as he stated. Whatever the deal, that timeframe was crazy unrealistic and appalling. The idea of a courtship, a little stuck in the past if you ask me.

And were there others like me, with the choice to either accept or deny? Who were they, and most importantly, were they happy with their decisions or did they regret them? Could I talk to them?

I needed facts. I needed evidence. How could I possibly agree to something like this without hearing from someone else who had been through it?

Oh god, was I seriously considering this? Why was it even an option on the table?

I figured a great fuck had made me delusional. I couldn't see any other explanation.

Releasing an agitated breath, I sat up and turned on my bedside lamp. I eyed the corner of my dresser where my foot had met the jagged edge last night and a suspicious thought emerged.

Something was off.

How had I not noticed it before? Yesterday I'd been in such a hurry for work that I hadn't paid any attention to how far out my dresser had jutted out from the wall. I stood so I could push it back into its rightful place. But how had it come to be so far out that I'd smashed my foot into it in the middle of the night?

I straightened myself out, smoothing my hands over my tank and lengthy pajama pants. I didn't normally opt for bottoms, but seeing as how my life was on display whenever a mirror was present, I'd wanted to cover up a bit more. His earlier words about watching me still rang on repeat in my ears.

Even if Kade was telling the truth, and I was meant for his eyes only, I didn't care. He had already seen enough.

I combed my fingers through my hair and cautiously stepped in front of the standing mirror, unlocking it so that I could flip it around to see its reflective surface.

Upon second thought, maybe I didn't want him back here. I marched away, only to stop at the foot of my bed.

Dammit, I had a question for him. Several, in fact. With

each piece of information he'd given me, more questions had come barging into my head. But I supposed I could always ask him to go away. It had worked the last time, and without any kind of argument or hesitation on his end. Did I really trust him enough to do it again? If I meant as much to him as he said, there shouldn't be any kind of argument.

These reflective surfaces around me hid whatever lay on the other side, and I had no idea if he was watching me right now as I battled the inner turmoil which no doubt registered on my face. I had never been able to hide what I was thinking or feeling, it was something I wasn't capable of no matter how much I fought it.

Now I realized I had over a dozen surfaces in my apartment that acted like cameras, exposing me. I was on display like some sort of caged animal at a zoo.

Keeping a watchful eye on the mirror that had been with me for as long as I could remember, I approached it once more. I studied it, biting on the tip of my thumb, wondering if I should really bring him back. *Summoning him* actually felt like the right words to use.

Who knew that my blood and a mirror could be used to actually summon…

I placed my hand on the stained wood and called his name as the gears in my head kept turning at lightning speed.

What the hell was he exactly?

The black eyes and blood elements didn't exactly make it seem like I was getting into anything good. It was more like the start of a horror film. I couldn't imagine that anything pleasant could come from this—although, the sex had a tight grip on me and my memory at the moment. I tried to push those images away to get into the headspace I needed to be in for his return.

I searched the mirror, nervously waiting. I even glanced back to see if he had magically appeared over my shoulder like he had the last time.

Nothing.

"Kade. We need to talk. Now." I didn't bother with pleasantries as I tried to gather what little gumption I could muster.

As I took a step back, his reflection suddenly appeared above my shoulder. Not letting it startle me this time, I swiveled to face him. He still wore the same jeans, and nothing else. His dark hair was still an unruly mess that I couldn't wait to get my fingers twisted in. I bit my tongue to try and reel myself back in before I began. I had to stay strong and keep my lustful thoughts under control.

"Did you have anything to do with my dresser being moved?" I gushed without delay, an accusation evident.

His dark brows furrowed and his reply was short. "No."

My eyes narrowed, unsure of him and his quick response.

He sighed, his square shoulders visibly lowering. "You have a habit of slamming your drawers. Your grandma used to get after you for that." He gestured toward the dresser.

I scoffed. "You're telling me you had nothing to do with my dresser moving, which led to my injury, which in turn caused my foot to bleed and release you from the mirror?" I paused for a moment, hoping that my drawn-out sentence made sense. I was a bit worked up and hadn't exactly planned out the conversation I was hoping to have. Now that the words were pouring out of my mouth, my accusation came across a little far-fetched, but how was I to know the extent of his…reach, from his world?

"When you first moved in, your mirror was over there." He pointed in the direction of the closet on the opposite side of the bed from the dresser.

He was right about that. It had been too close to the closet door and I kept hitting the dresser each time I opened it. That was why I'd made Brett assist me in moving it to the other side of my apartment.

"You slam your drawers so often that the dresser starts to move out from the wall. The floor in here isn't exactly level either, so you have that working against you. And while that was the first time you rammed your foot into the dresser, it's not the first time you had to move it back to its original place against the wall."

I clenched my mouth shut, recalling a time or two since I had been here when I had indeed moved the dresser back. I hadn't thought a thing about it. Now I'd jumped to a conclusion without thinking it through, and I didn't think I could blame sleep deprivation for my lack of reasoning. I had slept plenty of hours during the day thanks to him.

"I'm not allowed to interfere with your life, not until your blood releases me."

"So you just wait around in the hopes that I cut myself or do something stupid to let you out?"

"Exactly," Kade confirmed.

"Well, what if nothing ever happened? What if I went my whole life without summoning you?"

His face grew grim and his gaze dropped to the floor. "It has happened to others. I tried to remain optimistic that it wouldn't be the case with you. But even if you never summoned me, I am still only allowed one tethering to a human."

That rule, as well as the five-night courtship, was definitely crap. People could have multiple partners and marriages throughout their lives and yet he was only allowed one tethering? And—to a *human*? I had known there was something otherworldly about Kade, and his words only further solidified it.

"What are you exactly?" I had a few ideas as to what he was, but I was hoping he would prove me wrong. "You said you find the wrongdoers of this world and monitor others like me. Who—or better yet, *what*—would be responsible for doing that?"

"What do you think I am?" He sat on the armrest of my sofa and crossed his arms, his expression guarded.

"No, I don't want to speculate. I want answers." I placed my hands on my hips and spread my stance enough to balance my weight evenly.

His eyes bore into mine and a moment passed before the word escaped his lips. "Demon."

With that short reply, it was as if the world around me faded away and my ears started ringing in the silence between my four walls.

"Great, I summoned a fucking demon." I threw my hands up in irritation. What the hell had I gotten myself into?

"I'm not a demon trying to steal your soul or cause misery and strife." He seemed almost offended.

"Right!" I raised my voice, sarcasm evident. I fell back onto my bed and cupped my hands over my face. This wasn't going to end well. "You just want me to leave with you."

"I'm not evil, as you might define it, and I would never do you any harm. I have a purpose." His voice pleaded with an earnestness I tried not to fall for. While I wanted to hear him out, I was still hung up on my small victory—one of my guesses as to what he was had been right.

"But I'm no saint either."

"Is that supposed to make me feel any better?" I stared up

at the shadows cast on the flat white ceiling above.

I had let a demon come into my home. Even worse, now with my permission. Sure, the initial release had been unbeknownst to me, but I'd let him come back again. Twice.

Oh, dear god, I had fucked a demon. I had let him into my home and encouraged him to screw me.

How was this even a possibility? Demons were supposed to be things of movies and fairytales, not real life. If demons were possible, what else was?

"I know this is a lot to take in. No doubt it's overwhelming."

"You got that right." Overwhelming was just the tip of the iceberg.

"Just allow yourself to believe what I've told you so far is true. Could you answer me one thing?" Kade's soft voice was distant, and I couldn't tell if he was still in the living room or if he had crossed over to my bathroom.

"What?" I sat up to see him standing in front of me and I was confused by how quickly he had come to be there. I couldn't hide my surprise at his abrupt closeness.

He knelt down in front of me on his knees, and when he opened his eyes, I was captivated again by that black abyss. They managed to take my breath away and I noticed how they reflected nothing—not my own silhouette or the shine from my lamp. Intriguing.

"You accepted me last night as I am before you now. And now, knowing what you do…" He swallowed hard before continuing. "Would you allow me to see this courtship through, to be a part of your life so that you can finally get the chance to know me in return?"

My lips pressed into a line as I turned my head away, unsure of how to respond. In this moment he didn't frighten me, and I truly didn't want to believe that he was evil, as any demon mythology might suggest. He swore that he would never do me any harm and proclaimed that he even loved me. But the very fact that he was asking for my permission on the matter was a quality that I admired.

What exactly was I living for? What was my purpose in life? My goals? None came to mind, which made me feel pathetic. Was that a good enough excuse to cave and let him in?

At twenty-three years old I still had no idea who I was or what I wanted out of life. And here Kade was—taking tall, dark, and handsome to a whole new level with black eyes that I could get lost in for days if I allowed it. But for right now, all he was asking for was for me to get to know him.

Could I? Was it possible to entertain this and not find doom at the end? Would I regret not taking this chance to get to learn all I possibly could about him?

I should have asked him to leave the moment he uttered the word *demon*, yet here I was, allowing myself to be in company with him. I couldn't believe I was considering riding out this tethering courtship thing of his.

Returning my attention to him, I placed my hands in my lap and knotted my fingers together before realizing what I was doing and stopped.

My whisper might not have been the answer he was expecting, but a part of me wanted to explore what this was. Even if it was against my better judgment.

"Maybe."

CHAPTER 6

Violet

"So if I were considering this tethering thing..." I began as we sat across from each other on my bed. Fully clothed, I might add. Well, in my case anyway.

I'd asked him to stay a while in hopes that I might get to know him and this situation better. It wasn't like I was tired enough to sleep anyway. Might as well make good use of my time.

"Can I ever come back and visit? Or do I just vanish forever without a trace? Do I have to die or something?"

"You really know how to pile on the questions, don't you?" A playful smirk crossed his lips and I couldn't deny the ease it made me feel.

"I've got a lot to learn before I make an informed decision."

"Fair. Solid point."

Kade stretched out on the bed, elongating his torso and making his stomach dip, arms behind his head as he made himself comfortable. The pull of his muscles in the movement was a pleasing distraction and I reluctantly dragged my gaze away before he could catch my lingering stare.

"You can visit, yes. Once a year, humans can cross over to visit family and loved ones, should you desire. But you can only do so during a designated time. To answer your second question, you can leave your home here on good terms. Tell them you're traveling or whatever story you would like to construct."

Well that didn't seem so bad.

"And you must be living in order to cross over into my plane of existence."

"I don't have to die here or there?" I didn't do well at hiding my surprise, but I wanted it confirmed again, regardless. There was a demon on my bed, after all.

"No," he laughed. "You're still very much alive. When you cross over and accept the tethering, you'll stop aging too."

Stop aging.

The thought of it was a point of interest that I hadn't really considered the possibility of since I was a kid. Who didn't fantasize about that? It was probably around the same time I was mixing potions in the shower and had plans of becoming a popstar when I was older.

"That is always a cause of concern to those considering the tethering and the life it brings with it. You will not age as you will become immortal, but everyone you know here will still carry on in the game of life. And visiting doesn't come without its own dangers. I have to be honest with you."

"Dangers? What kind of dangers?" My eyes devoured his body once more before settling on his face. I couldn't seem to focus on anything else in my apartment for more than a few seconds.

"The most obvious danger is that the people you visit could realize you're not aging. And when you come back, you're vulnerable, a human in the human world. Thirdly, my kind may not reside here on this plane of existence, but there are others that do."

"Others?" I repeated after him as I lay on the bed beside him on my back. I had left the bedside lamp on and it was the only thing emitting light in my small living space. I focused on the circled shadow from the shade that was cast onto the ceiling.

"They call themselves saints. They try to keep all human souls here and, on this plane, regardless of what chaos or mayhem they might bring about. They also don't agree with our customs—like that of the tethering. They don't like how we remove a perfectly healthy body and soul from this world and move it to another. They believe that everyone should be born, live, and die here. Nobody is an exception or above that rule. Meanwhile they get to live and roam free here, as if they were normal human beings." He scoffed. "I shouldn't be telling you this but…you work with one."

I shot up in bed and twisted my upper half toward him. "What? Who? How do you know?" I rolled my eyes as I made the connection before he had to say anything. "Of course, you've had your eyes on me for years. Still creepy, by the way."

That earned a small curve of his mouth into a partial smile, but it disappeared as quickly as it came. "Over time they have come to realize just how easy it is for us to see them, but some have learned how to skate by with minimal detection. They use what we call deflections. Not only do they have the ability to change their appearance but they can project that of another in the reflections they cast. It's not an easy skill to come by."

My heart began to race, needing a name at this point. "There's only nine other people at my work besides me. Who is it?"

He stilled for a moment and I wondered if he was even breathing before he finally answered, "Your manager."

"What, Damian? My boss? No way, he can't be." I waved away the thought of it.

"It makes perfect sense. He is in a position of power and is able to keep tabs on you a guaranteed five days a week. I am also willing to bet you that there are no mirrors at your work."

"But why on earth would he need to keep tabs on me? It makes no sense."

"His kind monitors humans to some degree like we do, but more so the lives of people who cheat death. There's been a target on your back since you were a child and you had no idea. He will either try to claim you for himself or get you killed. You never know where you stand with them."

"That's crazy."

"I agree. He might never commit the act himself, but he can sure see it through."

I gazed into his eyes, still not accepting the words that were coming from his mouth. "The CEO, my manager, is not a so-called saint."

"Definitely not in the term you're used to."

Kade sat up and crossed his legs, facing me. "Believe me or not, you can't let him know that I'm here or that you know what you do. Not only are you in danger during our courting, but should you decide *not* to come with me, there will always be a target on your back."

"If you're trying to scare me into accepting this tethering, it won't work. I've been fine up until now."

"But you have been in the dark about our world until now. What you have learned in our time spent together so far, you can never, ever repeat." The seriousness of his tone made me want to believe that all of this was true, but it was still hard to fathom nonetheless.

"If anything, please trust that I do love you and I want no harm to come to you. Not now, not ever. I only want what's best for you. And whether it's with me or not, that's entirely up to you."

I couldn't afford to dwell on his declaration of love, so I attempted to bypass it and not acknowledge it this go-around. "I've worked with him for a year and a half. There's nothing odd or fishy or… How the heck do I know if you're telling me the truth now?" I was getting worked up again, frustrated.

"Hold that thought." He held up a finger, then crawled off the bed and took off toward the bathroom. Without turning a light on, I could hear him rummaging through the drawers of the vanity. What on earth could he possibly be looking for in there?

When he returned, he carried a small compact mirror that had to have been buried deep in my makeup drawer. It was a turquoise sequined compact that I'd found for about a dollar when checking out at the local grocery store. I mean, when it was that cheap, why not? The fact that he had known about it was once again proof of how long he had been watching me. I had purchased that thing before I'd even moved into this place.

He proceeded to walk toward the standing mirror and opened the dual-surfaced compact. What happened next had me inching toward the side of my bed. I had never seen Kade actually make contact with a mirror until now. It was always like a magic trick, appearing in a moment and then gone the next.

He stuck his compact-filled hand through the glass up to his wrist. I blinked hard, doing a double take to make sure I was actually witnessing this. His hand vanished from all visibility, leaving a water-like ripple effect on the mirrored surface. When he pulled it back out and within sight, my compact looked no different.

Well, that was anticlimactic.

I didn't know what I'd expected to happen, but I was disappointed with the fact that nothing seemed to have changed. The disappearing act of his hand, however, was a sight that I hadn't anticipated.

"Here." He held the compact out to me and I hesitated before taking it. "Use this if you don't believe me."

"What did you do to it?" I asked, examining it as I flipped it over in my hand, shutting it and then reopening it only to find my green eyes staring back at me. The metal was chillier than it should have been from being buried in my drawer.

"Absolutely nothing."

I turned my attention back to him. "What…"

He beamed adorably from ear to ear. Just like he had earlier when he had tricked me into hitting my heels together three times in the pretense of getting him to reappear.

"You jerk!" I launched myself at him, but playfully this time, remembering how my knuckles had felt when they made contact with him.

"I'm sorry, I just wanted to see your face when I did that." He laughed as he embraced my attack with a cold hug, locking me in place.

It made my nipples stand at attention to have him in such close proximity. His body temperature was another curiosity of mine. The cold radiated through the cotton fabric of my tank top as if I had walked outside in the dead of winter in below-freezing temperatures.

"Damn! Why are you so cold?" I giggled as I tried to separate from him. You would swear I was being tickled by my frantic cackle of a voice.

He stilled around me, and I allowed myself a moment to relax. Not only did we fit well together when we were cuddled close, but even just standing here it felt…right.

"I could ask you why you're so…for lack of a better term, hot."

I smirked as I turned my attention to his bare skin in front of me. I ran my hands across his chest and up his shoulders. It was as if he had been out shoveling snow in his jeans-only attire, but instead of turning purple from the winter weather, he remained gloriously beautiful.

Touching him was putting my head and body on the same track and all I could think about was last night. I wanted our coupling to happen again, and badly. My body agreed and I could feel myself priming and gearing up for him.

My heart sped up at the thought of connecting like that again. I'd thought I had concocted the whole encounter in my mind, but even knowing what I did now, I still wanted him. I couldn't deny it even if I wanted to. Only now we weren't surrounded in a cloudy darkness distorting my view. The glow of my lamp illuminated us and there was no hiding, no concealment. It was as if I were seeing him for the first time.

"I'd very much like to kiss you again," he whispered low, and I resisted my knees' urge to buckle.

I couldn't be certain, but the lowering of his eyelids made me wonder if he was focused on my lips. His confession made me clench my thighs together.

I'd already had sex with him once and I'd come out unharmed. Could I allow myself to submit to him again now, knowing the truth? Was it worth it?

"Where?" I was already breathless and I murmured my query for his ears only.

Reaching for the hem of my tank, I tugged it up and over my head and dropped it to the floor. I drew in an unsteady inhale, my breasts pressing up against him.

Kade drew a finger up the length of my spine, causing me to arch into him. He leaned in toward my ear, his response hushed. "Everywhere."

His chilled lips pressed into the nape of my neck and I surrendered to him. He lifted me as though I were weightless and gracefully laid me back onto my bed. He trailed kisses down, all the way to the top of my pajama bottoms, but those didn't stop him. It was almost agonizing how slowly he drew the material down, following it with his mouth all the way to my feet. When he reached the end and the last of my clothing was gone, he removed his pants with ease.

I now had no regrets whatsoever about having the bedside lamp on.

I was almost intimidated by the length and girth of his cock as it sprang free. I shouldn't have been, considering that he had already pounded his member into me last night, but nothing could hide my astonishment. I knew it read across my face when he approached me, crouching onto the bed with a sexy smirk. My mouth went dry and the sweet spot between my legs began to ache. My nether regions screamed that my body was ready, but my mind wasn't so sure.

Before he could fully position himself on top, I held out a hand, halting him. "Wait."

His smirk left and confusion followed. I rolled out from beneath him and pulled my hair to one side. "Sit up against the headboard," I instructed him as I held my breath.

Kade studied me for a moment before following my order and relocating himself. I contemplated what I wanted to do next, knowing that the quiet between us wouldn't last long.

A part of me wanted to straddle him and take the lead. After all, he'd said that I was in charge when it came to the decisions I had to make. It was my choice to accept or deny the tethering, and when I said I needed some time away from him he'd been gone in a flash.

Another part wanted to return the favor and kiss every limb and every muscle on his body, the way he had done with me. But then, maybe I just wanted to sit here and admire his body. Watch him for a change.

Swiveling to bring my legs around to my front, I hugged them to my chest. Resting my chin upon my knees, I let my eyes follow each curve and line on him. I was mesmerized as I took in the sight that he was.

His erection never faltered, and he was as still as a statue minus the occasional blink and the rise and fall of his steadied breath. I didn't think I could have dreamed up a body as perfect as his even if I tried. I marveled at the spectacle of him, tilting my head to the side.

There were things I wanted to do to him that I had never wanted to do with any other man I had ever been with. I hugged my legs tighter as my mind wandered. I would probably let him do just about anything he wanted to me as well.

"Enjoying the view?"

I grinned as I let out a sigh. "Seems only fair since you've had years to gaze upon me. Well, watch me," I corrected.

"You make it sound as if I watch you twenty-four hours a day and seven days a week."

"How do I know that you don't?" I countered.

"Because I have twenty-seven others that I am watching." He didn't miss a beat. "And as much as I would love to fixate on you and you only, I might miss other happenings if I were to gaze upon the curvy goddess that you are at every second of every day."

"Ha!" I burst out, real smooth and perhaps a bit over-the-top. I couldn't say that I had ever heard anyone utter that kind of sentiment when referring to me before though.

"I told you I would never lie to you." His lips pressed into a thin line as he leaned away from the headboard and my head popped up at his movement.

"Have you ever been with anybody else?" I asked before I could think it through. Did I really want to know the answer to that? He had never been tethered to anybody else, so on the human side of things I was sure the answer was no. But I had no idea about the others like him.

He stilled, face frozen. "In what sense? Sex?"

Hearing him say it out loud made me feel as if I were shrinking in size. Why on earth did I feel the need to ask him this? I wouldn't exactly be thrilled if the tables were turned and he asked me. Although, if he already knew so much, he would already know the answer.

I shook my head. "Never mind."

"I have not had sex since my request to tether to you," he declared.

My mouth twisted to the side and eyes squinted, unsure about his quick response.

"I promise you I have not. Others of my kind have tried to approach me, don't get me wrong. I just never felt the urge to engage in that kind of relationship with them. Once my eyes fell on you, nobody else even mattered."

He definitely had a way with words, I'd give him that.

Kade knew how to make a woman like me feel important, wanted, and needed.

"So last night was your first time in…a while."

I found that hard to believe. His control, his demeanor, the way he asked for permission to pleasure or kiss me—I didn't understand that a man of his magnificence could have waited so long, and for me for that matter. And the fact that he didn't explode the moment he entered me was another curious feat. My junior year though, had he really waited that long?

"That is correct," he confirmed. "I waited for you because you're the only one I wanted to experience it again with."

Well that was incredibly hot. But it also made me feel insecure about my past encounters. If I included the one-time fling with the jerk that I lost my virginity to in high school, I'd had four partners, and he had waited it out for me in that same timeframe. For years.

Guilt began to consume me as I realized he probably knew that number and worse, he'd even seen me with those other guys. A self-loathing began to settle in my gut.

"Was it hard? Seeing me with them?" Why did it feel like I had been cheating on him? Why did I feel so guilty for somebody who had been watching me with the hopes of claiming me as his own? It was bizarre that these thoughts were even crossing my mind.

"It was very…difficult."

Kade got that far-off gaze in his eyes again as if he were trying to look out the covered windows. Even though his eyes were completely black, I knew they were going off into an uncomfortable place—I could see it in his grim expression. I could only imagine the imagery springing to his mind.

Breaking free of my pose, I moved over to straddle him, certainly catching his attention in more ways than one as his shaft bumped up against my core between my legs. Putting my hands on the sides of his face, I stared into his eyes. Even though I was inches away, I still couldn't make out any kind of reflection in them. They were a strange and alluring part of him, one thing that visibly separated us as human and demon.

"I'm sorry." I spoke softly.

"Oh Violet." He turned into my palm and kissed it, cradling it with his own hand. "You don't need to apologize. You had no idea of my existence until last night. It's not like you did it on purpose."

"No, but I am sorry that you have those images in your head. Believe me, I wish I could erase them. All of them, in fact."

I shook my head. Some of those experiences I undoubtedly wanted extinguished from my mind. It was embarrassing and saddening to think of what he had seen. None of those encounters or relationships had led to anything of value; looking back, they felt more like learning experiences than anything else.

However, I didn't want to dwell on the past as I couldn't change any of it. For now, I just needed to do all that I could to make the both of us forget. I wanted the chance to see if last night was a fluke or if we could rekindle what we had experienced.

Rising slightly to hover above his shaft, I placed one hand on his chest and the other found its way toward his member. I positioned him at the angle I needed, gathering up all my courage to take him inside of me. His breath caught as my warm hand wrapped around him.

I shuddered just as I had last night; the temperature difference between his length and my heat were polar opposites. The shock wore off as I continued to take him in, and slow and steady we began to adapt to each other. His hands were on my waist, guiding me down with slight pressure but not tugging.

Capturing his mouth, I whimpered into him as I let him enter me fully. That same taste of liquor lingered on his tongue, a memory that I now knew was so much more than an erotic, fantasy-type dream.

I wasn't sure if I could even move at the moment. My body throbbed around him as I tried to settle and adjust to his presence.

"Are you alright?" His lips brushed against mine as I remained frozen in place.

I hesitated. "Mmm…" I let my forehead rest against his as I tried to slow my breathing.

I was hyperaware of everything between us. He was buried much deeper inside of me than I could recall. Granted, we were in a position that would allow for that, but I'd had no idea just how different he would feel.

Taking a deep breath, I began to move. Kade's hands relocated to my behind and his fingers dug into my flesh as I braced myself on his shoulders. With one long, drawn-out kiss and a few glides along his shaft, I was beginning to gain momentum.

My breasts began to bounce as I continued to ride him up and down. My hair swayed lightly across my back with each movement that I made.

Whether he was a man, demon, or the combination of both, I couldn't deny the connection we had. As much as I wanted to fight against this unknown territory, I also wanted to succumb to it. I knew I couldn't base our relationship off of this bed that we seemed to work so well in, but hey, it didn't hurt either. This was one area I had never been fully satisfied in until now.

Until him.

Kade's hands began to roam my body, kneading my flesh with his palms and working his way toward my chest. They weren't the perkiest, I would be the first to admit. But the way he cradled them in his grasp made me realize that he didn't care. I smiled, reflecting on the way he had teased them last night and the attention they had received. He could touch me anywhere and I think I would revel in the sensations he provided.

"Beautiful," he murmured as he placed a kiss to my clavicle. A blush overcame me and I didn't have it in me to respond to his compliment even though I enjoyed it.

Perhaps a bit forward, I led his hand down my stomach and toward my clit. I slowed down so I could guide his hand to where I needed him to go. I watched his gaze as he followed our hands down to the little bead that I selfishly wanted him to caress. I took his thumb and began to swirl it around in a circular motion. It had been a while since I had been touched there by a man, and he took direction quite well.

"Don't stop," I instructed as I released his hand.

The instant my hand left, he applied more pressure and I moaned. He was quick to accommodate and he moved with ease around and around as I began to rise and fall on him again. I began to climb quickly and I tried to brace myself on the headboard behind him.

Our breaths mingled in a frantic mess. I wanted to capture his mouth once again but I was afraid of ruining what I almost had. Ecstasy was just beyond my fingertips and I could taste it, the build was strong.

"I'm so close, Kade," I panted, my voice rising.

A few more swirls and he had me undone. My body began

to spasm but he kept going. My movements slowed as I rode out the waves of pleasure that washed over me. He all but bucked into me a few more times, and then found his release. Our bodies rocked into one another as we secured our limbs, letting our euphoric eruption run its course.

When the night had begun, I didn't think I would ever be able to get any sleep. And after another round on the bed with Kade, I still didn't have the urge to drift off.

For the first time in my life, I felt thoroughly fucked, and I was beyond thrilled and sated.

I thought it amusing when he disclosed just how many people had a kink for screwing around in front of mirrors. He said with some people it was almost the equivalent of a porn channel. I recalled the desire I had felt last night for a mirror, to be able to see his body move against mine in the reflection, but I was beginning to second-guess everything in my life right about now.

"Don't you ever feel like you're invading their privacy?" I inquired as my fingers intertwined with his. The soft glow from the bathroom night-light that I had decided at the last minute to plug in provided enough illumination for me to examine his long fingers—fingers that had explored about every inch of me tonight.

"Yes and no. It's complicated."

"How so?" I pushed, wanting to know more.

Kade turned to his side and propped our hands up on his chest, securing my fingers in his. "If they are recording themselves, they obviously want to be seen. Especially nowadays with social media so easily ready at their fingertips. If it's obviously a private moment with individuals that have no history of violence or abuse, I usually don't pay any mind and move on."

"You make it sound as easy as turning a channel."

He laughed a bit and the sound brought a comfort to my chest. "Actually, it is."

I propped myself up onto my elbows so I could look him in the face. "Please explain. Because I'm imagining a room full of televisions and a universal remote." Was it just like some sort of security room? Multiple views from security cameras that were actually reflective surfaces? "Would I be allowed to see it?"

He grinned at my inquiry as his eyelids drooped down as if he were looking down at our hands. At times, his black eyes made it hard to tell where exactly he was focusing, but the longer we were together, the more I was able to decipher. Or so I thought. "Should you choose to come with me, I would gladly take you into my watching quarters. You would be no stranger to it."

"Is that your job title? Watcher? Still sounds stalker-ish."

"Again, let me reiterate that my job is to find wrongdoers and monitor them. People who commit crimes and deserve eternal damnation. In some cases, we are called in to exact punishment ourselves, but—"

"Exact punishment?" I interrupted. "Have you ever done that?"

"I have."

"What do you do, exactly?" I could feel my heartbeat quicken. What was worse, watching people without their knowledge, or punishing them? Kade referring to himself as a demon came to my mind, and as much as I strangely admired his pitch-black eyes, it sent a shiver through me to think about him carrying out the latter of those tasks.

His brows furrowed as he sat up in bed. The sheet barely covered his member and I pushed away the thoughts of it penetrating me.

"Every situation is different. We might shift and moonlight as a civilian if punishment is to be done out in the open and in the public eye. Like a police officer, for example. Or, if the perpetrator is alone, we can collect them and stage it to look like an accident or self-inflicted."

"So…you've killed people." My throat went dry just thinking about him taking a life and I rolled myself onto my back. This certainly felt worse than the watching aspect of his so-called job.

"The people who get to the point where we have to intervene have committed much worse." His lips pressed into a thin line. "They would continue to do much worse until—"

"So you, and others like you, are playing God." I sat up and hugged the sheet around me. This was a lot of information to take in from a man I was screwing around with. A demon, to be exact.

"Think of it this way. There are two sides of the equation. We try to stop these people before they can do any more damage, cause any more unnecessary harm and lives lost. Saints like your boss try to keep these people—murderers, rapists, and so on—here no matter what terror or strife they cause. Their problem lies with the ones who cheat death, not the ones who are the very problem to begin with."

I mulled over this information in my head, thinking about how the roles of demon and saint seemed to be flip-flopped from what I would have believed prior to today.

But how could Damian possibly be a saint? I found it difficult to consider that he had a target on my back. And why would he be okay with killers on the loose that keep killing, but not alright with me surviving a car accident and an overdose?

"Look—" Kade leaned forward and rested a hand on my knee poking out from the sheet. "I can only imagine how much this is for you to process right now, but you deserve to know. I will try to answer every question you throw my way, and attempt to soothe every doubt in your head in the hopes that you might understand me and my world. I've had years to get to know you and I know it pales in comparison to the five nights I'm allowed to court you. It's not a fair trade, and I apologize for that."

I didn't want to be rendered speechless, but I was.

I wanted to be alarmed at the information he was sharing, but I was ashamed that I wasn't. I had more questions to ask, but the images I had concocted with the information given to me tonight already had my mind spinning.

He had a body count that I didn't want to acknowledge any further at the moment. Of course this man was too good to be true—that seemed to be my luck when it came to men in general. I supposed I could add demon men to that list now.

"Breathe, Violet."

I hadn't realized I'd been holding my breath, and I took in a staggered gasp of air. "I…I need a minute."

Leaving the bed, I crossed the short distance to the bathroom and closed the door with a click. The conflicted emotions coursing through me had me shaking and the temperature of the apartment had nothing to do with it. I tried to splash some water on my face but my hands still shook.

Demon. Watcher. Killer.

Why wasn't I running for the hills? Why hadn't I asked him to leave? Why wasn't I terrified of his very existence and the notion of him asking me to tether to him at the end of this courtship? This was insane!

I was only a human and a demon was asking for forever with me. How was I even considering this? Why was I so worked up over it all?

And—demons versus saints? This was too much to wrap my head around.

Deciding I needed more time, I turned the knob on the shower and cranked up the heat. I let the steam hit my face before I finally stepped in. The sting from the water radiated through me as I raised my forearms above and crossed them, letting my head rest against the tiled wall.

My back began to turn numb and I could imagine how red and inflamed my skin was turning. I struggled to focus on my breath and the blazing water, attempting and willing myself to focus on those two things and nothing more.

Flashes from our time together kept barging through and mixing with my preconceived ideas of his time spent away from me. The air in the shower felt heavier as I continued my slow and steady breaths.

He knew so much and I knew so little. How could I possibly get to know this man in five nights and make an informed and life-changing decision?

"Violet?"

Kade's voice broke through the downpour of water and the velvety sound made my shoulders sag. My mind was in turmoil because of him and yet my body craved his presence to settle down. I couldn't make heads or tails of any of it.

The metal shower curtain rings screeched to the side but he came to a halt. "Do you want me to leave?"

My eyes shot open as I turned to take in the sight of him. The night-light plugged into the wall highlighted his cheekbones and every rise and fall of his muscled pectorals. I reached for his hand and pulled him into the shower with me and he obliged. I half expected him to make a remark at the scalding water but he remained stoic, eyes fixated on me, guarded.

"Just be here."

My voice was barely audible as I closed my arms around him and placed my cheek against his chest. An arm settled around my waist as his other hand came to rest on my shoulder.

"I'm here."

CHAPTER 7

Violet

"I hate to be the bearer of bad news, but if you're going to work today, you'd better wake up."

I grumbled in protest as I began to stretch my limbs. My eyes were still heavy with lack of sleep; my nap during the day yesterday had messed with my usual routine and schedule. "What about you, do you have to work today?"

"That I do, but I thought I'd see you off first."

Kade peppered me with kisses as I tried to blink the sleep away from my eyes. As I turned, he found his way toward my lips.

"If I didn't know any better, I would say you're trying to get me to stay," I mused as I broke away.

A charming grin etched across his face as he responded, "Always."

I sat up and tried to clear my eyes of any sleepers that might have gathered. Glancing at my phone, I realized I had the bare minimum of time to get ready for work.

"Shit." I stumbled out of bed and darted for the bathroom. Making quick work of my hair, I braided it down the side and hastily applied some makeup to make myself presentable. Throwing on my satin green robe, I scurried out and toward my closet. Kade sat against the headboard observing me, looking mighty delectable as the sheet barely covered a quarter of him. His aroused member drew my attention, and I could feel my cheeks aflame.

"I do recall saying *if* you go to work today." He leaned forward, smirking. I rolled my eyes as I busied myself, trying to resist the urge to crawl back into bed and call in sick.

Once I retrieved my work shirt for casual Friday, I headed to the dresser and found my undergarments and denim capris. I gave the drawer a shove with my behind and the *bang* as it closed caused me to pause and glance back at it.

Damn, I really did have a bad habit of slamming the drawers hard.

I had a fleeting moment of embarrassment that I had tried to blame Kade for moving the dresser, but I pushed it aside and carried on. I scurried back to the bathroom and as I finished getting ready, a thought hit me. Once dressed, I rounded the corner and almost ran right smack into him.

"Sorry, um..." I tried to collect my thoughts as I examined him. I could have sworn he had arrived in jeans yesterday but now he was clad in sweatpants and—very clearly—nothing underneath that. I dragged my gaze up to meet his, heart still an erratic mess. "A date," I stammered.

Kade cocked an eyebrow and I spoke up, clearer this time and direct.

"Take me on a date tonight." I didn't even pose it as a

question, it was more of an order. "Whatever you want to do, let's do it. Don't even think about what I would like, just take me somewhere you want to go."

I was hopeful that he would take this opportunity and run with it. I needed to get to know who Kade was and what he liked to do and his interests. I crossed my arms and waited for him to respond, but quickly grew impatient.

"I need to know that we can get along and have enough in common outside the walls of this apartment. I can't base this, whatever it is that we are, on sex and sex alone." To be honest, it freaked me out in the best way how well we worked together when it came to that act, but there had to be more if I was seriously going to consider his proposal, and time was not on our side. Our courting would be halfway over by tonight and that thought was unsettling.

"And when should I expect to be summoned?" He took a step closer and pulled me into him by the belt loop at my hip, his erection pressing into me so hard that my knees almost caved.

"About six-thirty," I suggested. My heart never lessened in its pounding.

His mouth came down on mine and I returned his fervor. When I pulled away, I was breathless, but in the best way possible.

"It's a date." He kissed my hand and I leaned against the corner of the wall to brace myself. As he parted ways with me and started to make his way toward my mirror, he offered a small bow of his head.

"Have a good day at work."

He flashed his handsome smile and stepped through the mirror right side first, dipping a shoulder through the narrow frame so it would accommodate his height. The glass had a rippling effect as he departed, and my mouth dropped in astonishment. This was the first time I had actually witnessed him leave this way. I recalled him extending his hand through last night, but watching his entire body disappear into a solid object left me speechless.

I crossed my bedroom for a closer look and hesitantly reached for the glass. Would I feel anything after his disappearance? My eyes darted around, examining the mirror as I stretched an arm out toward it. A small ripple produced a hand that shot out of the mirror; its fingers latched onto mine and I yelped at the sudden contact.

"Oh my god, Kade!" His head appeared over my shoulder next to my reflection, but when I turned my head, he wasn't there. I couldn't put into words the fascination and curiosity that arose within me. "How did you...?" I returned to our combined reflection and stared in awe.

"You're going to be late for work," he whispered into my ear. The gust of air from his words sent a shiver down my spine. How could he possibly do that?

Releasing my hand, he faded away, and the mirror returned to its normal state. Lightly, I tapped the glass, but nothing happened. No ripple, just a smudge of my fingerprint that now tainted the clear reflection.

"No fucking way."

The changing of the time on my phone drew my attention and I grabbed it from the nightstand, making quick work of throwing on my shoes and retrieving my purse before running out the door.

Luckily traffic wasn't too bad and I made it into work at seven-thirty on the dot. Damian waved a hello from his office as I made my way in.

I stopped momentarily to return the gesture, an unease creeping in at the small act. I hoped it didn't read on my face as I tried to recover. I offered a polite smile and continued to my office.

Setting my things down and booting up my computer, I began to examine my surroundings. Kade had told me that there wouldn't be any mirrors around here and come to think of it, I couldn't recall a single one. I didn't want to start wandering around in search of mirrors or reflective surfaces, so I tried mentally running through each room in the building, trying to find something that would prove Kade wrong. I had once thought it odd there wasn't a mirror in the women's restroom, but then just shrugged it off and never gave it another thought.

I was so wrapped up in my own head and gazing at my computer screen that I hadn't even heard anyone approach my doorway. I jumped at the unexpected interruption of Damian clearing his throat.

"Have any better luck sleeping last night?" He stood in the doorway, arms crossed as if he had been there long enough to get comfy in his stance. I shook my head and let out an uneasy laugh. Deciding not to lie but not omit the truth either, I tried to keep it vague.

"Well, I slept the day away which kind of threw off my night schedule. But long story short, I am much better than I was yesterday, so thank you for the chance to go home."

Seeing as how I hadn't set my purse down under my desk yet, I opened it in search of my lipstick and found the compact mirror that Kade had given me. I nonchalantly took it and my lipstick out and opened up the mirror in my hand.

"No problem, glad you're doing better."

Damian shifted his weight before leaving and I flipped the mirror around in the hopes that if Kade was watching, he might catch a glimpse of him. But before Damian could completely disappear from view, his neck shuddered in an unnatural manner that traveled down the rest of his frame.

Panicked, I flipped the mirror around and acted like I was about ready to apply my lipstick. It had to be a coincidence, right? Maybe he had walked past an air vent or something. But an uneasy pit in my stomach opened up and I froze as my mirror fogged over.

It was as if someone was writing with their finger on the glass and a message began to form.

STAY AWAY FROM HIM.

I tried to swallow the lump in my throat but it felt stuck. There was no doubt that the message was from Kade and I could only assume that he was the one who had snuck the compact into my purse in the first place. I mouthed an "okay" before shutting the mirror and depositing it back in my purse.

The day seemed to crawl, which felt all wrong given how busy it was. I had people in and out of my office all morning, emails pouring in, and nonstop interruptions. I would briefly get the chance to think ahead to tonight, just to be pulled back into the present. I was responding to an email when I answered the phone without looking at the caller ID.

"Hi, this is Violet," I chimed as I continued multitasking, plucking away at my keyboard.

"Free for lunch today?" The voice on the opposite end stilled me into a frozen state. I peeked at the name I wanted to forget sooner rather than later. Brett was far too chipper considering I had just broken up with him yesterday.

"Why are you calling me at work? I'm *working*." I made sure not to hide the annoyance in my voice even though I became hushed.

"I figured you might not respond if I texted you and I thought it more appropriate to call and ask."

"Well you figured part of that correctly. And you knew if you called me on my cell I wouldn't have answered." A coworker passed my door with a stack of folders and I turned my chair away. I cupped my hand over the phone, hoping to quiet my voice from prying ears. "I broke up with you, Brett. It's over. Please don't call me here again. Or on any device for that matter."

"You can't just throw what we have away." The volume of his voice rose and I became annoyed. How was he not understanding this?

"Had," I corrected. I took a beat for myself in the silence that followed. "It really is over."

"DAMMIT VI—"

Perhaps a bit too rough, I slammed the phone down to end the call. The anger that had erupted last night at my apartment was rearing its ugly head once more.

Brett didn't like it when things didn't go his way, but that was his problem to deal with, not mine. In the time that we had been dating, I had never experienced the temper that he was apparently capable of and it shook me. I felt lucky to have dodged the bullet with him and his planned proposal, but I had an inkling of suspicion that this wouldn't be the last time I heard from him, and that worried me.

"Everything okay, Violet?" Trisha, a short redhead who had passed by earlier with the files, was peeping into my office hesitantly.

I pinched the bridge of my nose and blinked hard a few

times, trying to regain my composure. "Yeah, yeah, everything is fine. Sorry, I didn't mean to hang up like that." I leaned my head from side to side, trying to release the effect of Brett's voice.

"I know it's none of my business, but…" She looked around before stepping into my office. "Is it alright if I close the door?"

I nodded as her small frame did just that and she twisted her freckled arms around in front of herself to the point that it looked uncomfortable. "Brett called and asked if you were working earlier and I told him you were. I'm sorry if I did something wrong."

My eyes fell to my desk and I was unsure of how to proceed. We weren't exactly up in each other's business, but we knew enough of each other from small talk and working together. Trisha had been here two years prior to my start. She was quiet and reserved in group settings, but if you got her alone, she seemed let loose a bit. I didn't take her for someone to stir the pot.

"You're fine, no worries. Apparently he has no idea how to put on his big boy pants and handle a breakup."

"I'm sorry."

"I'm not. And his attitude toward me and the situation makes me very happy I cut things off now rather than later." I didn't have the slightest bit of remorse about ending our relationship, and as much as I wanted to be comforted by the fact that it was over, Brett and his actions so far were doing nothing to aid in that.

"Oh, well there's your silver lining then." She offered a soft smile.

"I guess so. But if he calls inquiring about me again, will you please let me know?"

"Of course." She nodded and began to open my door back up.

"Any plans for the weekend?" She was trying to move the conversation in a more positive direction in case any ears around us might tune in. It was a small building so privacy wasn't exactly easy to come by. Even with the doors closed, the walls were thin.

"I'm going to the lake this weekend with my family. Birthday party for my niece. Pray I don't get sunburned." She imitated praying hands as she looked up toward the almighty power that might hang in the sky above. Her porcelain skin had seen the harsh side of the sun a few too many times and I felt for her. She hadn't put on sunscreen for our work picnic last year and she'd practically turned into a lobster. She couldn't even come into work for a few days after the fact.

"Well, please lather up with SPF 300 and take a giant sun hat with you." I grinned. "Better yet, how many umbrellas do you have?" I teased, and she wrinkled her petite nose.

"As for me, I'm not really sure what's on the agenda. I'm overdue for a visit to my grandma so maybe I'll go see her."

I couldn't exactly tell her that I planned on getting to know a certain black-eyed demon over the weekend who wanted to steal me away in a few days' time, so I kept my response as plain and boring as possible.

My phone began ringing again and I held my breath as I looked at the caller ID. Letting out a sigh of relief, I waved Trisha goodbye and picked it up, returning to my seemingly menial tasks.

A short while later, an email notification came through on my screen from Damian, addressed to everyone at work.

Getting lunch from Jeri's and it should be here about 12:30. Let me know if you want anything.

It wasn't unusual for Damian to order lunch for us occasionally, but today I began to question every little thing involving him. Greeting me first off, the strange shiver that had run through him when I'd turned my compact mirror toward him, and now this email—it all had my brain scrambled. Mix that in with Brett and the demon-courting, and I wasn't sure why I wasn't headed for the hills.

Not once had I ever pegged that something was amiss about Damian prior to today, but maybe I was being overly critical. Perhaps I was looking for something that simply wasn't there.

Of course I was going to worry about it now that something like this had been brought to my attention. Kade didn't seem to have that much intel on him, so maybe that would be something that I could bring up tonight on our date.

Not only did I want to see what Kade was like in the real world, but I truly did want to get to know him. I couldn't explain the attraction and fascination I had with him, but with this short timeframe that we had, I needed to see where this led.

I glanced around my office as I tapped my pen to my chin. Is this where I planned to be in five, maybe even ten years?

In fact, now that I truly thought about it, I had done very little to make this office my own. The same black-and-white forest landscape photos still hung in the same spots from the previous occupant. The same vendor magnets were stuck on the filing cabinets and hadn't moved, nor did I use them to hang pictures like others around the offices.

I loved flowers and knickknacks but I had none of that. I liked splashes of color that drew attention, but the only vibrant things in here were items that donned our work logo.

It was kind of disheartening to make the connection that

maybe in the back of my mind, I'd never really imagined myself here long-term. Maybe Kade, and his proposal, was the answer to my future? I couldn't fight the intrigue and appeal he held over me.

It was convenient that food showed up just as I was ready to head downstairs to the break room for my lunch. The smell from Jeri's made its way into my space and my stomach began to growl as I snatched my purse and followed the delicious scent downstairs.

Jeri's was your typical run-of-the-mill American restaurant that had everything from burgers and salads, to the best milkshakes you could get in town. That being said, along with my Cobb salad, I'd also ordered a large banana milkshake. In my opinion, you could not go to Jeri's without snagging one.

I took my labeled container and drink and settled down on the couch, tapping around my phone in search of something to watch as I ate. I nodded and exchanged brief pleasantries as my other coworkers came and went, collecting their lunches.

"Thank you for lunch, Damian!" Theresa exclaimed. She was the eldest who worked here with glasses and graying hair that was straight as a board. She refused to cut it to the "old-woman bob" as she referred to it. The long gray hair suited her though, and instead of waiting for the gray to take over at its leisurely pace, she had gone straight to the salon to make the change on her own terms. I thought her actions to own her changing appearance, rather than fighting it off, were admirable.

I sat up straighter in my seat and made eye contact with my supposed "saint" of a boss as he rounded the steps and came into view. "Yes, thank you." I awkwardly raised my milkshake in his direction.

"Not a problem. It's been a while since we did something for lunch." He disappeared behind me but I couldn't shake the feeling that his eyes were still on me as he collected his food.

"Mind if I join you?" Damian rounded the corner of the couch with his items in hand. No doubt he had ordered a burger and fries.

"Um, sure."

"I can go upstairs, it's no trouble." He leaned his body in that direction as if to take a step.

Taking a breath before I responded, I set my phone down in my lap. I motioned him to the other end of the couch, which seemed too close for comfort at present. "Don't be silly, it's your lunch hour too."

"Thanks." He sat and retrieved the remote for the television and clicked through until he found reruns of a popular show.

My appetite seemed to have flown out the window and I was on high alert.

Dammit, Kade. I almost wished he hadn't told me about Damian. I was still at war with myself over whether the "saint" information was true or not, and after Kade's mirror message this morning telling me to stay away, here I was doing the exact opposite.

I sat cross-legged as I picked at my meal. I had been starving when I first came down here, realizing that I hadn't had time for breakfast this morning. Now, any desire to eat had evaporated, but I still did my best to go through the motions.

"Should have gone with a burger," Damian boasted as he pulled me out of my thoughts.

"Huh?" I threw a quizzical look in his direction.

Viewing his profile, I couldn't help but admire the clean-cut lines of his facial hair and hairline. Every slant was so precise, not a rogue hair out of place. But it was almost too perfect. The very thought reminded me of how anal Brett had been over his appearance. That alone became an enormous and instant turnoff.

"You've barely made a dent in that thing. Is something wrong with it?"

"No, it's fine." Any other day before today, it would have been. "Thanks again for lunch."

"No problem. Though I still don't understand how people can fill up on a salad for a meal. I feel like I'm hungry within an hour after eating one."

"Maybe it's just your metabolism," I quipped.

"Maybe," he chuckled.

"I've got a shake that will last me a while too."

"Seems counteractive. Salad and a milkshake."

"It's all about balance. Be a little good, be a little bad." Regret hit me instantly as I said it. I had struggled with my weight for some time, and that was the reasoning for my balancing act when it came to food.

But now, between Kade and Damian, I didn't know what on earth was good or bad anymore. Who was right and wrong. I could see both sides to the saints and demons and their reasoning; but then, I was getting one-sided information. Did I owe it to myself to get Damian's point of view if he really was a saint, or would that just be asking for trouble? I didn't think Kade would take kindly to me taking it upon myself to find out.

Deciding to change the subject, I glanced at Damian's loaded burger and redirected us. "What are you up to this weekend?"

I tried to take another bite of my food but it seemed to be becoming more and more bland. It was as if all the flavor had become nonexistent.

"Not sure exactly. Most of my weekends have been booked up and this is my first free weekend I've had in a while. With the heat dying down, I might have to enjoy the outdoors a bit."

Damian had served as a coach on some baseball league in town, but to my knowledge he didn't have a family of his own or any known ties to the kids on that team. I couldn't even recall seeing or hearing him ever talk about a significant other of any sort.

Honestly, Damian was easy enough on the eyes, so why hadn't he snatched anybody up yet? He was fit, well-liked, and easy to talk to. He was involved in the community and honestly, the best boss I'd had up to this point in my life.

"Don't have a hot date or anything?" I teased, but instantly wanted to insert my foot into my mouth. What the hell was I thinking? This was a territory that didn't concern me.

"No, but I guess I should be asking you about that. What about Brett?" He kept his gaze on the television as I tried to gather my thoughts to the point where I could respond.

"We're no longer a...thing." I took another swig of my milkshake to chase down my lackluster food.

Damian's head swiveled in my direction and I froze, mouth on my straw. "Oh?"

I blinked. "Yeah, I broke it off."

"I'm sorry."

Why did everybody always say that when a relationship ended? I wasn't even broken up about it. In fact, zero tears had been shed since I had decided to cut Brett out of my life. I wasn't in mourning over the loss of him, so why did other people react like I should be?

"I'm not." I remembered his brief assault on my door at my apartment and his tone on the phone earlier. *Good riddance,*

I thought.

"Well, it's his loss."

"It is," I agreed, although I was unable to tell if there was any underlying meaning to his statement.

I began picking at the meat in my salad and left the rest alone as we continued our lunch break in silence. Nothing but the sounds of the show filled the break room now.

I hated that we couldn't continue our conversations or banter as we used to. It seemed as if Kade had robbed me of one of the simplest relationships in my life.

He had to be wrong about Damian, right?

CHAPTER 8

Kade

Elated. I had never experienced a feeling such as this before, never of this magnitude. It was as if I could breathe deeper. My chest expanded and my heartbeat was pounding away at the excitement of it all. I knew I was grinning like an idiot but I couldn't care less.

Sure, Violet and I might have gotten off to a rocky start last night, but when we parted this morning, it had seemed as if we might be right on track and moving toward where we needed to be.

I had hope. Hope that she might consider my offer. Hope that she might accept me and my world.

Retrieving a shirt from my closet, I popped into my watching quarters instead of taking the short stroll down the hallway to get there. I swiped across the first mirror I came to, hoping that Elias was awake and ready for company. Tapping the glass to the rhythm we had used for years, I waited for him to respond. It was a series of beats reserved for our contact with each other, and no one else. Our own secret code, if you will.

Any other boring day I would have chosen to go for a jog to cover the lengthy distance to his living quarters. I had found multiple routes in doing so over the years through the interconnected castle-like structures of Darthou. Elias had taken the chance when it was presented to move into the newer construction on the west end, and was one of its first tenants. It was a bit too sterile-looking and modern for my taste, but it was what he wanted.

I glanced around my space, not bothering with any lights in the hopes that I wouldn't be here long. Now that I had been in Violet's presence, my home almost felt lifeless in comparison. Her apartment, albeit small, had life to it. It was evident that she lived there. No, it wasn't spotless, but it was *hers* and everything had her touch. From the coverings on her windows to her choices in decor and color schemes, she had made it her own, no matter what that piece-of-shit Brett had to say in the matter.

Everything had its place here, and the vast room of my watching quarters was split off into sections as if by invisible walls. A couch was centered amongst the wall of mirrors and to be honest, I rarely used it. I often paced when watching, or if I was having an uneventful day I would run on the treadmill to keep my body moving. My desk and home office area were clearly separated from my workout equipment and its zone, and musical instruments took over the far back corner. That area could use some sprucing up, but that was the last thing on my mind right now.

I had very few ideas for my date with Violet tonight and I needed to bounce them off of someone, preferably Elias. I was interested in what he might have to say and if he could provide any suggestions on his end. I had to get this right.

"I hope it isn't a bad sign that you're contacting me this early," Elias answered through the mirror, his voice coming in pants of exertion, and I took that as my invitation.

I left my darkened quarters for his, a substantial amount of light assaulting my eyes the second I arrived. In my opinion, he had too many damn windows in his place, but I had to remember that I wasn't the one living here. His apartment was one of the few that had double-hung windows that allowed the outside world to be seen without any distortion. I didn't understand his need to see the never-changing frosted tree line outdoors. That was one thing I envied from Violet's world—the changing of seasons.

Some days Elias was an early riser. He would squeeze in workouts while watching and today must have been one of those days as his platinum hair was gathered on top of his head and he wore a pair of shorts, body drenched in sweat as if he had already been at it for some time now.

"She wants me to take her on a date."

Elias cocked an eyebrow as if he didn't know where I was headed with this. I noted a few more sports jerseys that he had added to his collection on the wall behind him. The guy was a die-hard fan of human sports and this room was like its own mini-museum of memorabilia. "And this is a problem because..."

"Because she wants me to decide what we do, where we go." I ran a hand through my hair, the scent of her shampoo a reminder of our shower together.

"Still failing to see the problem in this. Wine and dine her. Dinner and a movie. Netflix and chill. Do what you have to do to sweep her off her feet. You only have three more nights."

Doubt started to creep in and my earlier high was rapidly evaporating. Did I need to keep my ideas of a date night confined to what she would like?

She enjoyed movies and restaurants, sure, but she would also gladly take a night in as well. Violet didn't like to be the center of attention and was someone who didn't mind fading into the background. She didn't care about expensive dinners, although they were nice to indulge occasionally, and I knew she enjoyed getting dressed up for special occasions. The courage and confidence boost it gave her to do so was insanely hot and attractive—but would she see this as such an outing?

"I don't know if that's the right move. Is it too predictable? What if she calls bullshit and she's not amused?" I began pacing the length of his mirrors, catching quick glances of familiar faces. We spent more time together in our respective watching quarters than any other place around here.

"I can't exactly fuck her into submission." Although the thought of doing just that was captivating, I didn't think she would appreciate that kind of move in the long run.

Elias snatched a towel from the handle of his treadmill and began dabbing at his forehead as the speed dramatically slowed to a snail's pace. "You've been drooling over her for years. Since before your tethering request, even. What would make the both of you happy? I'm sure you can find some common ground."

Something behind me snagged his attention and his head snapped in its direction. Elias leapt from the treadmill before it could roll to a stop, tossing his towel on the console. "You've got to be fucking kidding me."

Putting the pause on my dilemma, I met Elias at the mirror he was fixated on, zeroing in on one of his subjects. A man in glasses who looked to be in his forties was holed up in his car outside of what I could only assume was a strip joint. Posed and ready to leap from his vehicle with a knife in hand. There was a determination in his face that I recognized all too well. What was about to transpire wasn't anything good.

Elias swiped at the surrounding images to get a better look at the place, and retrieved his tablet from his chair. A scantily clad young woman who was more than likely barely legal stumbled out the back door of her run-down workplace in heels so high it was a miracle she didn't twist an ankle in the gravel she traipsed through. She didn't stand a chance with the predator across the dimly lit lot. The storm that was rolling in provided enough gloom to cover the early morning sun in its entirety.

"Is this the guy from Davenport you were telling us about?" I questioned him, already knowing the answer. Elias had brought him to the attention of the council just last week after his third victim.

This man had been on a downward spiral for months, and once his divorce from his wife had been finalized and he'd gotten himself fired from his job, things had taken a serious and deadly turn. He was now on to his fourth strip joint in the Midwest and about to claim the life of yet another woman. This one, however, was younger than the previous three.

"It is."

The man sprang from his vehicle as the woman's car door creaked open. The gravel shifted beneath his feet with each step and he was towering over her before she came to realize his presence. He stifled her scream with his hand as he held a knife to her stomach, instructing her to get into his vehicle.

Her eyes bulged with panic; he must have tilted the blade into her as she tried to elongate herself against the side of the car but she had nowhere to go. Her eyes began to glaze over as his frame kept her pinned.

These encounters never got any easier to watch.

I still hoped for the best, but knew all too well that the chances of her getting in his vehicle and sealing her fate were too great. If she entered the car, her survival rate diminished drastically. With the previous victims, he'd had his way with them and then disposed of their bodies in the Mississippi River within twenty-four hours.

"Get in the car or I will gut you." He spoke through gritted teeth, the harshness of his words sending tears streaming down her cheeks.

She nodded as much as his forced hand would allow and he granted her enough room to move. A small red spot began to form on her lacy garment close to her navel and I knew she was more than likely going to obey. Running wasn't an option—his speed and strength tipped the tables in his favor— and she was now injured, which only worked against her all the more.

I swiped across a few other mirrors, trying to locate images in and around the strip joint in search of some sort of security. Surely they had cameras around here somewhere. I knew the likes of these sleazy businesses—there had to be something in place to provide their assets with peace of mind. That, and they would want to protect their substantial amounts of cash.

Finally coming across an outdated camera without a live feed, I located what seemed to be a manager's office. An older man with hair dyed too dark for his age, was tipped back in his chair with his feet on the wooden desk. He was sound asleep with a ball cap sliding down his face.

By now the woman was being shoved into the trunk, instructed to handcuff herself, and I cringed. This lazy bastard didn't care about his employees and she was going to pay the price for it.

I wanted to wring his neck and shove his face through his computer screen. It's not like he was using it anyway.

Too many times to count, I had wanted to reach through and smack some sense into these humans, to give the victims who didn't stand a chance the upper hand for once. But even if I intervened and woke this shithead up, the killer would be long gone before his ass would even make it outside.

"Do you ever get tired of it?" I asked Elias as the trunk was shut with a thud, locking her away.

"Of what, watching?" He was poking away at his tablet, noting the time of the abduction, the location, and all of the logistics to this case.

"Of the inaction." My lips pressed thin as a familiar irritation came to the surface. It pained me to know I could have done something. I could have helped. It was these thoughts that plagued me more and more as time passed.

In my years of watching, it hadn't gotten any easier to watch these acts unfold. I never grew a thicker skin, to much disdain of the counsel. I cared too much, according to them. I thought they cared too little.

"What kind of question is that?" Elias shook his head as he swiped at the image before him so he could focus on the reflection cast in the man's rearview mirror. "If I had my way, he wouldn't see daybreak. But one task at a time, Kadriel."

I knew I wasn't alone in my thoughts. Most of the time, Elias and I were on the same wavelength when it came to these matters, but it helped to talk it out sometimes. Being able to openly admit and communicate these things within the confines of our apartments kept us in line with our future visions of change. We were ruled by an outdated and stubborn council that had no intentions of moving forward. Should

Violet accept the tethering, I was one step closer to my reign. Then they would have no choice but to listen to me.

"Even so, once she dies, I plan to petition the council again. He's escalating and I don't want to see any more bloodshed, unless it's his." I noted how Elias's jaw twitched, knowing full well just how deep this case was affecting him, and decided it was time for a segue.

"Speaking of bloodshed, any news on Aleena's mission yet?"

I figured my sister would more than likely visit Elias upon her return from seeking, since I was in the middle of my tethering courtship. She'd been planning to leave late last night to carry out an execution of a problematic wannabe cult leader who was moving across the southern states. Aleena's stealthy shifting abilities and combat training made her a force to be reckoned with in the seeking field, and when this case had come up for grabs, she'd fought for the right to snuff him out.

"Not yet. But you know her, she's going to take her time and enjoy tearing him down and into madness for what he did to those victims."

Aleena would do exactly that. She would torment him for as long as he could sustain it, make him face his crimes, and even when he began to plead for death, she would push even further. Even so, she would have to debrief first thing when she returned before she could do anything or go anywhere else.

Leaving Elias's side, I went to the end of the row of mirrors, to one that was empty. I swiped to find Violet arriving at work, only granted the view of her back as she entered her building.

I repeated the motion again and found darkness. The small compact mirror I had slipped into her purse this morning was emitting nothing but muffled sounds.

I wanted to believe that I could have gotten her to stay home today without it sounding like a demand. That I could have even persuaded her to think that the idea was hers. Time was not on either of our sides. After all these years waiting for her, now that we had touched, each time we parted ways—especially those times when she asked me to leave—was like a blow to my chest.

But this morning, the look on her face had made that ache almost nonexistent. She was equal parts fascinated and excited, and I knew that she was looking forward to tonight. Violet was without a doubt more than ready to see me again, and I couldn't wait. I just hoped that I didn't let her down with whatever expectations she might have regarding our date—and me.

Light filtered into view and I could hear rummaging, followed by her voice and that of another. I stilled, knowing that authoritative tone. I wanted nothing more than to go through and into Violet's office to confront him and shield her from the bastard. But I knew that if I did, it would put the both of us in jeopardy—not only in our possible tethering, but unnecessarily getting caught up in the crosshairs of a saint. Her close proximity to this unidentified man was more than I could bear and my hands balled into fists.

She opened the compact to reveal herself for a split second before the view whipped around to the backside of the lying and scheming boss who had held Violet under his thumb ever since she stepped foot in that place. A visible tremor ran through him, rooted from his neck, and I feared from this small involuntary response that he might be onto her—or worse, onto us.

I began to write out a message on the mirror, backwards. We had used this sort of communication long before the Navy did so on ships. It came in handy in times when we couldn't speak, and was taught to us demons at such a young age that I could write just as fast backwards as I could forwards.

STAY AWAY FROM HIM.

I had slipped the mirror into her purse as a reminder of me, not to get her to try and hunt down a saint with it. What the fuck was she doing? In hindsight, however, I could see how her curiosity would have won over her willingness to prove me wrong in matters she was only beginning to learn about. But even so, this was dangerous.

Alarm was written all over her face and it was evident that she'd picked up on the saint's reaction just as I had, but it did little to calm my nerves. She mouthed an "okay" and quickly shut the compact, leaving me in the dark, once again.

I despised technology for its electrical interference that wouldn't allow me to view Violet from her computer monitor. No one in that place could be seen, for that matter, and that had been the first major red flag when I started to research her workplace once she'd received an interview. That building and her boss were the biggest pains in my ass, and a constant worry.

If that saint ever tried to make a move on her, it would be game over for him, whoever the hell he was.

She is mine. Fucking mine.

How was I supposed to focus on planning an evening with her when I was concerned about her very existence with a fucking saint hovering around? He had been closer to her than I ever was before two nights ago, and the bane of my existence ever since she stepped foot through that door.

"You know if he was planning on killing her, he would have done it by now."

Elias spoke words I had heard time and time again as I struggled against the urge to punch something. We had talked in great length about this saint's possible agenda and the scenarios that might transpire from this situation. Both Elias and my uncle were always there on the sidelines to reel me back in when I was about to jeopardize everything I had been working toward. And their meddling couldn't hold a candle to my sister. She always found a way to weasel herself into my business no matter how hard I tried to keep her away from the drama that was my life, especially as of late.

"You look like you need to kill something. That can't be a good." And there she was. She had an annoying gift for showing up at the mere thought or mention of her. It was an unspoken and irritable talent of hers, and she knew it. "What did I miss?"

"You look like you did kill. Successful outing?" Elias lowered his tablet to his side as he spoke, and I begrudgingly angled toward my sibling.

Aleena was dressed in skimpy scraps of attire that somehow covered more of her body than the clothing of the Davenport victim currently in a trunk. Only Aleena had blood splatters and stains that made it look as if she had just come from the battlefield.

There was a gleam in her eyes that I had to admit I recognized. It came from the thrill of the chase and the ending of a life that had lived longer than it should have. From punishing those who didn't deserve to breathe and were a waste of space in the general human population.

The adrenaline rush that was still coursing through her veins, even after her debriefing, was evident from the bounce in her step as she approached Elias.

"Very," she mused as she put her finger to his chest. Their exchanged glances made me register that their on-again, off-again fling was having a very *on* kind of moment. That was probably my cue to leave, as I was well aware of how she liked to exert her energies after a successful mission.

The ringing of Violet's office phone sounded and she picked it up after the first ring. As much as I yearned to hear her voice and her part of the conversation, although faint, I swiped at the mirror to end the connection. She could read the weather forecast and I would hang on every word as if it were laced with an addictive drug.

"Things not going well with Violet? Why are you even here?"

"I was just leaving," I grumbled, irritated.

"Why is she at work and you're here?" Aleena pestered, unrelenting. "You should be with her."

"I wasn't going to force her to stay home from work, she still has a life separate from mine for a few more days."

"You blew it didn't you?" She flipped her brown hair over her shoulder and crossed her arms. For someone who normally donned unnatural hair colors, it was strange to see her looking somewhat normal.

I shot her a quizzical look. Did she really think I'd failed after only two nights spent with Violet? Why were Aleena and Elias both under the impression that me being here was such a bad thing?

"Not having sex in forever made you weak, didn't it? You literally blew it." She had the audacity to be appalled at the very mention of it.

"I am not talking about sex with Violet with you. Better yet, sex in general. End of discussion." Her line of questioning had me ready to bolt the moment she opened her mouth again.

"She wants him to take her on a date tonight. His choice on the date details," Elias interrupted.

I shot daggers at Elias for opening his mouth, and for

inviting Aleena into this conversation. I was a bit stunned that he wasn't rushing me out of here so they could do whatever the hell it was they intended to do.

"What? Your tethering affects us all. You need this to work. We need this to work. Aleena, even though she is your sister, is a woman after all. Maybe get her opinion on the matter."

My nostrils flared, not wanting to entertain any of this, and wanting to pop out of here and go somewhere else. Anywhere else.

"Kadriel, all joking aside, what's going on?" She took a step away from Elias, a calm coming over her as her breath slowed and her facial features softened. "How can I help?"

I understood that both Elias and Aleena were coming from a good place and were more than eager to help, but I wasn't much for discussing my personal life openly with these two.

I knew that my possible tethering would set in motion a slew of events that not only affected me, but everyone here. All eyes had been on me ever since I'd put in a tethering request, and there were scrutinizing ones around every corner, waiting for me to trip up and fail, taking a dramatic fall from my family's grace while doing so.

I decided to let Aleena in, even just briefly, to get her opinion on the matter. She had seen Violet from time to time as I watched her over the years; maybe her thoughts from the outside looking in could give me a different perspective.

I gave a quick rundown of our time together, and the worries that had seemed to plague Violet's mind regarding our world so far. I chose to leave out our sexual entanglements but I made a point to recognize that she had invited me back more than once. I wanted to believe her firing of questions and her inquisitiveness in everything we discussed was a good sign. I hesitated to mention it, but I did make note of how overwhelmed she had become last night. Even so, she hadn't asked me to leave again. I fully believed that we had parted on good terms this morning.

"I guess I don't really see what the big deal is. It's totally fair of her to ask this of you, but you need to take her request seriously. Don't think about her or what she would want to do. This is your chance to get out there and check out her world through the eyes of a human, and let her get to know you. It seems to be what she wants, just remember that."

I was dumbfounded that there wasn't a trace of sarcasm to Aleena's words, and no jabs or unnecessary comments. She was earnest in her delivery of the words, shrugging it all off as if it was no big deal, when minutes ago it had been very much the opposite.

"So go. Do some homework, figure yourself out, and don't wallow in your self-doubt for too long or you're going to fuck this up."

I crossed my arms even though I was practically gawking at her now.

"Don't fuck it up." She stuck her tongue out in a teasing manner, but I knew that she meant every word that came out of her mouth.

Elias had remained silent through it all, halfway listening to us and keeping the other part of his attention drawn to those he was watching.

It was challenging, but I tried to keep my line of sight away from the girl in the trunk. I couldn't travel down that rabbit hole again and it was Elias's case, not mine. If I did get involved, I might forget my place and send Aleena back out on another mission. Or worse, get involved myself.

The council would love any reason I gave them to scold me and question my authority, especially with my upcoming tethering. A part of me thought it would be totally worth it, but another worried that it might take away from what little time I had left with Violet before she had to make her decision. I couldn't risk losing any more time with her.

"That being said," Aleena interrupted my train of thought before I could speak, "you should get going, you're kind of killing my vibe right now."

I rolled my eyes. Elias and I both knew well enough what she was here for.

She strolled over and crossed her arms, eyes studying me as her head extended forward and she inhaled. Her sense of smell was one to be reckoned with and it was a quality that benefited her greatly in her role here. The corner of her mouth turned up as she picked up my scent.

"New body wash?"

I stuck out my tongue in the same manner as she had earlier, and vanished, not willing to confirm what she already knew. Talking about that area of life with my sister was absolutely off-limits.

With each hour that passed, my anticipation built.

I had pulled up a chair to a mirror in my watching quarters and had been scouring grocery store message boards and social media trying to get ideas for tonight. Setting a demon loose in the human world for a date was something I had never given any thought to. There was so much to do in and around her town—it was too overwhelming.

Not only did I worry about pleasing her, but I was eager to experience the world she lived in. Instead of being on the outside looking in, I would be present and at her side. It was the only place I'd ever yearned to be and now it was at her request.

I knew the concept of watching was a tough hump to get over—my aunt couldn't have stressed that enough—but for the most part, it seemed Violet had moved through it and accepted it. It was our world's familiarity with killing that had been a tough pill for her to swallow.

Strolling over to my makeshift mini bar beside the couch, I poured myself another double. It was probably meant more as a bookshelf, but I had collected various glass liquor bottles and had them displayed along its three tiers.

I downed the drink without pause. The liquid blazed a trail down my throat inch by inch and I welcomed the familiar fire as it came to settle in my stomach. Time slowed, even if only briefly, as I focused on this simple act and nothing more.

Movie theaters, concerts, food vendors, a traveling antique show. Baseball games, an art museum, movies in the park, yoga by the lake. The list went on and on. Just how many events were scheduled to happen on a Friday night alone in her hometown?

My head was soon spinning again with all of the possibilities. I needed to narrow it down somehow. The beer tasting at a local brewery was appealing, but I didn't want that to be our first date. That felt more like an experience I would haul Elias to if I ever had the chance.

My trips to her world had been limited so far. The council was reluctant to approve any travel for me due to my status, but I recalled the few instances when I'd been able to visit and what had caught my attention while there.

My mind wandered to my first trip with my father under a full moon, once I had mastered the skill of blinks—the changing of eye colors and the ability to sustain it for extended periods of time. We had walked silently through crowds of people as if we belonged, blending in among the masses. We were only there for maybe an hour, just sightseeing and people watching, but I could recall being so fascinated by all of the lights. I'd been blinded by their brightness and so many different colors that varied greatly from all of the stained glass windows back home.

Periodically I checked in on Violet, only to find that her mirror was still stowed in her purse in the darkness. I could hear the clicking of her keyboard and occasional mumbles. I tried not to linger, to give her some privacy no matter how maddened I was at the fact that a saint was so close.

Elias was right though. I had no doubt in my mind that if the saint had plans to kill her, he would have done so by now. So why was he waiting so long before making a move to claim her? Why keep her under his thumb for so long?

Leaving the connection open a while longer, I began to make my rounds and check on my other charges to make sure they were staying out of trouble. I retrieved my tablet from my desk, looking to see if I had any notifications or events that I might have missed in my time away. One name, however, drew all of my attention to it; I swiped at a mirror to bring up his workplace, knowing that he should have been there by now.

Brett. Not only did I have to worry about a saint around Violet, but this waste of space too.

Violet's douchebag of an ex had a history of abuse with women, some verbal and some physical, that I uncovered after he came into her life. Because of his family name and his parents' positions of power, nothing had ever made it to paper.

The women in his life before Violet had been blackmailed and shunned into silence before they could even breathe a word to authorities. One had even landed in the emergency room after an encounter with a flight of stairs, but not even she had spoken up about it. And how could she? Brett had taken her to the hospital himself. The only reason I knew about the matter was a therapy session I'd witnessed between her and her therapist where she had come clean. But when she was urged to take action, she'd never returned and had stopped going to therapy altogether.

I'd known it was only a matter of time before his true nature came to the surface with Violet. She had been growing frustrated and impatient with Brett for months before she was finally ready to openly admit that she wanted to end things.

It was to my advantage that it happened right as I was coming into the picture. The timing couldn't have been better.

I was more than prepared to serve him a taste of his own medicine should he choose to retaliate. I would more than gladly give him a shove down the apartment stairs of Violet's building if he presented the opportunity. I knew for a fact that the security cameras in the stairwells only covered the first, second, and top floor.

I had given it more thought than I probably should have.

Someday I would tell Violet of his past, but she already had enough on her plate as it was and I didn't want anything to overshadow our time tonight.

Finding Brett's office unoccupied, I scanned the rest of his work establishment. When it came up empty of his presence, I checked the parking lot. His truck was nowhere to be found, so I continued on to his apartment. He was already out of his routine—he was supposed to be at work currently—and the darkened state of his home did nothing for my nerves.

I zoomed in, eyeing something that I hadn't seen there before—a hole in the wall about the size of a fist, a blemish in the cream-colored walls. The drywall was broken and cracked, and yellow insulation could be seen peeking through.

Pulling up the notification on my tablet, I noticed a time stamp of 10:43 p.m. from last night. It was well after Violet had broken things off with him and I knew the hole in his wall represented a continuation of his outburst at her place. I went back in the recorded footage far enough to see Brett arriving home, slamming his door with such force upon his entrance that it shook the few items that hung on the surrounding wall. His suit jacket was missing and his collar was unbuttoned, a madness in his face as he headed straight for the wall and delivered a blow.

I clenched my jaw. Thank goodness he couldn't punch through Violet's door and had taken it out on his own wall instead.

"Making any headway on your date?"

Elias appeared over my shoulder, freshly showered and dressed for the day. His hair was neat and slicked back now, and hanging past his shoulders. I shook my head as I began to notate my findings on Brett, ignoring the fact that Elias had more than likely spent the whole morning with my sister. It wasn't that I disapproved of them together, but their no-strings-attached relationship was still a strange matter to wrap my head around.

"I'm more worried about the loose cannon Brett is right now."

"What's he up to?" He joined me at the mirrors and watched as I replayed the scene of Brett sending his fist through the wall. I only hoped he broke a few fingers in the process, but I probably couldn't be that lucky.

"Not sure exactly. I haven't located him yet."

"Thank you." Elias ended the feed on the mirror before us

and removed the tablet from my grasp. He plucked away at it briefly before dimming the screen. "Let me take care of this. I'll find him."

"I have some time, I can do it." I attempted to take the tablet back but Elias held it far from my reach with his lengthy arms.

"Nope. Date night. What are your plans?" He swiveled and plopped back onto my couch, making himself comfortable.

"Who's asking, you or Aleena?" I placed my hands on my hips, wanting nothing more than to be alone in my hunt for Brett. I wanted to be the one to find him and make sure he wasn't going to interfere with our upcoming evening together.

"Remember, we want this to work out just as much as you do. We're always on your side, no matter what. Which is more than I can say for the council. Minus your uncle, of course."

I eyed him, apprehensive as I considered telling him of an idea that flitted through my mind and begged for my attention. It went against his earlier advice, but I wanted to believe that both Violet and I could find our own sense of adventure no matter the venue or avenue of interest I chose.

"Do you have any cash?"

CHAPTER 9

Violet

By five I was ready to bolt from the building. Anticipation had been growing all afternoon for my date with Kade tonight and the wonder of what it might entail.

Was he the adventurous type, or a romantic? Would we have anything in common? What did he enjoy doing? Did he have any hobbies or favorite types of food?

With his so-called "watching" job, did he even have any time to do anything else? He'd told me he had twenty-some others he was watching as well as me. Realistically, how could he have the time or room for anything else?

And what if we didn't share any interests once we left the confines of my bedroom? What if we were polar opposites? I would assume, if that were the case, it would make my decision about his proposal easy.

But why did I find such solace in his presence?

Was I just rebounding because of Brett? Was it rash that I was considering a life with the demon stranger after a few nights of amazing sex?

Closing my car door, I kicked it on, letting the sounds of the engine and the air on full blast rush past my ears. Sitting in the hot sun all day made my small black sedan feel like a sauna and I regretted not cracking my windows. Luckily, the temperature was supposed to settle down this evening and level out over the next few days, which was a relief. I hated summer and the heat that it brought. The humidity that accompanied it made it hard to breathe at times, and I wanted nothing more than to sit by an air vent and bask in its comforts.

On my way home, I tried to make a mental note of everything I wanted to accomplish before six-thirty. Pulling into my usual but unmarked parking spot, I hopped out and made my way in. I checked my mail and awaited the elevator, nodding and offering a few polite greetings to others coming and going.

When I arrived at my apartment, I shut the door behind me and eyed my mirror. At this point, I had less than an hour and a half to get ready, but was wary of doing so, knowing that I needed mirrors in order to complete some of my tasks.

I crossed my arms and puffed an agitated sigh. Well, this might complicate things.

Did I need to throw a blanket over this one so he didn't sneak a peek? Even if I did that, I still needed the bathroom mirror if I was going to redo my makeup and attempt to curl my hair.

I took my place in front of my standing mirror, taking in my reflection for a beat before I called to the demon who had threw the world I thought I knew off its axis.

"Kade? Are you there?"

I paused, waiting for a reply. I swiveled around to make sure he hadn't popped in, and when it felt like it was taking him too long, I continued.

"Kade, I know I said six-thirty but I just need you for a few seconds."

"Yes?" His head appeared over my shoulder and I relaxed.

"I don't know if there's a good way to ask this, but—" I tilted my head slightly from side to side a few times. "I need some privacy to get ready and it's kind of weirding me out that you get a front row seat while I do the simplest of things."

Kade flashed his perfectly white smile. "I promise I won't watch you. I need to take care of a few things here before our date anyway. Just say my name when you're ready." I watched his reflection as he planted a kiss on my cheek, and I couldn't suppress the shiver that ran through me.

"Thank you."

And with that, he vanished. I didn't know what kind of magic he possessed, but the fact that he could plant a kiss on my cheek as if he were next to me was strangely hot—even though it was physically cold.

Checking the time on my phone, I rushed to the bathroom and made quick work of shaving my legs, brushing my teeth, and washing my makeup away just to reapply all new. I opted for winged eyeliner and darker eyes since we would be heading into the evening together. Afterall, who knew how long we might be out and about.

I curled my hair while I let myself enjoy tunes from my phone as it charged. Nervous excitement bubbled up within me and I kept arguing with myself about what to wear for the occasion. I probably should have asked him for a clue as to how to dress, but at this point I was just hoping he wasn't an extreme sporting type.

Granted, he was definitely in shape given the definition of his body, but if he really had been watching me since high school, he would damn well know that I didn't have an athletic bone in mine. I didn't mind walking, possibly jogging, and light weights, but that was the extent of it. My weight loss over the years was mainly a result of taking on my obsession with food and overcoming the comfort that I'd sought in it. I knew I wasn't the most coordinated, but the moderate exercise I had made a part of my routine was certainly a bonus in my journey.

Once my hair and makeup were complete, I stood back from the mirror and examined my work in my black underwire bra and matching undies. I smoothed my hands over my stomach and I admired how far I had come in my weight loss. However, I still studied every inch with a critical eye, wishing I were smaller and narrower from the side.

Kade had called me beautiful and a curvy goddess.

The color in my cheeks reddened harsher than the blush I had dotted them with. No man before him had ever uttered such a thing in my presence with such sincerity. As much as I wanted to believe it, I couldn't help but wonder if he had just been caught up in the heat of the moment. Men before him had complimented me when wanting something in return, and I noted how Kade was technically no different. He wanted me to leave and start a new life with him whereas others were hopeful for sexual favors.

Did I feel good in this present moment? Yes. But a little voice inside my head kept nagging at me, saying that he had just been telling me what I needed to hear in order to persuade me toward accepting him and his offer. I didn't know which way was up or down, left or right, and trying to make heads or tails of this ordeal was impossible. I shook my hands out as if I could shed the negative thoughts trying to invade my mind.

Switching the light off, I all but pranced out to my closet with a pep in my step and began to scan through its contents. I settled on a black dress with white carnation-like flowers scattered about. The low V-neck would show off the swell of my breasts, and I had to admit, they looked pretty damn good tonight. The flowy skirt was long enough to allow me to wear biker shorts underneath, just in case we would be more active, but still cut off well above the knee. I then opted for some slip-on sneakers, hoping they would be practical enough no matter the outing he had chosen.

I silenced the music on my phone and waited. At this point I had about two minutes until our date.

I entangled my fingers together in knots; all of my questions and concerns were becoming a storm cloud of worry in my mind. I should have been writing all of these down so I could organize and keep them straight.

My stomach was at odds with my body, nervous for what the night might hold. This date could probably make or break us and I had to be ready for the best- and worst-case scenarios. I had been on both good and bad dates before, but nothing that could lead to the possible outcome that came with Kade.

Would I be this nervous if I didn't want this to work out? Was I hopeful that it would? What did I want more at this point?

I admired my mirror and my own reflection in it while I approached it once again.

I had opted to pull my curled hair up into a messy ponytail with a few loose tendrils escaping. To think there was a time in high school when I'd wanted to dye my strawberry-blond hair to black was absurd to me now, and I was incredibly glad that I'd never followed through. I didn't think it would have looked right with my complexion, and I had since grown to truly appreciate my hair color. Some people tried and tried again to achieve this, but for me it was all natural.

"Alright, Kade. I'm ready whenever you are." I knotted my fingers together behind my back as I eagerly awaited his arrival. But a quick double-knock on my door drew my attention away. "Um, hold that thought."

I hadn't been expecting any company and glanced at my phone to make sure I hadn't missed any messages, but there was nothing new on my screen.

I opened the door to find Kade standing with one arm behind him, hair still unruly in a way I was sure only he could pull off without it looking lazy. He wore tennis shoes, blue jeans, and a button-up red shirt that was just tight enough to make my eyes linger slightly before meeting his gaze. I was lucky enough to know the sight that he was beneath it all.

Amused at his appearance, an unflattering chortle erupted from me. "Oh my god, you own a shirt."

Kade visibly relaxed as if he had been frozen in place and awaiting my reaction, his lips revealing a slight smirk.

"That I do. A few in fact. And you look stunning." I caught his gaze lingering on my breasts and I knew that I'd selected the right outfit.

"Thank you. Hopefully it's alright for whatever you have planned tonight?"

"Absolutely. But I would rather change my plans to keep you in that dress. If that weren't the case."

I could feel my cheeks flush at his remark. Before tonight, I had never had a good chance to wear this dress. While I loved it, Brett had said it was too revealing to be out and about in public. I had retired it to my closet to revisit again someday, and as of right now, I was certainly glad that I had saved it for tonight.

"These are for you."

A bouquet of prominently yellow flowers, accompanied by smaller white ones that were almost triangle-shaped, made its way into my view. My lips parted slightly, in awe of its beauty. It was unlike any floral arrangement I had ever seen before—peculiar and unusual, much like him.

"Side note, yellow is my favorite color, but I was hoping you would like them regardless."

I beamed as I graciously accepted them. "Good to know. I love them, thank you."

I smelled them before dragging him into my apartment and shutting the door. Retrieving a vase from beneath the sink, I filled it with water and unwrapped the binding on the flowers so I could set them in there. I inhaled their rich scent that reminded me of a crisp winter morning before returning my attention to Kade.

"One more thing, and I hope you'll accept it."

My eyebrow rose as he produced something from his pocket and held his hand out. A necklace lay in the palm of his hand—a silver chain with a black bar pendant about two inches long, almost cylindrical in shape.

"It's black obsidian. A protective stone that grows in abundance where I am from."

My hand floated out to touch the cold stone. "It reminds me of your eyes." I looked into the black pools that watched me.

I turned to allow him to place the necklace on me, his wintry touch grazing my skin. The pendant settled upon my chest, right between the swell of my breasts, and I examined it, turning back toward him. "It's stunning. Thank you. But I didn't get you anything."

Kade shook his head. "Nonsense. This date is a gift in

itself."

"We'll see if you still think that way after tonight."

"I don't think there's anything you could say or do that might persuade me otherwise."

He seemed so sure of himself, but not smug in the slightest.

I gathered my cross-body purse and headed for the door. "So, where are you taking me tonight?"

He blew out a breath and scratched his head, and for the first time, he seemed unsure of himself. Nervous even. "I know you said anything I wanted to do but, please don't laugh."

"Nonsense." I ushered us out of the apartment and locked up. "Where to?"

"If you want to go somewhere else, I'll completely understand. Elias thinks it's weird that I want to go."

"Elias?" I inquired as I pressed the elevator button to take us down.

"Guess you could say he's the closest friend I have. We've grown up and trained together. Practically the brother I never had. His words mean a lot, that's why I'm second-guessing my choice right now."

"Hey, I said whatever you wanted to do, and I'm standing by that no matter what. So spill."

I could see that he was toying around with words in his head.

"I was hoping we could go to the carnival that's in town." He shoved his hands into his pockets and shrugged his shoulders forward a bit as he spoke.

Of all the things he could have selected, I definitely hadn't been expecting that. I was pleasantly surprised by his decision and thought it strange that he would think it was weird to begin with. I was also grateful for the fact that my outfit would work out tonight after all.

"Then to the carnival we go." I beamed as I backed into the empty elevator that arrived. "Let's prove to Elias that we can go and have a good time.

"Really?" He followed me in.

"Really. Oh!" A startling revelation hit me like a brick. "Your eyes!" I hadn't even thought about him going out and about with his otherworldly gaze and the attention they would no doubt draw.

His laughter filled the small space between us but it did nothing for my rising concern. "What color?"

The elevator drew to a halt but we weren't at the main floor yet. I realized we must be picking up other tenants and I began to worry.

"What color?" I repeated, hushed as the bell signaled the doors opening. He moved over to my side to allow others access to the elevator. Within a blink, his eyes changed drastically to a blue-rimmed eye with a black center. It was the same hue from when we had finally met face-to-face without the cover of darkness yesterday.

I couldn't help the dropping of my jaw as a couple around our age from floor two joined us in the elevator.

"Good evening," Kade greeted them as he slipped his hand into mine. The two, whose names escaped me at the moment, exchanged pleasantries and we continued down to the main lobby. The awkward silence that filled the elevator made the time spent in the confined space feel longer than it took molasses to drip from a spoon.

It seemed like it took an eternity to exit the elevator and building as he led the way to the parking lot and directly to my car without asking for a single direction. The heat of the day was fading with the sun's slow descent, but I was still eager to get to the cool air my car could provide.

"What did you mean by what color? If I had said purple, what would you have done?" I knew we were out of earshot of any other people by now, but I still couldn't hide the surprise in my voice.

He blinked again, turning his eyes a deep purple, and my mouth went dry.

"That's…amazing," I said, astonished. "Would I be able to do that?" The words were out of my mouth before I even registered what I was asking. I really needed to stop that.

Blinking again, his eyes changed back to blue as he leaned up against my car. "I hate to disappoint you, but no. I can make changes to my appearance because I'm a demon."

"Oh." I pursed my lips. I had to admit, I did feel a little let down about that fleeting possibility.

"There is a possibility to transition, but that decision is not taken lightly and has to be brought to the council for approval."

I tried to choose my words carefully as I got in my car and kicked it on, cranking up the air. I buckled, then sat back in my seat as Kade mirrored my moves with a small delay as he settled in.

"First off, what exactly does the tethering entail? What happens?" I knew he had said that I had to be living to cross over, and that I didn't have to die, but I had no idea what else was included with the tethering.

"Think of it as a joining of two souls. Like a marriage, so to speak, but our version of it." He rested his hands on his knees that were almost touching my glove compartment. He looked a bit out of place in my small car with the length of his legs.

"Walk me through what happens." I began knotting my fingers again, but then splayed them out over my thighs to keep from doing it anymore. As if I could help it.

"Once you accept, you can cross through into my plane of existence. We would enter our 'chapel' of sorts and the elder council member, Staffan, would unite us with a few words and the tethering ritual." His hands fisted as he moved them up and down toward his thighs. "We then have to use a blade to…slice our palms and join them together."

His voice quieted as he spoke and I tried to stifle the gulp my throat wanted to emit as I was imagining all of this taking place.

Demon, a blade, and blood.

Was this a normal thing for him? Because it certainly wasn't here. It sounded more like a cult-type thing in my head.

"Then Staffan would take a rope-like cord and wrap us from elbow to fingertips, securing our union. That rope then dissolves into our skin, linking us together. Forever."

I waited for him to continue, but when he didn't, I gave the moment a longer pause.

That was it? Odd sort of marriage-ritual-type thing if you asked me.

"What, no rings?" I joked, nervously. Now I was trying to use humor to keep me afloat after the details he had just disclosed.

"If you want a ring, I would most certainly see to it that you get one."

I shot him a quizzical look. "So that's really it?"

"Were you expecting more?"

I was trying not to let the thought of the palm slicing get to me. I had to remember we were two different species with apparently two different sets of traditions. What was normal to me was not necessarily normal to him. That was clearly evident now.

"Not exactly a romantic way to enter into eternity with somebody," I acquiesced.

"Well, there are a couple of things we have in common," he continued. "After we consummate our union, the following day we have a reception type of party. Tetherings with humans are few and far between, so you have to understand it is kind of a big deal. It's a cause for celebration and a chance for you to meet everyone. It's really quite a day."

He smiled as if reflecting on some memories. The blue in his eyes made it easier to focus on his line of sight, but I began to long for his black gaze that I'd been growing unconventionally fond of.

"Have you been to a tethering celebration?" I was curious as to where his mind was at.

"I have, yes. But only two in this manner. The first time I was so young, I barely remember it. The second, I was about nine years old and my uncle had secured his other half, a human like you. Everyone was filled with so much joy, you could feel it in the air. I had never seen two people more in love, besides my parents. I have wanted nothing more than what they had and what my parents had, since then."

I had noted how he used the word "human" and while it wasn't at all in a negative light, it still made me press on.

"Do you not have tethering rituals among your own kind?"

He smiled. "We do, and they are still special in their own way, don't get me wrong. But for me, I can't say that anyone else back home has ever caught my attention in the way that you have."

Ah, again with the flattery. He sure knew what to say and when to say it. I tried not to get hung up on it.

"And what about your parents and uncle now? Do you have any siblings?"

I almost felt as if I needed a notebook and pen to keep up with the information flowing through Kade right now. I was grateful for the open communication and wanted to keep going and dive deeper. But I noticed that my questions stalled him, and he tensed. I could have sworn I saw his eyes flash to black, but I couldn't be sure if my own eyes were playing tricks on me or not.

"My Uncle Zan is actually on the council now and he and his wife Sarah have two kids. Absolute rascals, but I love them to pieces. I hope you get the chance to meet them." I became suspicious that something bad had happened, since he hadn't led with details on his immediate family.

"My parents, both born and bred demons, died by the hands of saints just a few years after my Uncle Zan's tethering. They were trying to collect a soul and were unsuccessful. They left my sister Aleena and I behind."

"Kade, I'm so sorry." I reached for his hand without a second thought, tucking my fingers into his hold. My heart ached, knowing the loss of parents was a wound that could never heal. Sometimes I wondered what life would have been like if the accident hadn't claimed my little brother too, as I'd never really gotten the chance to know him. But at least Kade wasn't alone in his grief. "And your sister? Tell me about her."

He cleared his throat as he shifted in his seat. "Older than me by four years, but I swear she has the temper of a toddler at times. That's probably why she turned into such an excellent seeker. They're the ones who go out into your world to claim those souls who deserve to be punished."

"But you have been a seeker on occasion." I was trying to understand his world and compare it to what he had already told me thus far about his dealings here in mine.

"I have, yes. But my full-time job, as you would call it, is watcher. From time to time, I can try to fill in elsewhere as needed."

I squeezed his hand, still hung up on the news of his parents and wishing he hadn't known the pain of such a tragedy. I didn't wish that upon anyone. It had messed with my head in so many ways I couldn't even comprehend it at times. My memories of them and my brother had faded over the years, and half the time I wondered if I even remembered correctly or if my brain was trying to form fake memories to help me cope with the sorrow of their absence.

Wanting to move on from this subject, I felt as if I needed to acknowledge his efforts in opening up to me. I knew the wounds that he was revisiting were without a doubt unpleasant and painful, and I didn't want that to go unnoticed.

"Thank you." I tried to be as gentle as possible and delicate in my demeanor. "I can't tell you how much it means that you would confide in me."

He kissed the back of my hand and held it between both of his. "I told you I would never lie to you. You deserve the truth, no matter what you ask. I'll do my best to answer everything you throw my way."

I bit my bottom lip, unsure of how to steer the conversation from the depths of despair and heartache into anything else but this. "Not the best way to start off our date night, is it? Sorry to drag it down."

"You don't have to apologize. Don't give it another thought."

Releasing my hand from his, I put the car in gear and began our drive to the carnival. It was only in town for a week and usually came through around the same time every year. It had been a while since I'd been there, although I was sure it hadn't changed too much. I was still excited to experience it with him.

"I have to ask, why the carnival? Color me intrigued by your selection."

"Would you believe me if I said I have never been to one?"

"Surprisingly yes, since it sounds like the few times you've visited my plane of existence have been when you were seeking somebody out." I was hoping that I was grasping the concepts of his world and using the terms correctly. "Is there anything in particular we need to see or do?"

He went rigid in the passenger seat, eyes wide and fixated intently on the road. I couldn't even tell if he was breathing. He was as still as a statue.

"Are you okay?"

"Great." The word came out quickly. Flustered, even.

"You don't seem okay." His knuckles turned white as he kept his fists clamped shut. I turned onto a side street to get away from the flow of traffic so I could slow down.

"What's wrong?" I urged for an answer.

"I think I just prefer my method of traveling."

"Is it my driving?" I was almost offended by the thought.

"Nope, no." He shook his head. "There's just a lot of…moving parts."

"Are there no cars where you're from?" Just how different was his world compared to mine? Was this his first time in a vehicle?

"No need for them. Do you know how many people die from automobile accidents in a single day? These things are…terrifying."

I slowed even more as I preplanned another less traveled route. We weren't far from the carnival by now, but I wanted to put his mind at ease in any way I could.

"Tell me about your home then. What's it called? Are jobs

limited to watchers and seekers? What would I even do?" I was hoping to get him to talk about something else, so I rapidly fired a few questions off at him.

"Darthou."

"Darthou," I repeated, drawing it out. It was a weird name that I would probably forget, and I would undoubtedly have to ask him to repeat it again later.

"Not limited to watchers and seekers, no. There is special training and some have family ties that date back for ages for those positions. There are teachers, cooks, and trainers, you name it. There are many positions available. Even if you were to settle on something that you like, you are not bound to that for your entire existence."

He seemed to relax now that we were out the hustle and bustle of the after-work traffic. "And if something piques your interest, you can attend training and schooling to help you get better acquainted with that field of work."

"Are there any student loans? Because I don't think I can take on any more debt if I decide to change fields." I rolled my eyes, thinking about the four years of college debt I had accrued. Finding out, after I had started my current job, that my degree wasn't necessary for my position had left a foul taste in my mouth. Sure, in some aspects it had helped, but knowing that the girl in the office next to me had no college degree or certifications for the job prior to starting was a tough pill to swallow.

"First of all, it's stupid that you have to pay to learn. And second, I am happy to report that we have nothing to do with them."

"Well if that isn't music to my ears then I don't know what is." I cast a glance over at him as I turned onto the road that would take us to our final destination, but I became distracted.

"Your blue eyes are—"

"Eyes on the road!" His words fumbled in alarm.

I suppressed a laugh as I returned both hands to their proper placings on the steering wheel and my sight straight ahead.

"I was going to say they are very distracting."

"How so?"

"I'm just not used to it. I'm sorry I said anything."

"You never need to apologize to me. But I am sorry for snapping at you. This death trap flying through a sea of other death traps is very intimidating."

"I thought you were immortal. Does that not count for anything?

"Ha! Just because I'm immortal does not mean that I cannot be harmed. And you are a much more delicate being than myself. Just try to remember that."

"So I'm going to take a stab and say no go-karts or bumper cars for you," I teased as I pulled into a parking spot.

Sensing his attention on me as I parked, I twisted to meet him. His baby blues seemed like those of a stranger now, but they still held his heated stare. As much as I appreciated the fact that he could blend in among the masses, I was already beginning to miss the black pools that matched the necklace he had gifted me.

CHAPTER 10

Violet

"I can't believe you've never had a corn dog, or any carnival food for that matter." I stole us a seat at a small table the farthest away from anybody else, hoping for a bit of privacy. The scents of fried foods and popcorn permeated the air around us.

Kade turned the stick in his hand, examining the corn dog with curious intent.

"Now we just have to find out if you're team ketchup or team mustard. Let's start with the latter but just a little bit in case you don't like it."

"Aren't you going to eat?" he asked as he gestured to mine.

"I don't want to have any influence over your decision on which is better."

Upon entering the carnival, I felt as if Kade was overstimulated. It was like he'd stepped into Times Square for the first time and was staggered by the chaos of the situation. Instead of rushing into games and rides, I'd figured I would try and ease him into it with some food first.

I kept catching him scanning the area and while I wanted to believe it was due to the environment and it being his first time here, a small, nagging part of me believed he was on the lookout for someone—or some*thing*. Be it saints or something else entirely, I wasn't sure. I just hoped that it wouldn't spoil the fun I longed for tonight.

The term "watching" had taken on a whole new meaning since meeting Kade and I felt at odds with myself, observing him as I waited for him to take a bite. I wasn't sure how I was expecting him to react, but he remained emotionless and I couldn't get a read on him. He had a great poker face, which I knew I didn't have. He went for the ketchup first, sticking the corn dog in his mouth, and he didn't give anything away as he bit into it and began to chew. I blinked away, afraid that I was being too overbearing.

"Just so you know, I have had ketchup and mustard before. It's just the corn dog that's new to me."

I rolled my eyes as he smirked and I playfully nudged him with my elbow. I dunked my corn dog into the ketchup and took a bite. The crispy coating on the outside made my mouth water as soon as I bit down. My taste buds came alive as I tried to remember the last time I'd eaten one of these.

"I think I prefer ketchup with these," Kade declared after having tried the other.

"I'll be damned, we have something in common already." There was more, of course—our lust for one another, among other things—but there was nothing that I wanted to openly admit out loud right now.

I took a swig of the freshly squeezed lemonade to wash

down the remnants of the corn dog. Its tart presence was a great combination with the fried food as the cold liquid cascaded down my throat.

"May I?" He gestured toward the lemonade before I could set it back down on the table.

"I have another question," I stated as I handed over the beverage.

"Shoot." I swore that the corn dog would be gone in two more bites the way he practically inhaled it. I had no idea if he was really even chewing the darn thing. He was disposing of it so quickly, maybe I should have bought two for him.

"Earlier when we were talking about tethering, you mentioned the possibility of transitioning."

He finished off his food and wiped his fingers on a napkin before taking another swig of the lemonade. It was almost as if he was putting off an answer. "I was afraid you might bring that up."

"Why?"

"Because it's dangerous."

Would my interest in the words that spilled from his mouth ever cease?

"Well the tethering doesn't seem so bad, minus the knife part." I tried to make light of the situation but his face told a different story.

"I don't want that for you. Not everyone who chooses it survives."

Oh. Well, this conversation had just taken a heavy turn. Some date night I was headed into. I guess I wasn't doing so well at this casual, get-to-know-somebody conversation. I really knew how to unknowingly bring in the depressing subject material. But our time together was limited and I needed to gather as much information as he was willing to give.

"Transitioning to…a demon?"

"Yes." His answer was short.

"But I don't have to. Like, it's not required after the tethering or anything?" I just wanted to clarify before we moved on from the subject.

"Definitely not. And I don't think it's worth the risk. I've seen what it does to the ones left behind. It absolutely destroys them." He placed a hand over my free one as he continued. "I would never ask that of you, so please don't let that be a determining factor in the decision you have to make. I would rather keep you alive and human than risk the chance of losing you."

I wasn't sure how to respond to that notion.

"I can assure you that you will not be the only human there. You can live your life how you see fit. Make friends and do what you want to do. Work or don't work. Think of it as moving across seas, to another country or something to that extent."

"Hm…" That was definitely an interesting way to view this opportunity. I stared down at my half-eaten corn dog. I had one last question before I would try to turn this night around. So far, we had been all talk and no play.

"How old are you, exactly? I mean, if you're immortal, am I courting an old man right now? How would I know?"

He broke into a small fit of laughter but I continued to wait for an answer, patiently. When he realized I was serious, his features softened and he cleared his throat.

"I'm only twenty-nine. I requested your watch and tethering at twenty-three, to much disdain and pushback from the council. They don't usually approve of such things at that age. My uncle didn't request his tethering until age forty-nine. But I hear he made a lot of rounds before he found Sarah. You didn't hear that from me."

"So, I guess children between demons and humans are possible." Damn me and my mouth running away from me. It wasn't that I was planning on children anytime soon; it was far off my radar at present, but maybe someday. I deserved to know if that was a choice that this tethering would rip away from me.

Kade supplied a wicked grin and my face heated. "Very possible."

Squirming in my seat, I suppressed the urge I had to fan myself with our extra napkins. I wished I could blame the weather on the fever coming over me, but with the sun setting shortly, the temperature was already on the decline.

I pushed the corn dog down the stick so I could take another bite before we could move on. I offered the rest to Kade and he slid off the remainder, dunking it into the remains of his ketchup and finishing it off. I rotated my position to straddle the bench we sat upon, letting my dress fall between my legs where it thankfully still covered any view of my biker shorts beneath.

"So." I lightly slapped my hands on my thighs. "What do you want to do now? You wanted the carnival, what's caught your eye so far?"

I had to admit, I'd thought for a Friday night it would have been busier, but I didn't mind the smaller crowds. Although some changes had been made and new attractions added since the last time I had visited, I was ready to have some fun and do some exploring. After all, how many times would I get to experience this with a demon?

Kade scanned the area and settled on something behind me. "The bumper cars can't be that bad, can they? They seem slow."

I jumped up and at the ready. "Nope, you'll be fine. Press the pedal to go, turn the wheel, and make sure you're braced for impact."

"You make it sound like that's a normal thing." He stood and collected our trash and I followed him to the nearest trash receptacle.

"It is, it's bumper cars." I took his hand in mine as I led him toward the loud clanging of the cars.

I thought his blue eyes were going to bug out of his head when I told him to hop in one of the cars by himself. I gestured for him to put his lap bar down and when the music started, I put my foot down and let the mini car do its thing.

I had almost made a lap around Kade when another vehicle struck him. I let out a laugh as pure shock registered on his face, an amusing emotion that I hadn't witnessed from him until now.

I shouted to remind him to hit the pedal with his foot. He held on to the wheel with such a tight grip, I started to wonder if he was going to snap the thing in half with the amount of pressure he seemed to be putting on it.

Offering him a teasing wave of my fingers, I began to put some distance between us as I skirted around the perimeter. When I turned to head back in search of him, my vehicle was struck from the rear, blocking me in a corner with a jolt. Before I could get back in the game, I witnessed a teenager heading in Kade's direction, intent on colliding with him. They made an impact on their way toward me and I couldn't hold back the laugh that ripped through my throat. Kade was appalled at the entire situation as the giddy teenager with braces retreated, pumping his fist in the air.

"This is a complete clusterfuck!" He shook his head in disbelief.

"Welcome to your first carnival!" I beamed as I weaseled my way out and made a quick swoop, whizzing past Kade as fast as my little red car could take me. His steering was so stiff that I wondered if I should have just ridden with him to give him a quick lesson first before throwing him into the den of wolves; but it was far too late for that now. And judging by the angle he had to position his legs to accommodate the vehicle, I may not have had that much room.

The cars soon came to a halt and the music faded. When we exited, he began scratching his head as he looked back at the scene that had just unfolded. "I didn't even know any of those people and they just ran right into me."

"Yep. Doesn't matter who you are. Everyone is fair game. Not a fan, I take it?" I adjusted the strap at my shoulder and looped my thumb through the metal ring connecting to my purse.

"Jury is still out on that one." He let out a heavy sigh. I thought I already knew the answer.

I dragged him over to the Ferris wheel and hopped in line. "Are you afraid of heights?"

He shrugged. "Not that I'm aware of. But I guess I'm going to find out."

He took in the sight of the giant wheel before us and I handed our tickets over to the worker. I let Kade follow me in and the lap bar was lowered for us, clicking into place with a loud clunk. The sun was beginning to meet the horizon to our right as the wheel began to move. The mechanics of it creaked as it roared to life and I half wondered if this was any safer than the death trap that I'd driven to get us here. The grinding gears didn't help either.

I felt for the necklace that lay on my chest and rolled it between my fingers as we began lifting up and into the sky. I leaned on Kade's shoulder, taking in the sight of my hometown that went on for as far as my eyes could see from here. I adjusted as his arm came around to rest at my side and his fingers grazed it. His body relaxed as we curved at the top before coming back down.

"Maybe I should have eased you into all of this with the Ferris wheel first. I'm sorry." I pursed my lips, regretting my choice to break him in with the bumper cars first without much of an introduction.

"Don't be." His fingers drew up my arm as we passed the loading dock and made it about three quarters of the way up before we came to a stop. "I am on my first adventure with you. Hopefully the first of many."

I didn't want to provide any false hope or lead him on, and if I were being honest, I didn't know what the hell I wanted right now. I tried to focus on the carnival and that alone.

We were here to have fun and get to know each other. And after our earlier conversations, I had to make more of a lighthearted effort to bring the mood to something more playful. I needed to take a step back and see what he was attracted to around us. Judging by his reaction to the bumper cars and the drive here, I decided that go-karts were out unless he made the decision himself to give it a go. But I wasn't going to be the one to bring them up.

"Tell me, what should we hit up next? There's lots of swinging rides, games, more twirling rides, and food."

Straightening my back, I studied him, trying to memorize the face of the man before me, lit by the setting sun as the sky turned to hues of pink, orange, and blue. He was here and among other people. Being *seen* by other people.

Only yesterday I'd fully believed I was losing my mind, but this was very much real and happening. Here he was blending in among humans like he was one. Kade was not just some strange dream or figment of my imagination.

This courting, and the decision I would have to make, was all becoming too real.

"How about the basketball game?" he finally answered.

"Only if you win me a stuffed animal." I gave him a teasing wink as I continued. "But don't get your hopes up. Those games are almost impossible to win."

"Challenge accepted."

Once we were able to exit the wheel, I let Kade take the lead. To be honest, I wasn't sure where he had pinpointed its location, but I had no doubt we would find it eventually strolling down the gaming alley.

We arrived at the booth he had selected, manned by a young man who I might have guessed was a high schooler by his young and adolescent complexion, looking miserably bored. He was furiously typing away on his phone with his thumbs, only to put it away the moment he realized we were approaching him. Kade handed the man a five-dollar bill and I shot him a look of disbelief.

"Wait, you have money?" I quickly piped down, realizing that my blurting was a bit too loud. I didn't mean to embarrass him, if I did.

"Elias hooked me up." The worker gave an underhand toss of the ball to Kade. His referee outfit was too big for his slender body and he was drowning in it, even with it tucked into his slacks. "You didn't think you were going to have to pay for everything this evening, did you?"

Kade toyed with the ball in his hands for a few seconds, inspecting it. Did they even have money where he was from? Did he get paid for his watcher duties? Surely, they had some sort of currency even if it wasn't the type that I had grown up with, yet here he was handing over cash to play the game. It was hard to imagine a world without cars, so the idea that they may not relate on the money side of things wasn't that far-fetched.

I offered a wish of good luck and took a step back to allow him some space. He widened his stance and extended his arms with a flourish that sank the ball in the first shot. His feet never even left the ground, just a slight raise of his heels.

The worker who'd only halfway been paying attention to us now had his sights set on Kade as he handed him another ball.

Beginner's luck, I thought.

Kade examined the ball once again, firmly pressing his fingers into it before taking his stance and sinking the second ball.

I did a double take, not believing that he would actually be able to pull this off. Was I seeing things? I had never witnessed anyone play this game before with such ease; the ball didn't even bounce or hit the rim.

"Third one and you win your choice of a small stuffed animal," the worker spoke for the first time. His voice was so deep it didn't seem to match the body that it came out of.

Kade made quick work with his ball and sank it into the hoop once again without a single touch to the backboard on any of the three shots he had taken.

"Well, that wasn't so bad after all." Kade elbowed me playfully in the arm, a smug look registering on his face, but one that suited him well. One might think he was proud that he had the chance to prove me wrong. "Now what animal would you like?"

I let out an exaggerated sigh as I scanned the wall of plush and gestured toward a little yellow teddy bear with black beaded eyes. I supposed I should be more careful in what I asked for. Now I would have to carry this thing around for the rest of the night.

"Flowers, a necklace, and now a teddy bear." I sighed as I admired Kade's face, alight with a warmth that made my heart skip. We soon exited from view of the deep-voiced basketball worker and the hoop Kade had claimed victory over. I had to get him out of here before he won anything else. I studied the little bear as we made a right turn in our stroll, trying to plan another move that didn't involve any chance of toys.

"Violet, Violet!" A little girl's excitement rang through the surrounding noise of carnival-goers and I swiveled in its direction, recognizing the voice and searching to locate its owner.

Charlotte, otherwise known as Lottie, was my youngest cousin. She was obsessed with me for some unknown reason; I couldn't fathom why. Her blond curly hair was a twisted and tangled mess. She had no doubt been on rides having the time of her life tonight. I scooped her up without a second thought as her parents came into view.

Shit.

Lottie's parents picked up speed to follow after her. My aunt's gaze locked in on my companion for the evening and I froze.

Last they knew Brett and I were still together, and here I was with Kade, stuffed toy in hand and dressed up a bit more than my usual jeans and tee attire. I highly doubted my grandma had spread the news of my impending breakup yet. Little did she know, I had already followed through with it and cut ties with him.

Lottie's panda-bear grip on me didn't lessen as her parents caught up.

"Fancy seeing you here," my aunt greeted us, guarded as she glanced between Kade and me. The tone of her voice made it seem like she was awaiting an introduction to the man I was spending my time with tonight.

"Hey." My greeting was drawn out, knowing how this looked. I didn't think it painted me in a very good light. I gave Lottie a light squeeze and then pried her away from her hold on me to set her on the ground between us adults. "Um…Aunt Cindy, Uncle David, Lottie—this is Kade."

"Nice to meet you folks." Kade outstretched a hand and shook both of theirs, starting with my uncle who was the closest.

"Likewise," my uncle said, his firm handshake a stark difference from that of my aunt. While they were polite, I could sense their silent judgment.

"Mommy, I have to go potty." Lottie began doing her little tiptoe dance.

"Of course you do," my aunt groaned.

"But I want Violet to take me." Lottie pouted her little bottom lip out as far as she could.

"Well I think Violet is busy, sweetie."

"It's okay." I figured I could use this as a chance to relieve myself as well. "You'll be fine, right?" I glanced at Kade, offering a reassuring smile.

"Sure, go ahead." He didn't even skip a beat. I was hoping he was becoming more comfortable in our surroundings at this point, but then I guess I'd never asked him how often he had visited my world before our courtship began. Apparently not enough to ever warrant the use of a car.

"I'll come too," Aunt Cindy piped in. Her dark blond hair was pulled back, but the humidity had taken a toll on her and it had grown in volume from its usual sleek tresses.

While I was relieved that my aunt wasn't staying behind with Kade, she undoubtedly wanted the inside scoop as to what I was doing here without Brett.

Kade would be alright with my uncle, as he was pretty chill about everything and everyone in general. He was just an inviting and warm person who seemed to genuinely care about whatever you had to say. You had to give him a pretty good reason to dislike you.

It was my aunt who concerned me as she made everybody's business, her business.

"Where's Brett?" she asked as soon as we were out of earshot.

"History," I spit out without giving her a glance. Lottie was skipping along beside me humming a tune I didn't recognize, her small hand tucked into mine.

"Oh?" She seemed surprised.

"Yeah, it just wasn't working anymore." I really didn't want to talk about Brett, especially with her. In fact, I'd thought she would be drilling me about Kade by now.

"Is it because he popped the question?"

I stopped dead in my tracks and glared at her, but she was unwavering in her deliverance of the words and without regret. She wore a tank top from her college days, and shorts, her tanned skin a lucky blessing she had bestowed on all of her children. She looked tired and run-down for her age. I could only assume that having a five-year-old would be tiresome after raising two other kids who were well into their teen years. Lottie was an oops and my uncle had apparently gotten himself fixed after that ordeal.

"Who do you think your grandma called to vent?" She raised an eyebrow and I was struggling to stay level-headed.

Did it have to be Aunt Cindy? Anybody else but her.

I knew she visited my grandma regularly, more than I had been since moving out. At least I knew my grandma would be taken care of if I decided to take up Kade on his offer. She wouldn't be alone. She still had family.

I continued on to the park's indoor restroom facility. "I didn't give him the chance to do it."

Letting that information settle, she and Lottie went into a bathroom stall and I entered another. I finished up long before them and toyed with the idea of waiting for them or fleeing and heading back to the boys before she could ask anything else.

"But I want to ride it agaaaain," Lottie started to whine, and I chuckled. She must be getting tired. I wondered how long they had been here tonight and figured it had to be getting close to Lottie's bedtime. I listened to their exchange, my aunt trying to bribe her with excuses to leave and things to look forward to this weekend, but still she carried on in her struggle to triumph over her mother. "But I don't want to leeeeeaave!"

When they exited the stall, I could see the strain on Aunt Cindy's face—she appeared worn out to the hilt. The fluorescents in our enclosed space highlighted the dark circles beneath her eyes that had gone unnoticed outside.

"Is this a date that we crashed?" I was questioned as she lifted Lottie to wash her hands since there was no step stool of any kind to give her a boost. She was oblivious to the other women that came and went, asking as if we were the only people in here.

"I wouldn't say that you crashed it."

Aunt Cindy narrowed her eyes. "Does your grandma know?"

"Do I need to tell her about every date I have?" I countered.

I couldn't help it, but I felt like I was in the wrong, trying

146

to justify a date so soon after breaking things off with Brett. And apparently, a relationship that he had thought to be serious enough to warrant a proposal.

I just hoped he hadn't gotten as far as buying a ring. Sure, what had been in his pocket last night had looked like the kind of box that could hold something like that, but I never saw it to verify and I had only heard about a proposal from my grandma. Hopefully I'd squashed that hope of his before he had gone too far with it.

"No, but she cares about you as if you were her own daughter. Just be careful, is all I'm trying to say."

Lottie reached up, opening and closing her hands, and I lifted her up, letting her secure herself to me. "I like your teddy bear. What's its name?" She rubbed her eyes as she reached for it.

"I don't know, Kade just won it for me. What do you think its name should be?"

She pondered for a moment, eyes fixated on the plush toy. "Dottie!" She giggled as we exited the bathrooms and made our way back outside. I hadn't realized how boisterous the carnival was until all the commotion welcomed us back.

"On a side note, I'm not sure where you snagged this Kade, but he's really easy on the eyes. Kind of puts Brett to shame."

"Aunt Cindy!" I scolded her at the admission.

"What? I might be married, but I can appreciate a good-looking man when I see one. And those eyes of his, swoon."

I laughed at her remarks. If only she knew what his eyes really looked like, I highly doubted she would think the same.

We returned to the row of games and I was suspicious of the scene that was unfolding. People had gathered around the basketball hoops and as a ball dipped into the basket, they started to cheer. Making our way through the crowd, we made it to the front to find the men we had left behind.

"One more, you've got this!" Uncle David's face was alight with enthusiasm as he clapped his hands awkwardly. I couldn't recall him having two bags of cotton candy and another full of caramel popcorn when we had left, and now he was attempting to cheer on Kade with the sweets in his grasp.

"What's going on?" my aunt questioned the onlookers around us.

A skinny, teenage brunette answered back, "This guy has made nineteen hoops in a row!"

Kade was handed the ball one more time. As if he could sense my presence, he turned his head in my direction as he repeated the winning stance I had witnessed earlier. His pearly white smile flashed at me as we made eye contact, and within seconds, he sent the ball flying through the air and landed another shot to perfection.

The small crowd that had accumulated erupted into cheers as my uncle patted him on the back. They all began to disburse as the excitement of his spectacle died down.

The teenage worker, who now appeared to be enjoying his job, retrieved a giant pink unicorn from the side wall. My eyes bulged at its magnitude. "Oh god, I do not want to carry that around for the rest of the night."

Aunt Cindy scrambled to hold back a cackle of amusement at my plight and she began making her way up through the parts of the crowd that opened up. "I think David might have a new best friend. He's practically drooling. Look at him."

"I leave for a few minutes and you've got an audience full of admirers," I stated as we met back up.

Lottie's eyes landed on the pink unicorn and her little mouth popped open. "It's so pretty!"

Kade accepted the unicorn and held it out to Lottie. "I

heard that you like pink." He held it out to her and she leapt from my arms and into the stuffed animal, squealing with glee. She bounced up and down, giddy, as a second wind seemed to breathe new life into the tired little girl. The unicorn was practically double her size.

"You really don't have to do that." My aunt cleared her throat.

Kade shrugged it off as he put his arm around my waist. I couldn't help but be flattered by the small gesture and I leaned into him.

"Well, clearly there's no taking it back now." I looked to Lottie who was now trying to hoist the massive toy over her shoulder but failing. She might topple over backwards if she kept at it.

"Here, have some cotton candy." My uncle tossed a bag at us and Kade caught it with his free hand. Uncle David then took possession of the unicorn from Lottie and threw it over his shoulder, a narrow miss from hitting a person behind him.

"Thanks, David." Kade nodded as he examined the bag.

"We should probably head out. It's getting late." Aunt Cindy seemed even more adamant to race out of here now that they had a giant plushie to carry around. By now the sun was at the brink of disappearing and all the carnival lights were illuminating the grounds. "We'll let you guys get back to your date."

Lottie rushed over and gave Kade a squeeze around his legs. "Thank you, thank you, thank you!" She grinned from ear to ear before coming to me. I knelt and gave her a squeeze as she whispered in my ear before letting go, "I like him."

"I do too," I whispered back, my heart feeling full. I hadn't known what to expect from sharing my time with Kade with others around, others who happened to be my family. I was glad to say that he didn't disappoint.

We all exchanged goodbyes and let them go on their way. I let out a drawn-out sigh through my parted lips, relieved that our encounter had come to an end. "That went surprisingly well."

"Did you have doubts?"

"About you? Not so much. My uncle is harmless. It's my aunt who I was concerned about," I admitted. "And what about you? Are you some sort of basketball star back home? In Dar…"

"Darthou," he finished for me. I knew I was going to forget the name. "Not in the slightest. I've observed occasional games in your world, sure. We've made courts modeled after yours, played various sports and experimented with them. It's a hobby for some, I just go along for the ride sometimes."

I took his hand in mine and began to walk away from the scene of his victory. The basketball worker might run out of stuffed toys if Kade remained in this one spot tonight. It made me speculate just how much money he had bummed off of his friend as these carnival games weren't exactly cheap.

"What do you do in your downtime? Do you have any hobbies or anything?"

"I like music. I've even dabbled with a few instruments myself. I train with Elias quite frequently though, be it dueling or just working out. I try to keep busy when I'm not watching. Sometimes it's hard to switch my brain off."

I could understand that feeling, wanting to keep busy so my mind didn't have a chance to dwell on my past and my anxieties. I always had to be doing something. Working, walking, reading, watching a show or movie.

"What is this exactly? It looks like a giant cotton ball."

Coming to a stop, I snatched the bag from his hands and

opened it. I stuck my fingers in and pinched off a piece of the pink fluff and pulled it away. I acted as if I was going to feed it to Kade, letting it graze his lips before popping it into my mouth. It dissolved instantly and I let out a small moan as the delicious treat melted away against my tongue.

I twisted my mouth to the side, playfully.

"Just testing it out." I pinched another piece between my fingers.

Kade's eyes flickered for a fraction of a second and this time I knew I hadn't seen incorrectly. I wondered if it was hard to keep up the facade of the blue eyes.

When I slipped my hand from the bag, his hand closed around my wrist, raising it toward his mouth to make sure I didn't pull a fast one on him again. His lips closed upon my fingers as I released the cotton candy and he slid them out. I swore my heart skipped a beat at the encounter and my breath caught.

He released my wrist only to clasp onto my hand. The same poker face returned, giving nothing away as to what he thought of the pink treat.

"I found something I want to do." His voice was low, seductive even, and it had my body responding in ways I wasn't expecting it to in a public setting such as this.

"Then by all means, lead the way." Dottie and cotton candy in hand, I followed beside him, wondering what had caught his eye this time.

When he made a right turn, there was no mistaking where we were headed.

I observed his profile, curious about his decision to enter the Maze of Mirrors. Few people were in this part of the carnival, most opting for the rides and food vendors that had set up shop here. We made our way up to the entrance as a bunch of teenagers exited the attraction. Some of them were exclaiming how they never thought they would make it out of there, and another laughed at how one of them ran into a mirror and they all erupted into fits of laughter.

For someone whose life revolved around mirrors and reflective surfaces, I wasn't sure what about this place begged his attention.

Techno music filled the space as we entered the off-centered doorway. The neon lighting was low but cast shadows upon us and our path sporadically. Kade removed the cotton candy and Dottie from my hands, leaving me with my cross-body purse. He then backed into a mirror, a mischievous grin on his face as he rippled away.

"What..." His vanishing act caught me off guard. I searched the mirrors around me, waiting for him to turn up again, fearful of the entrance we had just come through and if anyone else might catch the sight I had just witnessed.

"Over here." It was as if I could feel his breath on my neck as he announced his location. I caught a glimpse of him in a mirror to my right before he left again.

The tumultuous music sent me down a row of wobbled and odd mirrors, changing my shape and size with each one that I passed. Fingers brushed from the side of my knee and up under my skirt, closing in on my shorts not far from the hem. My heart began pounding in my chest with excitement.

Kade had an unfair advantage in this game he was playing but I didn't care. I caught sight of him again as lips planted on my collarbone, and as much as I wanted to release a moan, I tried not to give him the satisfaction.

I had no sense of direction in this maze, and I searched high and low for any sign of movement. Arms reached out from behind me and Kade's reflection appeared, pulling me flush against the hardened surface of the glass as he locked me into place.

"Watch me," he instructed seductively as his eyes bore into mine.

I followed his hand as it made its way down between my breasts, slow in its descent down my stomach, continuing down to my nether regions which began to pulsate at the scene unfolding before me. The mirror pinched our reflection in the middle, his hand almost disappearing before the image grew larger again and he made contact at the apex of my thighs. Applying slight pressure, the lower his hand dived, the enjoyment came to an abrupt halt when he vanished again.

The remnants of his touch lingered after he had gone.

Breathless, and a bit agitated at the tease, I scanned my surroundings and found a glimpse of him ahead and I took off. Well, as fast as I could without running into something.

A hand caught and pulled me from my pursuit as I came face-to-face with him. He placed a piece of cotton candy through my parted lips, only to follow with a harsh kiss. His tongue explored mine aggressively as the sweet substance melted between our mouths. I grabbed a fistful of his shirt, willing him to stay as I backed myself up against a mirror to block any exit strategy he might have his sights set on.

Our hands roamed each other in a feverish state, consumed by the heat of the moment and lack of air movement in here. My forehead began to perspire and I raised a leg, eager to feel his arousal at my core. Kade grasped my leg behind my knee and ground his hips into mine. His lips left my mouth and he continued down my jawline, creating a trail down my neck. The way in which my body ached for him caused me to whimper, longing for the chance to connect.

A cackle of laughter caused us to break apart and my leg

went weak from the sudden and unwelcome interruption. I gasped for air as I tried to collect myself, smoothing out my dress and readjusting my bra. I wanted to exit before we became trapped in here with its new guests.

"Not to break up our date, but..." I panted, trying to recover.

"I've seen enough of the carnival," he replied, a fiery intensity to his facial features. He had my insides all askew as I recognized the need in his eyes that I also harbored.

I took his hand and let him lead me out of the mirrored maze without a single wrong turn.

CHAPTER 11

Violet

The entire ride home, Kade's hand lay on my exposed knee. The contact kept my body on high alert and I struggled to remain calm as I took the less traveled roads and slower speeds back to my apartment. What I really wanted was to put the pedal to the metal and take the quickest way back, but given his earlier reaction to traffic and other vehicles, I fought the urge to do so.

Once on my floor, I made the connection as to how Kade had arrived tonight without entering his usual way. The opening elevator doors revealed a rather large and modern framed mirror and I gestured toward it. "You know you could have used my mirror for tonight, you didn't have to use that."

He offered a shy smile as he replied, "First date. I was trying to be polite."

I paused outside my door and decided to have a little fun

with him. "I guess this is me. I enjoyed our date tonight."

Apparently, his poker face was limited in its displays, because the dumbfounded expression that overtook him had me in a fit of laughter. I, on the other hand, couldn't get away with anything of the sort. My face spoke volumes even when I didn't want it to.

His mood darkened as his head dipped down. My amusement came to a halt and I stiffened.

"Got any more of that cotton candy?" I bit my lip as I recalled his exploration of my mouth and the sweet pink treat that had led to our exchange earlier. I entered my apartment and let him follow before I began locking the mechanisms and released my purse to the floor with a light thud.

"I can retrieve it if you like." He began unbuttoning his shirt and I leaned up against the door, letting my feet slide out of my sneakers.

I shook my head, changing my mind. I didn't want him to leave, not for a second, as even that would be too long.

"Another time, maybe." My breath quickened and the rise and fall of my breasts seemed rather exaggerated even though I wasn't trying to do it.

With his final button free, he took a step forward, but I stopped him.

"Wait." I didn't want him to lay a finger on me before I could make one small request. "Change your eyes back."

Kade's falsified blue eyes were gone within a blink and I was more than pleased to see his normal ones again. "Do you really prefer these?"

I nodded my head slowly. "I said I accepted you as you are, right? Eyes and all."

My hands gently pushed his chest and I walked him back toward the bed. He watched me intently as I freed his member and clasped my hand around it, working it from root to tip a few times before I lowered to the floor. A small bead of cum began to form at the end.

The black pools that I had missed this evening followed me down and, looking up through my lashes, I took him in my mouth. His body visibly sagged and his head rolled back slightly as I began to move on him. I devoured him as far as I could take, and a hand came to rest at the base of my ponytail as I continued my work.

He became vocal as he moved against me. His hand, tugging at my hair and my body, was responding to the sounds his throat emitted. When I glanced up and met his stare, I showed my teeth along his tip and smiled.

"Fuck." He removed my head and pulled me up to standing, and his lips crashed onto mine.

My body was aflame with my need as the ache between my legs throbbed. I longed for him to fill me and consume every inch of my being.

Unzipping the back of my dress, he peeled it away and I slid his shirt off of his arms, letting our garments fall to the floor. His lips grazed past my necklace and the swells of my cleavage. I took a sharp intake of air as he continued down my middle, then he dragged my biker shorts and panties down all in one and I stepped out of them.

"Lie back," he instructed, and I obeyed without hesitation, letting my feet stay on the ground only to be scooped up and sat upon his shoulders.

His fingers parted my flesh and his mouth made its way to my sweet spot. I arched my back at the speed of his contact. He flicked and sucked and I was soon spiraling. I gripped the bedspread with one hand while the other took hold of his hair. I couldn't stop moving—no, writhing—against his attack on my clit.

Long fingers began to explore my insides and I moaned at their entrance. But as much as I reveled in the intense pleasure he was providing, it still wasn't enough. I needed him inside me. I wanted to feel his length fill me until I screamed.

"I need you." I rolled my hips as he withdrew at my pleading rasp.

He lowered his jeans slightly down his muscled thighs and I let my knees fall toward me and away, granting him all the access he needed for a swift entrance.

"Please," I begged as I sat up on my forearms. If he didn't come down here, I was prepared to launch myself at him as I couldn't wait any longer.

I didn't think I had ever craved anyone as much as I did him. Every fiber of my being hungered for the connection.

At an agonizingly slow pace, he bent down to cover my body, his member hovering around my swollen opening. My hands made a feeble attempt to pull him in closer and his face delivered that wicked grin that promised everything I needed to know.

"Eager, are we?" he teased as his member brushed against me with a slow roll of his hips.

I nodded. "Only for you."

Our mouths met as he slammed into me and I couldn't suppress the sound that left my throat on the impact. My eyes pricked with tears and my nails dug into his back as his hips pounded into me, unrelenting.

This. This is what I needed.

My breasts were slowly working their way out of the confines of my bra with each thrust and I was lost to the sensations consuming me. It was hard to admit, but I was beginning to think I wanted to end every day like this. Tangled together with Kade and screwing around for as long as our bodies could possibly stand it. I liked to think that I would never tire of the chemistry created between the two of us, that we would never get enough of each other's bodies and what happened when we came together.

Seeing him at the carnival tonight, giving us a chance at an ordinary date, made me think that we might be able to work this out. I wanted to give this, give *us*, a chance. Maybe it was selfish of me to want this and the unknown world and life that Kade offered, but I didn't think I could live with the choice of not seeing where this could possibly go.

Kade was nonstop in his drive, and we soon found ourselves at the finish line, uncontrollably releasing as our bodies spasmed around each other. Kade rolled onto his back, his body slick with sweat as he pulled me atop him and held me tight.

Kissing his chest, I let my head rest against it as I came down from the high that he had provided. I closed my eyes and let my mind wander, thinking about accepting his proposal, about the tethering, and anything else a future with him might hold. I wanted to meet his family and see his world.

Maybe it was foolish and naive of me to think this way, but I couldn't fight the feeling that this was where I was supposed to be.

With Kade.

I must have drifted off at some point. It didn't feel like it was that long ago that I'd been snuggled into Kade but now I awoke to the darkness of my apartment and I felt oddly cold.

Images of our entangled limbs and heated exchange flitted through me and I longed for his touch. I hugged my blankets in close and I realized the bed was empty when I met no resistance. I sat up, searching my surroundings for him, but couldn't make anything out.

"Kade?"

Loneliness crept in as I didn't hear a reply and I reached over to turn on my bedside lamp. I muttered a curse as the harsh light blinded me. His shirt and shoes still lay on the floor among my clothing and I got up from the bed deciding to check the bathroom. When it came up empty, I retrieved my robe and went to collect my phone from my purse. It chimed as I pulled it out, and Brett's name caught my attention.

Oh good grief. What the hell did he want now?

It was almost one in the morning and I had eleven unread messages and three missed calls from him. Was I really so out of it that I hadn't heard a single one of these notifications go off until now? I hadn't bothered silencing my phone at the carnival since it was so loud that I wouldn't have been able to hear it anyway.

I had every intention of blocking his number without reading anything he had sent, but what popped up on my screen knocked the air right out of my body.

A picture of myself feeding Kade cotton candy at the carnival tonight sent an unsolicited shiver through my entirety. I cupped my hand over my mouth as I began reading the messages calling me a slut and a cheater. Threatening me, telling me that I would never find anything like what we had and I would be sorry for the choices that I had made.

Brett's face lit up the screen with an incoming call as it began to ring.

I was more fearful about this possible interaction now that

he knew about Kade. I could only imagine how this picture had added more fuel to the fire in his hostility since the call I'd experienced at work. I trembled uncontrollably, not wanting to answer but also fearing what would happen if I continued to ignore him.

"Violet, what's wrong?"

Kade came up from behind me and looked over my shoulder. He swiped at the screen to answer it and replied with a rough "wrong number." He ended the call and tossed it on the bed. "Violet, are you okay?"

My eyes searched the ground before me as I attempted to find the words that were jumbled about inside my head.

"Speak to me, Violet. Please," he urged as his voice rose and his outstretched arms held mine at the sides. His wintry touch went right through the thin sleeves of my robe.

"I've never seen him act like this." I was rattled to my core as I thought about the image on my phone. A moment that I had remembered so fondly was now tainted because of Brett.

He acted as if I was his, and his only. The possessiveness and entitlement made my words shake. "He was there. At the carnival. He had a picture of us together." I gulped as Kade ushered me to sit on the bed. I retrieved the message history and showed it to him, not able to bring myself to look upon it another time.

"You watch people." I turned my attention to him and not the phone. "Brett wouldn't do anything stupid, would he?"

Kade's face turned grim as his lips pressed into a thin line. My stomach dropped at his small movement, his silence speaking volumes.

"Would he?" I urged, louder.

"He has some tendencies that haven't gone unnoticed."

"What does that even mean?" I stood to put some distance

between us.

"It means that he now has a full-time watcher assigned to him since you two have split. I could keep my eye on him while you two were together. But seeing as how I'm now in the middle of this"—he gestured between us—"I can't watch him to the extent that he requires right now."

Wrongdoers of this world. Murderers. Rapists. That was what Kade had told me about his work and the duties of others like him. Brett now fell into that category to be watched.

"But he wouldn't actually act on anything, right?" I couldn't help the downward spiral of worst-case scenarios that were flooding my brain. "You've been watching for some time now. In your expert opinion, would Brett try something?"

He stood and tried to level his gaze with mine, dipping his chin down. "As long as I'm here, I won't let any harm come to you. I promise."

He might as well have said yes with a response like that. Who the hell did I just break up with? How had I been dating a man for eight months without knowing what he was capable of?

"Don't make promises that you can't keep."

Kade took a step back in confusion. "What do you—"

"Where were you? I awoke and you were gone." My voice came off harsher than I had meant for it to, but my emotions were raging and all over the place, getting the best of me.

He held his hands up in defense. "I swear I wasn't gone for long, maybe half an hour at most. I was dealing with this exact situation."

"And?" I needed more information than that.

"And I don't think Brett is acting alone. I never saw him once at the carnival tonight."

I opened my mouth to speak but quickly closed it again.

Who the hell would rat me out to Brett? Perhaps one of his buddies? Did they really have nothing better to do? I understood that the short amount of time between breaking up with Brett and being seen with Kade might be problematic in itself, but it was nobody else's damn business.

"I can't exactly prove it yet, but I think he might be working with a saint, and he most likely wouldn't even be aware of it. I sensed one at the carnival tonight but they have shifting abilities just as we do. It could have been anybody."

I pondered that information for a beat. I'd thought he was just overwhelmed at times tonight and taking everything in, but in reality, he was on high alert due to the possibility of a saint in our vicinity. "How could you tell that there was one there?"

He sighed, his head hanging low. "I'm not sure how to explain it, in all honesty. But I've spent a large enough part of my life watching others to know when I myself am being watched. If my eyes had been my kind of normal, I might have been able to pick up on their location better. Narrow them down, but I—"

"Is that why your eyes changed? It was brief, but I saw it." The realization hit me that it hadn't been a weakness in his upkeep of his appearance at all. He'd been trying to scan our surroundings in search of the saint.

That caught Kade off guard. "You noticed?"

I nodded. "It was brief. The first time I thought I was seeing things. The second time I knew I wasn't." I resisted the urge to talk about the first time I'd thought his eyes had flashed, when we were parked outside my apartment building. I was afraid of knowing the truth about how often he was examining the area and when he suspected a saint of being nearby.

"Huh, and here I thought I was being discreet."

Silence came between us and we stood for a while. I resisted the urge to let my fingers tangle themselves and decided to ball them into fists instead.

"I'm sorry I wasn't here." His apology made my heart ache. I hadn't meant for it to come off like that, but I didn't know how else to react. I hadn't exactly been put in this kind of predicament before.

"I'm sorry, I wasn't in my right mind when—"

"Don't even finish that thought." He pulled me back with him to lie on the bed. My left thigh lifted up on top of his legs, snuggling into place against him, cold again from his return.

I could feel myself grow heavier as I relaxed in his presence. Reflecting on our time this evening and the course of our quick courtship so far, I watched his chest rise and fall and tried to memorize the citrus scent that came with him. It was unlike anything I had ever experienced before and not one I ever wanted to part with. It was almost like an aphrodisiac that both calmed and excited me.

I was falling for him. The speed at which I was left little doubt in my mind on my decision to accept this tethering thing. Even if I wasn't quite ready to admit that out loud just yet, my answer was becoming clearer. Only last night, I'd been beside myself with the introduction to him and his world, and now here I was, head over heels for him.

"Do you have to work this weekend or am I limited to evenings with you?" I didn't want him to leave in the morning if he didn't have to. Sunday night, I would have to make a decision, and I wanted to spend as much time with him as possible before I had to officially make that call.

"Elias and his father are splitting my work as we speak, so unless a situation arises, I am all yours until you tell me otherwise."

"Good. Because Aunt Cindy has no doubt alerted my grandma by now about us, and I would really like for you to meet her."

"I would be honored to meet her." He agreed immediately and I raised my head.

"Are you sure? Because she isn't aware that I broke up with Brett already, and here I'll be strolling in with a complete stranger on my arm."

"Ouch, a complete stranger?" he poked fun at me. I nudged him with my hips, seeing as my arms were curled up between us.

A strange and faint tapping came from above me and I glanced up at Kade quizzically. I didn't recognize the sound, but he sat up on the bed and scooted off.

"Cover up," was all he said, and I scrambled to gather the comforter around me as he rounded the mattress. He swiped in a downward motion on the surface of my mirror and it fogged over.

"What's wrong?" Kade's stern reaction had me inching forward in the hopes of catching sight of something in the mirror, but I couldn't hear or see anything. Just a one-sided conversation.

"Are you sure?"

I peeked a little further forward. Kade cast no reflection in the mirror; its surface remained unchanging and foggy and I could only view him from the side closest to me.

"How much time do we have?"

My heart sped up. Time? Time for what?

Whatever news was being delivered didn't sound too promising. Was it Elias, his unnamed father, or both? The two were taking charge of his duties while he finished out his time here with me. If those two took care of the amount of people that Kade did on the regular, hopefully splitting up his twenty-some wouldn't be a huge undertaking. But for my peace of mind and the comfort that Kade's presence brought me now that Brett was an unpredictable threat, I made the mental note to thank them both should we ever get the chance to meet.

"Thank you." Kade parted from the mirror and began picking up our clothes from the floor as I scurried to the mirror. Just as quickly as it had fogged over, the fog vanished within about two seconds.

"What's going on?" My heart was beating so erratically I clutched my robe together at its front. "Is everything okay?"

Kade took our clothes and deposited them in my linen basket just outside the bathroom before returning. "Everything will be fine, but we should be expecting company."

"At this hour? Who?"

Kade looked toward my phone on the bed that had been silent since Brett's last call.

"Brett?" My voice quaked at the thought of him coming over after all of his attempts to contact me. The headspace he must be in right now was petrifying.

"Tracking him has been no easy feat and some of his whereabouts this evening are unknown, which solidifies the fact that he must be working with a saint. No one can place him at the carnival, but he has since been barhopping and now he's on his way here."

I felt so small and vulnerable within the confines of my apartment. There was only one way in and one way out. I wouldn't even trust the fire escape outside my window if my life depended on it. If Brett lost his mind over a photo of Kade and me, I didn't want to imagine how he would react to a bare-chested Kade in my place.

"What should I do?"

Kade pulled me into a tight embrace and I didn't move. "Just breathe. I'm here and I will take care of it."

I hated that I had no way to defend myself, but up until this point in my life, I had never felt that I needed it. The only times I had even touched a gun, or any type of weapon for that matter, were out in the country at my Uncle Steven's farm, but that had been years ago.

I'd never thought I would see the day that my situation would warrant protection like this of any kind. If I had been here alone and Brett showed up unannounced, if I didn't have the knowledge of his impending visit, I would have opened the door ready to fight with my words.

Now, I didn't even want to see his face at all.

A thought dawned on me and I darted to my closet, pulling out a tattered box. I began rummaging through it as I knew it had to be in here somewhere. Some people, like my grandma, had a junk drawer in their kitchen full of miscellaneous items that they were always afraid to get rid of because they might need it someday. For me, I guess that junk had accumulated in this box.

A series of three slow bangs on my door sent a chill through me and I visibly shook at Brett's arrival. Finding the item I had been searching for, I made sure my robe was securely tied before hiding it behind my back and rejoining Kade.

Two more harsh bangs caused me to jump as they seemed to echo through the space I called home. The deafening sound reverberated in my head and I began to worry about the other tenants in the building. Hopefully they didn't become a part of this ordeal; I didn't want anyone else to get involved.

"Open up, Violet." Brett's apparent drinking combined with his anger had him spilling loud and slurred words.

Practically soundless, Kade swiftly approached the door, unlocking the set of mechanisms, and swung it open.

My ex and my current…whatever he was, were now face-to-face and I could only imagine the look that Kade had met him with. Brett was disheveled, his shirt askew, and his perfect hair was all wrong and out of place. His face, red with anger and no doubt liquor, caused me to take a step back, drawing his attention to me.

"You slut!" he practically spat in my direction, avoiding Kade.

"That's enough." Kade tried to block Brett's view of me, but Brett poked his head up and over Kade's shoulder.

"How long?"

I took a step back, bumping into my bed.

"How long have you been fucking him?" His voice rose as his face distorted into that of what I could only describe as a monster.

What had I ever seen in him? I didn't recognize the man looming in my doorway.

"I said, that's enough!" Kade's voice boomed and both Brett and I winced at the demand in his tone. Even at the intensity of Kade's order, I still didn't fear him in the way that I did Brett.

He made a feeble attempt to take a swing at Kade but missed, almost toppling himself over.

Finding my voice, I took a step forward. "Stop it, Brett, you're making a fool out of yourself." I tried to widen my stance to steady my footing. "You need to leave before you wake up the entire apartment building."

"What makes him so special?" he sneered as he tried to step through the doorway but he faltered.

"She asked you to leave," Kade intervened.

Brett tried to swing again and this time as he missed, Kade delivered an uppercut so swift to Brett's stomach that I swore his toes left the ground. He slumped over, trying to recover, and gasped for air as if he were trying to replenish it all in one swoop. It sounded agonizingly painful.

"Leave," I repeated again as I approached. "I don't ever want to see or hear from you ever again. This is the last time I will tell you this. It's over!"

His face twisted into an expression of revulsion, hatred spewed from every pore and I could feel it in the air. "I oughta—"

Releasing my secret weapon from behind my back, I unleashed a stream of pepper spray, coating his eyes until he began to shriek and retreat. The sense of relief that flooded through me as he backed into the hallway was a high I had never experienced before.

I was able to defend myself after all, and it felt pretty damn good. I'd been given this little can back in high school and had been unsure if it would really work or not, but the fact that it had made it all the more satisfying.

"You bitch!" Brett wailed as he clawed at his eyes and the effects from the spray. The veins in his neck were seemingly about to burst as his skin reddened on the upper half of his body.

By now my closest neighbor had opened her door enough that I could make out her face and the chain that was still intact. The look of fear in Ms. Vanders' face was evident as her view settled on Kade, clad only in sweatpants, grabbing Brett by the back of his shirt as he began to drag him toward the elevator.

"Can you please call the police?" I kept my voice as low as I could but loud enough for her to hear. She nodded and shut the door with a loud click of her deadbolt.

Rushing to my dresser, I pulled out the first pair of pajama bottoms I saw and I almost tipped over in my attempt to yank them on. Grabbing Kade's shirt, I threw on some sandals and bolted from my apartment.

I blazed down the hallway toward the stairwell, hoping I wouldn't be too far behind as I didn't want to wait the time it would take for the elevator to return. Leaping down the last couple of stairs, I could hear Brett's cries as I opened the door onto the main floor lobby. He was a crumpled mess on the floor where Kade must have deposited him.

Within minutes, the police showed up and escorted Brett to their car. I only hoped that getting them involved would help convey the gravity of this situation, that it would make Brett understand that I meant business and I wanted nothing more to do with him. His actions were unacceptable and I wasn't going to tolerate it.

I'd like to think that a run-in with the police might sober him up in his shitty efforts to pursue or keep me, but knowing that he worked for a law firm, even in a minority position such as his, I didn't have high hopes.

Kade remained by my side throughout the ordeal, never bothering to button up his shirt. He remained quiet unless spoken to as we delivered our statements to the officer that stayed behind with us. The other was standing outside of the police car on his phone and periodically he would talk into the radio attached at his shoulder.

The ease with which Kade answered the officer's questions surprised me, and I hoped that my face didn't give anything away. From our conversation and for the police report, Kade provided a last name of Thomas. Given the names I had heard so far from Darthou, the generic name didn't seem to fit. He'd no doubt plucked it out of thin air because of how common it was. He also declared that he was only here visiting and picked the sunny state of Florida as his home, noting that he worked for a private security firm. It was a bit comical, considering what he actually did for a living.

We thanked the officer and began our retreat to the elevator. With a glance over my shoulder, I checked the police car one last time, almost afraid that they would let Brett out if I didn't pay attention. But the officers entered the front of the car, illuminating the backseat as they did. I could see Brett's silhouette facing my direction as the elevator doors closed on the scene.

I let out a shaky breath, knowing that I was no longer on display for him. Under that demeaning and ugly scowl that I couldn't rid from my memory, the thought that things could have gone much worse tonight plagued me.

I hadn't stopped clutching my robe closed since Brett had arrived, knowing I wore nothing beneath it, and my hands were sore from doing so.

When the elevator reached my floor, Kade swooped me into his hold and exited, heading down the hall. I let my head rest on his chest as I nuzzled into him.

"Remind me to never get on your bad side." Kade spoke softly as he kicked the door closed behind him. He sat me down on the bed and then returned to the door, locking all three sets of mechanisms before running his hands through his hair.

"Would pepper spray even affect you?" I inquired. "I know you said you could still be harmed even though you're immortal."

"I have felt the effects once but I did not have the experience that he just had. You might have doused him with the whole can."

I stifled a laugh as a sense of pride came over me, realizing that I had sent Brett into a crippling state. Funny how fast he could be taken down to the size of a toddler by a small little can and its contents. I felt powerful, and my body was alive and primed for action.

I stood from the bed and let my bottoms fall to the floor. Untying my robe, I let it do the same. Kade's eyes changed from blue to black in an instant and I grinned in approval as we neared each other.

Grabbing the opening of his shirt, I closed the distance between us. Hands grasping and bodies grinding against each other made it difficult to remove his pants to meet my naked skin. My heightened emotions, and the high alert I had been on, were now melting away as I focused on nothing more than what came so naturally between us. I craved our connection as my selfish need arose between my legs.

I yanked my hair free from its hold and it fell in waves down my back, gliding across my skin and I grinned. God, I loved that feeling. The light sway of it compared to Kade's grip on me, a contrast that had my body singing.

His long fingers curled into my sweet spot and I moaned into his mouth as his palm cupped me. My body turned on for him like a light switch, ready at a moment's notice.

I rotated in his hold, his hand retreating as I bent over the bed, urging my entrance toward his cock. His fingers parted me and I braced for his arrival. He sank into me and my shoulders sagged at his presence as he penetrated me. I fisted my hands in the covers before me as I adjusted to his member, my hair creating a halo around my head.

I was already panting before he picked up speed, and I thought he might tear me apart in this position. I was reeling in our connection, oblivious to anything around me and solely focused on us.

Kade drove into me over and over, the speed of each thrust promising a grand release if I didn't pass out from the intensity of it all first. He became vocal, joining me on the chase for the explosion that would no doubt await us at the end.

CHAPTER 12

Violet

Whether he meant to do it or not, I burst into a fit of laughter as Kade ran his fingers along the soapy suds on my side.

"I love that sound," he admitted as he captured my mouth with his. "Almost as much as I love the sound of you coming."

"Kade!" I playfully smacked his chest, pretending to be appalled at his confession.

To be honest, the sound of him coming undone inside of me was something I never wanted to go without. Which begged the question, what would happen to my birth control if I crossed over? Obviously, kids were a very real possibility, whether demon or human.

"Not to dampen the mood…" I looked around the tight confines of my shower, cluttered with too many products that I seemed to never touch. I avoided eye contact as I lathered him up way more than I probably needed to, although he didn't seem to mind in the slightest. "How does birth control work…there? Because I'm not ready to have kids yet."

He enclosed his hand upon my wrist and stopped me, using his other hand to lift my chin, forcing my attention to his gaze. "Believe me, I'm not ready to share you with anyone just yet. But if and when you are ready to have children, we will take the appropriate steps to make that happen. You don't need any birth control."

I eyed him, disbelieving. "You're trying to tell me we can fuck like rabbits over in Darthou and I don't have to worry about getting pregnant? Sounds too good to be true."

Letting the water wash through my hair behind me, I tried running my fingers through it but they kept getting tangled. I was peeved at myself for not running a brush through it before entering the shower.

"Should we decide we want to pursue that avenue of interest, we would pay a visit to Staffan's wife."

"Do we need permission to get pregnant? Or is there another blood-related ritual that I need to be aware of?"

"Not exactly, but the decision is all ours. Rafina and her family are the greatest healers our kind has ever known. But she in particular specializes in, I guess you could say, blessing us with a child. She has done so for generations and she takes great pride in it but somehow, she remains so humble. She is one of the kindest in Darthou. I think you would like her."

"You make her sound like a goddess of fertility or something."

"I guess you could say that she is. And I should mention that there is a ritual, but not a drop of blood would be spilt." His fingers traced down my sternum and my stomach before he pulled me in close.

"Oh?" He'd startled me with his quick movement. I could feel his breath on my face as he spoke again.

"When we are ready, we request her presence. She would bring a cord of her own making and wrap our bodies together, like so, and say a few words." We were flush against each other and the air we breathed became one. "She then leaves us with well wishes and then…" He protruded his hips into me and my mouth went dry. How did he make having a baby sound so sexy? Even with a third person who I had never met in such close proximity to us? "I think you're well aware of what comes next."

I let out an unsteady breath, imagining the day that we might make that decision to start a family. But one thought still bothered me, lingering, and I had to speak up.

"It still sounds like we need permission though, if there's another rope or something involved." I pouted as I couldn't understand why it had to be anybody else's business whether we had a child or not. It didn't matter how fondly he spoke of this goddess of fertility or how long she had been doing these blessings.

I then got sidetracked, thinking about the names Kade had disclosed in the little time we had known each other. So far, the only ones that had stuck with me were his Aunt Sarah and his friend Elias. The rest of the names he spewed were practically Greek to me, but his sister's name was on the tip of my tongue.

His expression changed, his features softening, pulling me out of my own head. "There have been rumors," he began as he swapped places with me in the shower. We brushed past one another to switch places so he could rinse. "I don't know if anyone would ever flat out admit it, but people like to talk. We're not excluded from rumors, politics and so on in

Darthou, and we are far from perfect. But to go against tradition would be going against the council's wishes. Even if they seem impractical and outdated."

"Tell me how you really feel," I poked fun at him. "So spill, what do demons gossip about?" I might not be one for rumors, not when I had Aunt Cindy in my life who liked to meddle and get in the middle of everything. But hearing how demons and humans were alike was appealing.

"It's an unspoken rule that the bonding between the two consenting adults goes through this process each and every time they want a child. But apparently, all it boils down to is that—consent."

Kade had to lower himself to get beneath the falling water to rinse his hair. And while he did so, I admired his physique— his machine of a body that worked so well against mine.

I cleared my throat as I tried to push my dirty thoughts away and I resisted the urge to help rid him of the remnants of soap trailing down his torso. The confines of this shower made me think that sex in here would be more of an accident waiting to happen than a good idea, no matter how tempting it was to try.

"Under that logic…" His so-called rumor didn't sit right with me. "If you and I consented right here and now to have a baby, could we?"

His lips turned up at the corner, amused. "No, because we haven't tethered yet."

I continued on, adjusting my question. "Okay so after we complete the tethering, if we decide we want to test this theory out, we just, for lack of better terms, go for it?"

"You make it sound as if you might accept my proposal so we can find out." He raised a brow and the hope that filled his face made my heart flutter. I was still afraid to confess out loud that the possibility of that happening was very likely at this point.

"Maybe," was all I could utter. I had five nights to decide and I wasn't going to cut that short for any reason. I would take advantage of the time that I had here for as long as I could, and I would not take it for granted.

"Answer me something," I said as I reached for my towel on the hook just outside the shower curtain. "Please tell me you have a bigger shower than me because if not, that might be a deal breaker."

His laugh filled the small space as he cut the spray of water. "Happy to report that it is much bigger." That wicked gleam returned to his face and I could feel my cheeks heat beneath his gaze. "But I'd like to think that I could accomplish a lot, no matter how small the space."

Keeping in mind Kade's aversion to traffic, I took the long way to my grandma's house.

I let him pick the music in the hopes that it would ease his mind, and it seemed to have that effect on him once he located a channel that was playing music from my high school days. He began drumming his fingers on his legs as we moved along, and as cute as it was, I tried not to let it distract me. I was overly cautious about every move I made, acting as if I were in the middle of a driving test in the hopes that we could avoid the reaction I had witnessed yesterday.

On his own, he began to talk about his experiments with various instruments. Come to find out, he had dabbled in quite a few from each family. From woodwinds and strings, to brass and percussion, he had tried many, to my surprise. I had attempted and failed miserably at the flute many years ago, so I could appreciate the patience and dedication it took for him to learn to play so many different ones.

He also showed disdain for those who willingly destroyed instruments for entertainment purposes, and it was adorable how worked up he became as his voice rose. I even joked that he would have to serenade me someday—if time allowed in his watching schedule. I was curious just how busy he was with work on a regular day.

"Crap," I muttered, pulling into my grandma's drive as I noticed Aunt Cindy's red van parked out on the street. I half wondered if she and my grandma were in cahoots, trying to figure out the man situation that had taken control of my life by now.

"Showtime." I cut the engine and Kade took hold of my hand, kissing my knuckles.

"Everything will be fine. Your grandma adores you," he tried to reassure me.

"Me? Sure. Decisions I've made past and present? Not so much."

He smoothed his thumb over my knuckles and kissed them once more. When I met his gaze, the blue irises had returned. Showtime indeed.

Grandma had insisted that I not bring anything over for lunch but I didn't listen to her. I had grabbed a container of macaroni salad that I had bought the last time I was at the grocery store, seal still intact and well before its expiration date. With the unexpected addition of guests, I was glad I had made the executive decision to pitch in even if it was only a small dish.

I hesitantly opened the side door that everyone used as the

main entrance only to be met with a familiar squeal erupting from little Lottie who leapt not into my arms, but Kade's. I was equal parts jealous and delighted as her little arms tried to latch onto his shoulders. He picked her up with such grace, as if her abrupt outburst didn't faze him.

"Did you bring me anything?" Her voice was loud with excitement, her ruffled sundress with little smiling suns and rainbows a bright and cheery pattern that matched her disposition.

I couldn't help but laugh that Lottie had found a new best friend in my demon boyfriend. Could I call him that? Boyfriend?

"Lottie!" Aunt Cindy made her way into the room, scolding her daughter.

"It's alright," Kade tried to reassure her, but the look on my aunt's face didn't sit well with me. I was sure I'd been the topic of hot debate long before our arrival.

He set her down on the ground and kneeled so he could level with her. "I'm afraid I haven't won anything today so I'm empty-handed. I'm sorry."

Her nose turned up slightly and I decided to butt into the conversation as I bent down. "Be thankful you have that giant unicorn. It could have been Dottie that he gave you instead."

Kade's confusion didn't go unnoticed in my periphery as I saw Lottie register that thought. She pursed her lips as she pondered the information for a few seconds before her eyes bugged out.

"I like Ms. Sparkles much better!"

Aunt Cindy swiftly ushered her out of the room and into the bathroom, hopefully just to wash up for lunch. Just yesterday my aunt had been drooling over Kade's appearance, now the cold shoulder? I wasn't going to pretend to understand her.

As I tried to suppress my laughter, Kade leaned in and whispered, "Dottie?"

"Yeah, Lottie named the little bear you won me." I tried to tease him with my emphasis on *little*.

Grabbing his hand, I led the way out of the pastel-infested living room and into the kitchen. My grandma was about done setting out food, condiments, and all the fixings. I could see my uncle in the backyard at the grill with their two eldest children, busy with their cell phones on the outdoor furniture.

"I thought this was just going to be a small lunch thing, Grandma," I said as I set the container of macaroni salad on the counter.

She turned toward us, and paused as her eyes fell upon Kade. I froze instantly, unsure of how to move forward with the introductions.

Demon. Friend. Boyfriend. Friend with benefits. Possibly betrothed?

I didn't see how I could put a positive spin on our relationship, whatever it was, without lying. I knew how this looked and I felt guilty for bringing him along even though I had invited him in the first place. I had cast us both into a terribly awkward situation.

I removed the casing from the top of the container and popped open its lid, knowing full well my grandma was judging me in this very moment. I couldn't even attempt to look at her straight on. I didn't normally jump from one man to another so this was unusual and unfamiliar territory. The time that the two just so happened to overlap was a tidbit I didn't want to divulge to anyone, ever.

"Grandma, this is Kade, Kade this is my Grandma Margaret." I stuck an oversized spoon into the dish and tapped my fingers on the counter.

Kade took the opportunity to step forward and held out his hand. "Nice to meet you, Margaret. You have a lovely home."

She accepted his handshake but I could tell by her stiffened posture that she was leery of him. "You as well, young man. Now how do you two know each other?"

I held my breath as Aunt Cindy and Lottie entered the kitchen. Another set of scrutinizing eyes met with mine and I was ready to run for the hills.

"Our paths crossed many years ago, but just recently we ran into each other and, well…"

"We're just taking our time, enjoying each other's company. Not putting any labels on anything," I finished for him, trying to keep things somewhat vague.

Aunt Cindy wasn't buying it and it read all over her face. There was a very good chance she had seen Kade and I closer than the friend zone at the carnival last night. Luckily, they should have been long gone by the time we made it to the Maze of Mirrors.

"Although I wouldn't mind wearing the label of bodyguard."

I shot Kade an incredulous look as I whipped my attention toward him. How could he bring that up right now?

"What is that supposed to mean?" My grandma's voice wavered and her face came to rest with worry, her thinning eyebrows pinched as she kept bouncing her focus between the two of us.

"You used to live here, right?" Kade directed this at me. "They probably need to be up to speed on what happened. Just to be on the safe side."

"What's going on?" My grandma urged as she crossed her

arms, dotted with more age spots than I could recall her having.

"Lottie, why don't you go outside with your father." Aunt Cindy ushered her out the door.

"But, Mooooooom…" She dragged out her words as the door closed behind her. Of course Aunt Cindy wasn't going to step outside too. I was sure she wanted in on the drama that had become the center of my life.

"Look, I know that this might not look the greatest right now. The timing isn't ideal." I gestured between Kade and myself. "I did break things off with Brett but he is not taking it well."

I went into minimal details about the breakup, the calls to work, the messages, and the stalker-esque photo he had sent me. When I started to get into the events of last night, my grandma and aunt's faces were almost identical but decades apart. They were stunned into silence, which kept them quiet long enough for me to make sure to include Kade's role in the situation and the conclusion that the night had led to.

"If Kade hadn't been there, I don't know what he would have done." It was a statement that couldn't have been more true, and it sent a chill through me thinking about what could have transpired had I been alone. The thought had been plaguing me sporadically ever since, and I wasn't sure if I would ever be able to shed the grip it had on me.

The kitchen fell into a muted state that made my ears ring and Kade discreetly looped a few fingers into the palm of my hand. The kitchen island allowed us this small comfort, hiding our link as we let the information we'd unloaded sink in.

"The police officers did say that if he continues down the road he's on, we could file a restraining order, but I know that's nothing more than a piece of paper," Kade added.

I decided to butt in. "But if he calls, or attempts to contact you in any way, please let me know."

"Well, I haven't heard from him since that last time I told you we spoke. He wasn't in the best of moods after that conversation. I suppose I could have aggravated him. Made things worse." My grandma's admission broke my heart.

"No, Grandma, none of this is on you."

"Well, regardless. Thank you for being there for Violet." She nodded in the direction of Kade and his chin dipped slightly in acknowledgement.

"Even if it was in the middle of the night." She shrugged and turned away. "Now, where are those burgers?" Her petite frame and slightly hunched shoulders headed toward the door and out.

I could feel my eyes go wide. I had no words. I might as well have told everybody point-blank that Kade and I were fucking. Why else would he have been at my apartment at one in the morning?

"Well now that she's gone…" My aunt eyed the door before continuing. "Thank fuck Brett's gone and he had better leave you the hell alone. And you—" She pointed at Kade. "Whatever this is? Treat her right."

"I will." Kade didn't skip a beat or cower at the sudden change of her demeanor. She was putting on her mama bear persona that I had witnessed a few times since she became a mother, and even I wanted to shrink from her parental voice. The stern look on her face softened ever so slightly, then she followed her mother to join the others outside.

Not realizing how shallow my breathing had become, I took in a large intake of breath. Well, all of that dirty laundry was out in the open now.

"Why did you have to bring that up? And now?" I turned

to Kade with a hushed voice. I was a bit upset from the intensity of the moment, but also a little relieved that it was over.

"I figured what better way to break the ice than to give them something to focus on, like a shitty ex."

I pinched the bridge of my nose and closed my eyes. "You don't think Brett is stupid enough to do something to my grandma, do you?"

Kade pulled me in close. My body reacted to his touch and my limbs loosened. "I already have Elias on it. I know you grew up here so I wasn't taking any chances."

My head slanted back so I could take in his face. "You're really taking this bodyguard thing seriously, aren't you?"

"You have no idea."

He kissed my forehead before the screen door opened and the kitchen became alight with noise. We separated but remained in close proximity as I instructed him to help me put two leaves in the table since our gathering required more room and seating. We then set the table with disposable utensils and napkins to ensure a quick and easy clean afterwards.

I introduced him to my other two cousins, Torrance and Troy, who exchanged pleasantries but then returned to their screens once they collected their plates of food. I began to keep count of the times my grandma threatened to take their phones away, only to result in them trying to hide the devices under the table instead. My uncle, who had greeted Kade with a solid pat on the back upon his entrance, ended up taking the phones from them in the end. But it was to everyone's benefit, as it made them get involved in the conversations that thrived at the table as we ate.

Kade defaulted to the story of Florida and his work with a security firm. The ease with which the table talk flowed made the time pass quicker than I wanted it to. Brett never once came up in conversation again, and for that I was grateful.

Kade fit in with everyone in the room and he was very personable, relatable even in our group setting. His laugh was infectious and I recalled this morning when he had told me that he loved the sound of mine. The feeling was entirely mutual.

On the other side of Kade sat Torrance, and once the topic of music was brought up, they were thick as thieves. I knew that Torrance had a garage band and I mentioned it to Kade, and then the two of them hit it off from there. If I didn't know any better, I would have thought they were going to set up a jam session sometime.

If only we had more time. If *I* had more time.

Realization began to set in as it registered that this might be my last meal here with them, like this. Kade had said that I could visit, but that time would be limited as I would stop aging. I wondered how many years I might have before I wouldn't be able to make it back at all.

I examined little Lottie, munching on her chips and strawberries, imagining her changing and growing up. She could practically be a different child the next time I would have the chance to see her again.

There was a big possibility that I would miss all of my cousins graduating from high school, college, or both. My aunts and uncles, present and not, who weren't graying yet, would show their age in the blink of an eye.

The birthdays, anniversaries, and holidays that I would have to forego had a lump forming in my throat and I couldn't get it to go away no matter how hard I tried to swallow or chase it down with my punch.

Everybody seemed to be getting along so well and I wished that this moment could last.

Why the hell was I only allowed five nights? Whose barbaric decision was this?

Just because I was ready to say goodbye to this life in high school, didn't mean I was ready to go now. My life had changed drastically in the years that had followed that horrible event. I wished I could forget, but I knew my memory would never do me that service.

Kade's hand fell upon my leg under the table and he gently squeezed. I wondered if he could sense my tumultuous thoughts spiraling out of control as they so often did. I tried to keep my expression light and pleasant as I excused myself to go to the restroom. Everybody was finishing up and the eating had slowed, so I had no doubt that we would be cleaning up soon anyway.

I made my way to the bathroom and in doing so, passed my old bedroom. The twin-sized bed that I had occupied was still made in its black duvet and red sheets.

I could see in my head all the posters that had once lined the now bare walls. Some had been torn from magazines, others from the local movie theater, plastered about with that weird putty stuff as my grandma had been adamant about not having holes in her walls.

Sometimes they would fall in the middle of the night and scare the shit out of me. Grandma would just shrug it off and tell me it wouldn't happen if I kept the walls bare in the first place. She probably thought I was in some kind of cult with the images of the bands I listened to. But even so, I had made it a point not to be able to see any blank space if at all possible.

Remembering how it once was made the space feel so vacant now.

My white bookshelves still held some memorabilia, such as movie tickets and movies, along with some of the books I had left behind. My grandma's romance novels had begun to creep in from the bottom up, and were growing toward the height of my hips.

I grinned. She loved those damn books—the men with their shirts ripped open and the women with elaborate dresses, the wind sweeping through their hair. For as long as I could remember she had loved these types of novels.

My grandma never remarried after she lost her husband, and he had passed long before my parents and brother died. She was alone before I moved in, and she was alone again now. How would she manage if I dropped off the face of the earth? Would I be able to call or text? Just an occasional visit here and there as time went on wasn't enough.

What kind of impact would that have on her?

Would Kade be allowed to keep tabs on my grandma and the rest of my family? What if something bad happened and I wasn't here? What would I do if I returned and she was gone? Would I just be shit out of luck?

I hugged myself as I made my way through the room and toward my old bathroom. Mentally, I was transported back to high school, waking up in a mess of my own vomit. My vision had been blurry, my head had hurt like hell, and my stomach had been in an unrelenting squeeze-like grasp that urged me to continue to expel whatever else I could.

I'd been too scared to tell my grandma what I had done and I didn't want anyone to fuss over me. I didn't want to go to the hospital or cause a scene. I had just wanted to forget my failure.

"Are you okay?" Kade approached from behind me and placed his hands on my hips, his chin on my shoulder.

"My heart really stopped that night?" I muttered. Even though I could still hear voices in the kitchen, I couldn't be sure that anybody else wouldn't walk by unexpectedly.

Tears managed to escape in streams even with my eyes wide open. How could I have been so stupid? The life that I had taken for granted then was the very one I was spiraling over potentially losing now.

"Hey." He circled around me and tenderly swiped away at my wet cheeks before pulling me into him.

I wanted to let it all loose and sob but I knew if I did, I would draw more unnecessary attention, and that was the last thing I needed right now. I really didn't want to be the source of any more worry for my family on what might be my last day with them. It was already bad enough they would have to be on alert regarding Brett and the situation I was in with him.

This morning I had been so sure about leaving with Kade, and now I was at war with the very idea. He had been nothing but kind and considerate of everything since arriving here. He had never once pressured me, even though he had to be feeling it himself on his end since he was only allowed one request for a tethering to a human. I felt responsible for his happiness, and it was too great of a load to carry when I thought about what I would be trading it for.

But, could I even be happy here after knowing Kade?

Now that I had tasted a life with him in it, it seemed like I knew the answer. It was as if I was already mourning the loss of the life I still had yet to live here. Would my yearly visits be enough to satisfy me?

"Let's go outside and get some fresh air." He led me out of my old room and through the living room toward our earlier point of entry. We bypassed the kitchen chaos as we met the outside heat that hit us like a wall. It was a stark difference from the central air at work inside.

We sat on the concrete steps just outside the door, under

the awning so we were shielded from the sun, and I rested my head on his shoulder.

I placed my hand upon my chest to feel the stone that Kade had given me, but my neck was bare. Evidently, I hadn't put it back on after our shower and I missed the weight of its presence. A small pout formed on my lips, feeling silly for missing something that I'd only been given last night.

"Do you need to talk?" Kade asked after some time had passed and my breathing began to level out. My eyes were sore from clenching them and I was afraid my face had gone puffy.

"I just wish I had more time," I mumbled as tears threatened to spill once more.

He laced his fingers with mine and kissed the top of my head. "You don't have to accept the tethering if it is too much." His voice lowered and I swore by the subtle crack in it that he was struggling to get words out. "I would understand."

The fact that he was willing to let me go after our time spent together caught me off guard. He had been waiting years for the chance to even meet me, and now that he had, there were only five nights to get me to accept his proposal.

Would he really just part ways without some sort of fight? Did I want him to do that? Fight for me, convince me to leave with him? I had mixed feelings about what actions I wanted him to take.

"Believe me when I say that I have tried to persuade our council to allow more time, since we have nothing but an eternity on our end. But they are strict and cling to their outdated ways, believing any more time would be a danger to both us and our possible tethers. But I would understand if you can't part with your family."

We sat in silence a while longer, his thumb brushing across the back of my hand over and over again in an attempt to soothe me. It was working, to an extent, as I focused on it, until I felt Kade go rigid.

I raised my head, concerned. His eyes were now black and his hard stare was towards the road and unblinking.

"You should go inside." His mouth barely moved as I followed his line of sight. My stomach twisted, knowing that he would only change them to get a better look at his surroundings in case a saint was nearby.

I focused on the road before us and then the houses across the street. A small figure in the yard of a two-story blue house came into view. Half of their body was hidden by its frame but even so, I recognized the man staring back.

I could tell by the driveway that nobody was home. The elderly owners had owned a red van for as long as I could remember, and its parking space was vacant. They would trade it in when necessary just to get a newer model, but they never strayed from their usual preference of a vehicle.

"Damian?" I spoke as I began to stand, not really needing an answer. I would recognize him anywhere.

Kade took a step in front of me, guarding. "This is mighty ballsy of him. Please, go back inside," he urged once more.

I pushed past him. If Kade was right and Damian really was a saint, was he the one working with Brett? If he'd been keeping tabs on me all this time, was he the one at the carnival last night? I marched off without another thought, heading down the pavement in his direction.

"Violet, wait. What are you doing?" Kade's hushed voice was raised in alarm as his long strides caught up to me in a flash.

"Getting answers." I balled my fists together, trying to muster up whatever courage I could find.

Did Damian really have a target on my back this whole

time? Was he manipulating Brett to make our breakup worse?

Kade had said a saint could work behind the scenes, orchestrating schemes and deaths to make sure the ones who had cheated death didn't get the chance to do so again. Having cheated death twice, I didn't want the moment to come when I might encounter death a third time, and I certainly didn't want any harm to come to others I loved if I could help it.

Damian rounded the dark blue-sided house and began his path toward us. We came together to meet on the sidewalk on his side of the street.

His scoop neck tee was too tight, showing off his muscles that were rarely seen at work, and his athletic shorts cut right above his knees. The eerie demeanor in which he approached almost sent me into retreat but I stood my ground. Surely he wasn't stupid enough to try and pull something out here in the middle of the day.

"It's true," I spat at him, almost reaching my boiling point. I glanced at Kade and his eyes remained black, so that alone was proof enough for me. If he hadn't bothered to change them back, he knew. "I'll be damned, he was right. You really are a saint."

"You say that as if it's a bad thing." He tipped his head to the side, almost charmed by my newfound awareness.

"Is your name even really Damian? Who the hell are you?"

I knew that Kade hadn't even known for sure who he was. The shifting that both parties were capable of made that difficult enough.

"For now I am. Until I decide otherwise." His response made my blood run cold even in the heat of the day. His admittance had me doubting everything I knew about him. Was it all really a lie?

"Until you decide what, to kill me and move on to

somebody else?" My words escaped with no filter.

Damian shifted his vile attention to Kade. "What are we on, night number four tonight by my calculations?" He shook his head as his tongue clicked in a disapproving manner. "You should have just stolen her away by now."

"I am nobody's property to be stolen away." I wavered in my retort, shaken by the fact that he was aware of the courting Kade and I were currently in the latter half of.

Kade took a step in front of me in a protective stance. "Who are you?"

Damian unleashed a villainous laugh that I'd had no idea he was capable of. The amount of humor he was finding in this confrontation made me want to run for the hills. I didn't know anything about this man, this saint, standing before me.

"That's the million-dollar question, isn't it?" His demented grin faltered and, as if a lightbulb had turned off, he replaced it with a kind expression. My fingernails dug into my palms.

"Damian, is that you?"

I whipped my head around at the sound of my grandma's voice. Fear crept into every fiber of my being as she began waving at him, making her way out of the darkness of the carport and into the sun, still wearing her kitchen apron.

"Hello, Margaret!" He waved as he called to her, sidestepping around us. "Excuse me."

"I—" I shot a weary look at Kade, who had already shifted his eyes for company. He grabbed my hand and we followed after Damian.

"Are you hungry? We just had lunch but there's plenty of food left." My grandma, the kind soul that she was when in the presence of others, offering the chance for Damian to enter her home, had my stomach in knots. I thought I might lose its contents if he accepted her offer.

"Oh, I wouldn't want to impose." Damian's charismatic side came out with such ease that my stomach lurched. I had to keep my temper, actions and face of mine under control.

"He was just passing by," Kade tried to insert himself into the conversation, but Grandma interrupted.

"Nonsense, come and fix yourself a plate." She waved Damian to follow as she turned to go. "What brings you around here anyway? Haven't seen you around the neighborhood before."

Damian glanced over his shoulder at us. The look on his face made my stomach bottom out and I stilled. His smug look made me want to vomit as Kade's enemy was welcomed into the house.

"Stay calm." Kade's voice was barely audible behind me as he gently pushed for me to follow.

"Well hi, stranger," my aunt's voice greeted from the kitchen. She didn't come to my place of employment often, but she had met Damian a handful of times, enough to know who he was.

My grandma bustled around the kitchen, removing lids and handing Damian a plate. He greeted everyone with such ease and explained away his presence today by saying he was exploring a new route for his daily workout.

It was a real effort to resist the urge to roll my eyes, but I was afraid that with all of the room's occupants, someone would take notice. As of right now, as far as anyone else was concerned, we were still boss and employee.

I was spiraling with numerous questions firing at rapid speed and they were ricocheting around inside my head. Had he ever cared about me as an employee? Did I really deserve the job that I currently held? Was it all just a part of an elaborate ruse to keep me under his thumb and watchful eye?

The lengths to which Damian had gone to keep me in his view seemed worse than Kade's observations from the sidelines. Kade had never interfered with my life, and told me that he hadn't been able to do anything until I released him. He knew that there was a saint in close contact with me, but I could only imagine the turmoil that knowledge had put him through.

"Not to be a killjoy but, where's Brett?"

I didn't miss a beat as I answered, "Hopefully still sobering up in jail."

The kitchen went quiet as Damian's eyes met mine. The fact that he tried to feign shock made me want to spit at him. I'd told him in the basement of our work yesterday that Brett and I had broken up. If he was doing this to get under my skin, it was working.

"Awkward." Troy glanced up from his phone as he made his way out of the kitchen, excusing himself from the room.

"I'm sorry, what?" Damian pretended to choke on the food in his mouth a bit.

This fake performance of his had me madder than hell. I'm sure he was well aware of Brett and his current situation, but I couldn't say so, and I was livid about my inability to speak freely.

My family might have been in the dark at the moment about everything that was really going on. But I, on the other hand, was coming out on the other side, seeing things more clearly than I ever had before.

Aunt Cindy butted in and tried to shut the conversation down. "Let's just say a restraining order might come in to play if he doesn't clean up his act."

Lottie began whining of boredom and Torrance took her by the hand to lead her outside.

"Wow, I'm sorry." Damian's apology seemed sincere but Kade and I knew better. "And you think you know somebody." His eyes bore into mine as if this comment was meant more for me than for Brett, and the rising urge to punch something—or better yet some*one*—was all I could think of.

CHAPTER 13

Violet

What should have been a small and intimate lunch between my grandma, Kade, and me had morphed into something else entirely.

Kade joined me outside a few minutes later after excusing himself to the restroom. We had slowly begun filtering outside after our unexpected guest had finished grazing on our feast.

"Brett is out of jail and home right now." Kade sat beside me on the back porch swing, the tips of my toes skimming the ground.

I had no doubt in my mind that he was checking in on things when he left my side. I knew he would only leave me if absolutely necessary, especially when we were in the company of his enemy.

The thought that Brett was already cut loose did nothing for my nerves and I stared dead forward at my manager, attempting to shoot daggers.

Damian was on the small patch of cement next to Grandma's gardening shed and out of ears' reach. He was joined by Troy and my uncle, alternating taking shots here and there with the basketball they had brought with them. The basketball hoop attached to the shed had seen better days, but it seemed solid enough for them to use at present. If anyone tried to hang from it, I'm sure it would come crashing down.

Grandma came out of the house, scooted her wooden rocking chair up next to my side of the swing, and sat, hands on the armrests. She cleared her throat, indicating that she was about to speak, and I tensed.

"What's he really doing here?"

Kade and I both glanced over in her direction in unison. I wasn't sure how to respond and raised an eyebrow.

She shot me a look that said she wasn't buying into the bullshit that was taking place; I was partially glad she could see beyond Damian's little act.

"There wasn't a lick of sweat on that man when he showed up." She scoffed as she shook her head. "Does he take me for a fool?"

"He's a fool if he thinks you are," Kade stated, very matter-of-fact.

"Ah, you flatter me." She grinned as she watched the boys up ahead. "Look, I'm not going to meddle in your life like Lucinda, and I'm not going to pretend like I know what's going on when I clearly don't. But I am happy to see you here today. Even with all this Brett nonsense." She puffed in aggravation.

"I'm sorry my life has been such a mess lately." I let my head drop down, not wanting her involved in any of it. I felt incredibly guilty that she was being dragged right through the middle without being able to divulge all I had learned within the past few days. I seemed to be at an unfair advantage in that aspect.

"Oh, stop it. I don't care who you are. Life is messy. There's no stopping it, it's going to happen." The ease with which she uttered those words made me wonder what all she was referring to. Certainly nothing that could match the caliber of my situation. "Well, if he's going to stay and play, he might as well take his shirt off and get sweaty."

"Grandma!" I couldn't hide my shock, and it earned a few turned heads as I squawked. She offered a shrug as if nothing that came out of her mouth was wrong. She had never hidden the truth that she appreciated Damian's looks, but hearing her talk about him in that way had me wondering if she was alright in the head.

My uncle, whose attention was on us now, must have noticed that my demon/bodyguard/boyfriend had joined us out in the open air. "Hey Kade! Join us!" he called over, and I warily looked in his direction.

"Wish me luck." Kade stood, the swing shifting at his exit. "Ladies." He nodded in our direction and I bit my tongue, afraid that anything I said might not be understood by the ears closest to me. As he left, he sprang off of the porch steps and landed without a sound at the bottom, making his way toward the others.

"Kade's gonna kick your butt, Daddy!" Lottie was playing with her toys in the grass as he passed. Her remark earned a few chuckles from everyone, including her mother who was seated beside her. But even though Aunt Cindy was amused, she hushed Lottie shortly after.

"Wine cooler?" My grandma produced a glass bottle and I could feel the tension of my body shift. It was the only alcohol you would find in her house. She knew what she liked, and there was no persuading her otherwise.

"God, yes." I thanked her as I accepted it. The exotic flavor was one of my favorites and I knew she was well aware. I was hoping that a little alcohol might take the edge off even if it was minimal.

Kade was paired with Troy, and Damian with Uncle David. They began strutting about, the bouncing ball picking up speed as they played. The swiftness of Kade and Damian's moves came so easily to them, I could tell now that it was mainly going to be a game played by the two of them. After last night's events, I knew Kade could successfully land several baskets in a row when uninterrupted, but I was about to find out the extent of his basketball abilities.

"Are you alright, Vi?"

Grandma's question struck a melancholy chord in me. I was afraid if I looked at her, I might lose it. I couldn't tell her just how messy my life really was right now. How everything I knew was being turned upside down, and how it was questionable at the moment if that change was for the better.

My internal struggle was not for her to deal with.

Kade passed the ball to Troy, setting him up for a shot, only for it to be blocked by Damian. *Dick move*, I thought. Let the kid try. Troy was on the varsity team at his school and I wanted to see him make it. I hadn't been to many of his games since his school team traveled a lot, but I still appreciated the chance to witness him doing something that he enjoyed.

"I don't know what I am right now." I tried to be as honest as I could be, even if vague.

We both took swigs of our drinks and I reached to fumble with my necklace only to find once again that my neck was bare. I let the fingers on my left hand curl under the hem of my denim shorts and held the icy drink with the other. Sweat was already rolling off of the bottle, leaving a ring on my lap.

"It's alright not to be okay. I had no idea what Brett was capable of. I could never quite put my finger on it. He was always a kiss-ass but I never would have imagined he would go to such lengths." Anytime I heard a curse word spill from my grandma's mouth, it still jarred me after all this time as it was a rare occurrence.

"Me neither." It was only a matter of time before she led into the situation with my guest today, and I decided to beat her to the punch. "And I know how this looks with Kade, I can't imagine what you might think of me right now."

Damian made quick work of a layup, scoring the first points for his team. I wanted to roll my eyes at his performance.

"You know all that matters is that you're happy, right? You don't have to have a man for that either." Her voice was quiet as she spoke, but not condescending in the least. It was more concerned than anything else.

"But I want to be happy with Kade."

This damn mouth of mine was going to get me into trouble. I was head over heels for this man, and feeling hopeful about our possible future together. Yet, I still had an endless amount of questions, more than I could fathom or possibly put down on paper. It was time consuming and overbearing. I wasn't sure if I was any better off now than I'd been a few nights ago.

Kade reached for the hem of his shirt and pulled it off, throwing it off to the side. His abs shone in the sunlight and I felt a pang of jealousy that he had caught the attention of both my aunt and grandma.

I wanted those abs on top of me and beneath me. Against me, and for my eyes only.

Which also begged the question—did he ever wear a shirt back home? The only time he had graced me with his presence while wearing one was last night for our date. He'd only parted briefly this morning to collect his clothes for the day, so I knew he had them. So why did he always come shirtless? Were they optional in Darthou? What kind of dress code would I possibly be walking into?

"Well, I'll be…" My grandma slowed her words as she took in the sight of him. "I think I would want to be happy with him too."

I couldn't help but grin at her reaction, as ridiculous as it was. "It's more than just his body, I promise."

Damian followed suit, shedding his shirt and discarding it. My uncle tossed the ball to him and he dribbled it at a leisurely pace.

"Where do you find these men?" My grandma fanned herself before she let her drink rest against her face. I had never seen her act like this before. Aunt Cindy looked up from Lottie's toys and in our direction, her jaw dropping as she peered above her sunglasses.

"They found me."

I was almost breathless as Kade moved quickly, stealing the ball from Damian and setting himself up for a shot. His muscles pulled and stretched as he sank the ball with ease. I resisted the urge to jump up and holler my approval but nobody had clapped or cheered after Damian's basket so I stowed my enthusiasm.

My uncle placed the ball on his hip, perhaps a bit winded already. He wasn't by any means out of shape, but compared to the teenager and men surrounding him, his physique was definitely not up to par. That combined with the heat and food we had consumed, probably did nothing in his favor.

"Sorry to disappoint you ladies, but this dad bod is going to remain fully clothed." He chuckled as he tossed the ball away. His statement earned a groan from Troy, and his wife snorted the most unflattering sound I had ever heard come out of her.

"He was a sight of his own when he and Lucinda met. I don't know what's in the water these days but these boys are bred differently or something."

I wanted to say that they were more otherworldly, but refrained. The grace with which they moved was certainly that.

"Is there anything I should know about Damian?"

I was conflicted on how to answer that without telling her to stay away from him and Brett at all costs. My time working for him now felt like a big lie, and I didn't know what he really looked like or what he was truly capable of. I didn't know him at all, and that was alarming. I still didn't know all the ins and outs of demons or saints.

Deciding on my path, I answered with the closest thing to the truth that I could. "He's been acting weird since I told him that Brett and I broke up. It came up yesterday at work, so I'm not sure why he brought it up today like he did."

I could hear Uncle David ask where Damian had played hoops as he took another shot. Kade blocked it and passed the ball back to Troy after a few strides dribbling the ball. What I couldn't make out was the answer. Damian's voice was too muted for me to make out what he was saying.

Downing the rest of my drink, I folded my legs up onto the swing and set the empty glass bottle in between them. My face was feeling warm at this point and I was sure the sight of Kade shirtless, paired with the alcohol, was to blame.

Although, I didn't need a drop of that stuff to appreciate his good looks. I observed Kade mention something to Troy and he widened his footing to show him something. I had been so wrapped up in them that I hadn't even realized my grandma had left and brought back another cooler. I offered my thanks and cracked it open.

"I think you might have two different boys vying for your attention. One is being cocky about it, and the other is being a team player."

"Ha." I took another long swig. "I don't think my boss is trying to do that." I shook my head. The thought occurred to me that if I accepted the tethering tomorrow, Damian wasn't technically my boss anymore. He was nothing more than a stranger to me now.

Troy released the ball and scored a basket. Kade patted him on the back and my uncle hollered his approval even though he was playing on the opposing team.

"Why else would he show up here with a half-ass excuse?"

Because he had ulterior motives that I couldn't possibly discuss with you.

"Grandma, if you don't like him, why don't you just ask him to leave? It's your house." Torrance had appeared almost out of thin air. Last I knew she had wandered around toward the front of the house before the boys had started their game.

"She's got a point," I agreed with her as she came to sit with me on the swing, phone firmly in her grasp as if it were an extension of her arm.

"Enough about me and my problems." I leaned against the back of the swing. "Who has you glued to your phone today?"

I tried to get involved in any subject that wasn't about me, and it worked for a while. Torrance confided in me about a boy in school who she had only had the chance to hang out with in group settings, and it wasn't until this summer that they had started talking one-on-one through messages and social apps.

I could tell that she wanted more from it, but she seemed to err on the side of caution. She had never been on any dates to my knowledge and this was all new territory for her. Then her brother was the total opposite—I couldn't keep track of how many girls he hung out with. Torrance and Troy were the closest cousins I had to my age, but there was still an age gap that kept us at arm's length.

When I'd finished my second cooler and Torrance had gone back inside, I retrieved some bottles of water. The boys were drenched in sweat at this point and Lottie had passed out on the blanket she had been playing on, perfectly shaded by the house. Aunt Cindy seemed to be suntanning an arm's reach away from her, but I couldn't tell if she was asleep or not. Her shades were dark enough that I couldn't make out her eyes even as I passed.

"You guys about finished out here?" I asked as I started to toss bottles at my uncle and Troy. I purposefully went a little short on Damian's, hoping it would fall to the ground, but he swiped it before it could, thwarting my plan.

I took my place next to Kade and opened the bottle for him, and he murmured his thanks. I tried not to let his body distract me even though I wanted to run my fingers along every inch of him right about now. My wine coolers had given me enough of a buzz that I was starting to feel its effects in my nether regions and I had to reel myself back in, pushing my lustful thoughts away.

Now was definitely not the time.

"Well, I think I'm tapping out." Uncle David began to leave their makeshift basketball court, patting his son on the back.

I could hear him utter a few words about how he was getting too old for this and I smirked. He had kept up until this point, and for his age, I thought that was pretty impressive. This was the most active I'd seen him in a while and I was sure with two teenagers and a toddler, he was about at his limit. But you could never say that he didn't get involved in his children's lives and their extracurriculars. He couldn't even carry a tune to save his life but that didn't stop him from trying to join in on the garage band his daughter started.

"Can you help me with my jump shot?" Troy asked Kade after he downed about half of his water, swiping away at the loose streams of water that escaped down his chin. His auburn hair, which matched that of Torrance, was short on the sides but longer on top. The height that he usually had in it was almost nonexistent now due to their game and the heat of the day.

"Gladly." Kade grinned. "Unless we need to get going." He looked at me as if awaiting my approval. I thought it was cute that he was being considerate in that small way.

"Go for it, I've got no plans. Although, you should probably get going." I zoned in on Damian, who eyed me with a cocked eyebrow. "You have quite the trek home since you didn't drive here. I'll see you out." I didn't want to give him the chance to enter my grandma's house again—I wanted him gone.

"Violet." I could hear the edge on Kade's voice at the notion that I would be escorting Damian away on my lonesome, but I chose to brush it off and ignore it.

"You guys enjoy. I'll be back shortly."

"Good game, boys." The emphasis Damian placed on the word *boys* reminded me of a bully. I turned to lead the way out of the backyard and I could hear his faint footsteps behind me as we crossed over to the driveway.

I waved to my grandma in the kitchen window as we

passed, making sure that Damian took notice that we were in view of another. Surely, he wouldn't try anything. It wasn't like he had a vehicle here. Or did he? I had just chosen to believe that he'd walked here, but who was to say that wasn't a lie itself?

Scanning the street as it came into view, I didn't see his truck anywhere. I hoped I was in the clear and he wasn't going to try and make a quick escape with me. He couldn't be stupid enough to try and pull something like that with so many people within earshot.

"What's your angle?" I pivoted around to face him.

His demeanor had changed and softened, and he was almost beginning to look like the man I knew from work again. It was a night-and-day difference from when he had arrived here and it was mind-boggling. I had to remind myself that he was Kade's enemy and a fraud of a boss. I had no idea who was really looking back at me.

"My angle?" he questioned, trying to play innocent. It wasn't going to work. I had seen another side of him that I wished I hadn't, but there was no turning back now. He rounded me and I swiveled until my back was facing the house.

I crossed my arms, waiting for his features to change into what I had witnessed earlier. But it seemed he was going to keep up with this act. I was curious if someone inside the house was keeping tabs on us and perhaps that was why he was keeping his nice guy routine. I resisted the urge to turn my back on him to find out.

"I don't even know who you are anymore," I stated, perturbed.

"And you know Kadriel any better?" He became defensive.

The sound of Kade's full name coming from his mouth stunned me as I had barely even used it myself. He knew Kade's real name, and knew about the tethering ritual down to the night that we were approaching. Just how much did he know?

"Do you believe every word that comes out of his mouth? He's a *demon*."

"And it's *my* understanding that both of you have your own agendas when it comes to me, so out with it. What the hell is it that you want?" My nails were digging into my fists as I tried to quell the rage building within me.

"You," was all he said.

I couldn't make out if he was trying to play the game as if he wanted me for himself—or if he wanted to kill me. His one-word confession gave nothing away. Kade had declared that as a saint, he would choose one of the two. Judging by how he'd reacted earlier when Kade and I met him across the street, I was beginning to think that he might have death on his mind.

"I'm not yours to take." I stared him dead on. Maybe that little bit of liquid courage was giving me a boost, but I wanted to make sure that I put my foot down.

"Kadriel will steal you away tomorrow. Just wait and see."

I took a step closer. "You don't seem to understand. It is *my* choice and my choice alone."

"Keep telling yourself that." His face hardened as he pivoted and left the driveway at a jog.

I didn't budge until he was out of sight. I was waiting for my body to calm down after the edge it had perched itself upon, but my head began to spin.

Seeds of doubt began to creep in and I could feel my heartbeat quicken. Kade wouldn't steal me away, would he?

I knew no other demons so it wasn't like I could ask anyone or verify any details on the matter. All I knew was what he'd told me, and I had no reason to believe otherwise. He had been right about Damian so far, so why would I doubt him now?

Why was I letting Damian get under my skin like this? Was this his goal after all? Get me to say no to Kade and the tethering ritual altogether and stay here? I had no idea how to protect myself against a saint, if I even could.

What about my family? Would he go after them if I were to leave? I didn't know the extent of his knowledge and what all he was capable of.

I had worked for him for five days a week for the past year and a half and in that time, I had probably given him an arsenal of information about me. And since Kade couldn't view me at work due to the lack of reflective surfaces, it made me contemplate if Damian knew me better than he did at this point.

I couldn't get a read on if he wanted to hurt me or something else. If he was trying to take the relationship path, then he was delusional. I could never trust him after this, no matter what. And if he tried to make any kind of advance, it would be in vain. If I were to turn him down, would his resolution then be to end me?

"Vi, are you alright?" My grandma's voice seemed so distant, I couldn't be sure if she was calling me from the house, the backyard, or across the alley. Raising a foot to take a step back toward the house, my leg gave out.

The next thing I knew, I was falling.

CHAPTER 14

Violet

A constant cool breeze was hitting the side of my face, but my shirt was clinging to me as I drew in a breath and exhaled. The rest of my body was still warm and I wanted to strip out of everything in an attempt to rid myself of my soiled clothes.

Better yet, a shower felt like the superior option. That would feel amazing right about now.

"I'm sure the heat just got to her. She really didn't have that much to drink." Grandma Margaret's voice was faint but I knew she was close.

"Should we take her to the hospital?" Aunt Cindy chimed in.

"She didn't even hit the pavement thanks to Kade."

"Those were some spidey reflexes," Troy stated in appreciation.

I could picture everybody swarming around me, and the fuss they were creating was making me uncomfortable. This was exactly what I tried to avoid, being the center of attention for any reason.

Kade's familiar hand closed over mine and he squeezed gently. I felt the fog from my head lifting and my body temperature began to level itself. Was he doing that freaky healing thing on me again that he had done on my foot the first night we'd met?

My eyes fluttered open and I came to on the plush couch in the living room, staring up at the white popcorn ceiling. Several heads began to come into view and my grandma began shooing everyone away, telling them to give me some space.

"Vi?" Grandma returned and the concern etched on her face had me sitting up a bit too fast. My hand shot up to my head at the dizzying motion.

"Woah, easy." Kade released my other hand and attempted to steady me as I wobbled into an upright position.

"What happened?" My voice was small as I spoke, trying to remember how I got here.

"You passed out in the driveway after Damian left. Luckily, Kade was there and caught you before you could smack your head on the driveway," my grandma said.

"Oh…" I was starting to remember bits and pieces that had led up to that point. "I'm sorry, I…" Words failed me and I didn't know what to say except to thank Kade for his quick rescue.

"Here, have some water." Kade took the bottle from Grandma and removed the lid with a snap, handing it to me.

To be honest, I was rather thirsty. I couldn't remember having any water so far today, and I could only assume that downing two coolers in today's heat was probably what got the best of me. I wasn't a lush by any means, but since when had I become such a lightweight with alcohol?

"Perhaps we should get you home?" Kade recommended gently.

I nodded my head slowly before letting the frigid water cascade down my throat. It wasn't even supposed to be this hot over the weekend. The weather needed to make up its mind.

"Well, take your time. It's no rush. I'll pack you some food to take home."

"You don't have to do that," I tried to discourage her from doing so.

"Nonsense, there's too much left." She was apprehensive at first, but then she left and everyone else began to dissipate behind her.

Kade's eyes went black and he examined me from head to toe.

"What are you doing?" I whispered in alarm, afraid that someone might stumble back into the room and catch him.

"Did he hurt you?" His face was hard as he clenched his jaw, and the jerk of the motion made me wonder if he popped something out of place in doing so.

"No, he didn't even touch me," I tried to assure him as he gave my body another pass. I leaned forward and let my head rest on my hand, placing the bottle on the back of my neck. "I promise."

"Then what's wrong?" he asked, unbelieving.

"I am human, remember." I rolled my eyes, embarrassed that I had caused such an ordeal over something so stupid. "I'm sure Grandma's right. It's just the combination of alcohol, the heat, and not enough water. I'll be fine."

"Are you sure?" His face was now mere inches from mine.

"I'll be fine," I repeated, my voice laced with a touch of

bitterness that surfaced without my trying.

He slowly backed away and his eyes flickered to blue before Lottie came to stand in the doorway. She rubbed her eyes; no doubt she'd been awoken from her nap by my fainting spell and I felt to blame.

"Mommy says it's time to go." Her bottom lip protruded as she hugged her princess dolls into her chest. Their tangled hair was in disarray much like her own.

"I think we're getting ready to head out too. Come here, Lottie."

Kade allowed enough room for her to crawl up into my lap for a giant hug. She smelled of the outdoors and chocolate and I worried about what she had gotten into to make the sweet smell so fragrant on her.

She retreated from me and went right into Kade's arms, taking him off guard. He relaxed momentarily into a hug before she left him too.

"Be good for Mommy and Daddy, okay?"

I could feel my face betraying itself in my goodbye, not knowing if this would be the last I would see of her for a while. I hadn't expected the company of any of them here today, so I guess I was lucky that their unannounced appearance granted me this.

Aunt Cindy returned, containers stacked in a reusable bag, and gave me a hug before she departed. Uncle David, Torrance, and Troy offered their farewells before they all piled into their van to leave.

Grandma met us in the driveway with another sack full of food to send home. It was a mix of plastic containers that she reused as needed. That way she never had to worry about tracking them down or getting them back. Some were from butter, others whipped toppings, cottage cheese, and so on. She never recycled or threw them away unless they were broken or stained.

"Thank you for today, Grandma." I pulled her into a hug that I feared was too tight, but I couldn't ease up on it. "I love you." My voice cracked, betraying me and my troubling thoughts pertaining to the goodbyes today. Out of everyone, this one hurt the most.

"Well I love you too," she returned, speaking into my ear and then taking a step back, the first to loosen our embrace. I could tell that my words were making her weary.

"I'm sorry if I don't say it enough, but I do." I shrugged as I looked into her crinkled eyes that only served as a reminder of all the laughs we had shared together. I thought she might break me into a fit of tears if I drew this out any longer.

"I know, Violet."

Kade took the bag from her hands and put his arm around me. "It was nice to meet you, Margaret. Thank you again for lunch today."

"Of course. And if you ever leave hungry, you're doing something wrong, not me." She beamed as she stepped up to him and waved her hands toward herself, signaling for him to come down to her level for a hug. He bent slightly and let her do so, offering a slight squeeze in return as he towered over her. "You take care of my granddaughter."

As they separated, Kade nodded. "I will."

He had given me no reason to doubt that he wouldn't. I just didn't know how it would be possible if I ended up saying no tomorrow. How would he be able to protect me from Damian if I stayed? How could I protect myself?

"Are you sure you're okay to drive?" he asked as we began entering my car. I regretted that I hadn't cracked my windows as it was well above the boiling point inside.

"I'm fine," I assured him.

Now I only had a minor headache since the fogginess I'd felt earlier had lifted. There wasn't a doubt in my mind that Kade was responsible for that relief.

"I think my grandma prefers you to Damian." I tried to create conversation as we made our way back to my place. I wasn't sure how to navigate into the discussion that I really wanted to have, so I thought I might start with how well he seemed to rub off on her.

"I didn't know it was a competition." His statement was a curveball that I hadn't intended. I couldn't tell if he was more annoyed or angered.

"You both seemed to be playing games of your own." I gripped the steering wheel a little tighter. "Only he came off as a showoff and you, a team player." I offered a nervous laugh as I repeated some of my grandma's words. "Not quite sure how you have my three cousins wrapped around your finger like you do though."

I glanced in his direction. He was stiff as a statue, bracing himself against the door as if he was about ready to bolt. Surely it wasn't my driving; I was being overly cautious in everything that I did, every move I made. Did Damian really get him this riled up? Or did he not believe me when I told him that nothing had happened between us before my embarrassing fainting spell?

I tried to recall my brief conversation with Damian but was still a bit hazy on some of the details. He didn't lay a finger on me, I knew that. I remembered waving to Grandma inside the house, and I never turned my back away from him once we came to a stop because I didn't trust him out of my sight even for a second. He'd admitted that he wanted me, but it was still unclear for what purpose.

"Have you two met before today? You and Damian? Or whoever the hell he is?"

The only thing that budged was his lips as he replied. "I can't say. But something about him felt…familiar."

"Well, somehow he knew your name was Kadriel."

His head whipped in my direction so fast that I jumped in my seat, causing my foot to hit the brakes in my response. Luckily, there was no one else around on this side street I had turned onto.

"What?" I gaped at him, heart pounding.

The blast of the air vents directed at me was the only sound that filled my ears. I couldn't even hear the engine with the air going at full force.

The grim expression on Kade's face told me that nothing good would come from this knowledge.

"What exactly did you two talk about?"

I skimmed past his question. "Is it really that weird that he knows your real name?"

"Violet, please," he urged, ignoring my inquiry in return. That in itself was unusual.

As I continued to drive, the image of Damian in front of me outside the house went cloudy. In fact, any memory I had of him prior to today felt off. He was a faceless man in the doorway of my office. A figure at the grocery store, and nothing more. If I didn't know any better, I would have said he was fading away.

"Why do I feel like I'm forgetting him?"

A sense of dread began to form in my stomach at saying that out loud. If he could have this effect on me, then what about my family?

If I was having trouble recalling him now, what would tomorrow hold? What if he did something serious and a short time later, nobody would remember it? Had he already done something prior to today and I had lost the memory?

"Did he do something to me? What can a saint do?"

I knew that we had talked, we had to have talked, right? Why would I lead Damian away from the house without saying a single word? It didn't make any sense. My brain was trying to put puzzle pieces together that didn't fit.

"Get us to your apartment as fast as you can," Kade ordered, and I hit the gas.

Twenty-five minutes.

It had been twenty-five minutes since Kade had left, and the urgency with which he did had me in a tailspin.

I picked up a book to read, but after repeating the same paragraph four or five times and unable to retain any of the information, I slammed it shut and tossed it onto the couch. I turned on some music, hoping it would get me in the mood to tidy up and do some dishes, but it did nothing of the sort.

I normally kept my door locked up tight when I was home alone, and Kade was adamant that I would not touch it no matter who knocked. He'd instructed me not to answer my phone or leave under any circumstances. I thought he was being unreasonable, but his actions told a bigger story that I didn't understand and he apparently didn't have the time to explain, which was annoying by itself.

I wasn't sure when he'd decided to make me a prisoner in my own home.

"Violet." His voice sounded like an echo as I spun around to meet him and he was almost flush against me. "Where's your necklace?”

"My what?" I shot him a brief look of uncertainty before my hand shot up to my bare neck.

"Your necklace that I gave you." He began searching around the bed and the surrounding areas only to dart off toward the bathroom.

He trotted out with a silver chain dangling from his hand and he rounded me, securing it into its place upon my neck. I sucked in a sharp breath as the black obsidian touched my skin and my head began to spin.

Scenes came flooding back and I almost collapsed to the floor, but Kade caught me with ease, gathering me into his arms. He laid me down on the bed as I got a crash course in the recent memories I'd lost.

I could feel my eyes darting back and forth and side to side erratically as Damian and all of today's events came tumbling through. Even moments with Kade seemed to have been fading, and now they were coming to the surface at full force. It was as if every memory that had taken place with Damian, the so-called saint, was being zapped from existence, and now the past few days' events were coming back in droves.

My emotions were all over the place and I was experiencing them at such extreme levels I couldn't help but let loose in the only way I could.

I lost myself in my sobs as Kade cradled me into him. It hurt. The world of demons and saints had brought my life to a screeching halt and a crossroads that I hadn't asked for.

I didn't want to run to Kade and his world out of fear, but I also didn't know what kind of life awaited me here if I didn't. My boss and my workplace, what would become of it? Would he make my life a living hell, or try to keep me as some sort of consolation prize? Why did he even want anything to do with me? What made me so special? The very thought was sickening.

Would I have been better off to forget all of this? Or would Damian have used this to his advantage, spinning the tables in hopes of getting to me once Kade was out of the picture? The endless game of what-ifs was harrowing. I was angry and confused and so, so lost.

When I finally settled down enough to find my voice, I sat up, leaving his side.

"I don't know what I'm supposed to do." My eyes stung and I felt drained. Exhausted and at the end of my rope. Desperate to seek an end to the madness of trying to make this major decision about my life and future, all while trying to keep myself together even though I was falling apart.

I was tearing apart at the seams.

Kade sat up and took my hands in his, stilling the shake that I hadn't been aware of. Concern was etched upon his face, and a sadness I could read that made my chest hurt. But I had to carry on. I owed it to myself to have this discussion, no matter how difficult.

"If I don't come with you…" I couldn't bear to look at him any longer as tears threatened my eyes once again. "How can I protect myself? How can I protect my family?"

I knew the answer was that I couldn't.

I didn't have any special talents. I couldn't be in several places at once, and I was only a human. I didn't know the extent of Kade's abilities, but with him out of the picture, I felt like I was helpless. I didn't think pepper spray could aid me when it came to dealing with a saint.

If I didn't go with him, I would be nothing but a lamb to the slaughter, or worse. If Damian had other plans for me, even some notion of romance, I didn't really want to know.

"You said it yourself. Should I choose not to accept the

tethering, you would leave and I would be transferred to someone else, but that doesn't help me. That does *nothing* for me. It's the same as getting a stupid restraining order against Brett. It's pointless."

"And if I go, what if Damian retaliates somehow and takes it out on my family? He told me, point-blank, that he wants me. For what, I don't know. But he…" I tried to suppress the lump in my throat but fought through it. "Either decision I make has unknown consequences that could potentially hurt me."

Kade swiped a rogue tear away from my cheek and I let the side of my face fall into his hand. I wanted to get lost in his comfort, but the roaring storm inside of me about my decision tomorrow wouldn't let up.

"I will start off by saying that today's events were not in vain. But even though our time with Damian was short, I think we might have a lead on him."

"What does that mean?" I finally turned my attention toward him. "What did you find out?"

"The mind games alone come from elder saints. That is a skill that takes decades to master, and since he never laid a finger on you, even longer."

"How old is he then?" I was at full attention now, pulling out of my sorrows even if only momentarily.

"I can't be certain just yet, but we have him narrowed down to a handful of saints in our records. But he's no younger than one hundred." I didn't relish the way that he spoke of his age. It was as nonchalant as telling me the sky was sunny today. As if he could just skim over that fact like it was nothing.

"Oh my god, ew. He's that old?" I could feel disgust on my tongue.

"Neither demons or saints age once they hit adulthood,

and the number of our years doesn't really matter to us. With shapeshifting you can take on whatever form, age, or shape as you please."

"If that's not a form of catfishing then I don't know what is." I turned my nose up.

"If I do recall, one of your favorite fictional characters was over a hundred years old and in a teenage body when he met the love of his life. She was what…seventeen?"

My eyes narrowed on him. "Different scenario. And no shapeshifting."

"Okay, well should you meet my uncle and his wife, you can ask them about their feelings on the age gap. And while we're at it, should you meet my people, I think you will find that they don't get hung up on age the way humans do."

I shook my head. "I know your normal is nowhere near my idea of it, but I can't help but think he's some sort of elderly man in a young twenty-something-year-old body."

Kade shifted so his feet hung off the bed and he placed them flat on the floor. "The fact that he knows my name is unsettling. Any time we are here, we go by an alias. Before you and I met, I had never spoken my real name in your world."

"So how did he know it then?"

Kade rounded his shoulders and stilled. "I told you my world is not without its problems. Our own politics. We are far from perfect."

"Okay," I acknowledged, reluctantly, suddenly unsure of where this was going.

"We take our identities and some of our traditions very seriously. My sister and I are starting to suspect we have a traitor in our midst. Someone who wants me out of the way."

Why on earth would someone have a target on Kade's back? What was I missing?

"We think Damian has been on my tail since last night. I am somewhat vulnerable while I'm here because I have not tethered yet. Still strong, don't get me wrong. But if you accept, not only would that bond make me stronger, but you as well. It seems as if someone doesn't want that to happen."

"Do you have any ideas as to who it could be?" I searched his face, worried for his very existence. Not only did I have to worry about him being alone if I rejected the tethering, but now his strength too?

"I do, but I have no proof. Aleena and Elias are the two I would trust with my life. I was delegating the task to them to try and see if they could find anything out."

"Sounds like Elias needs a raise. He's doing a great deal while you're away." The fact that he mentioned his sister as well made me happy that he had another in his corner, especially in matters such as this.

"He is a man of many talents." Kade grinned, but it didn't make it to his eyes. "But to answer your earlier concerns, because of you we have been able to build a better profile on Damian. We have narrowed him down greatly just since our encounter today. We plan on dealing with him sooner rather than later."

"Oh?" I shot him a look.

"Whether or not you choose to come with me, he will be dealt with. I will personally see to it."

"What do you mean, like kill him?" Worry became evident in my voice. Would Kade really try to carry something out like that himself?

"Yes." He turned his attention back to me and I froze. He was so certain of himself. "You and your family will never be safe until he's out of the picture."

My mouth went dry at the thought of Kade carrying out

an act like that on my behalf. "But you wouldn't do it alone, right?"

He cocked an eyebrow. "Afraid for my safety?" He tipped his head to the side, a small smirk on his face.

"Just as you are with mine." I didn't skip a beat.

He offered a half-hearted chuckle as he shook his head. "I would not be alone, no. In some instances, if someone were to go against the likes of Damian alone, it would be a suicide mission. In this case, it would require two to three of us demons since we intend to interrogate before we end him."

"Well that doesn't make me feel any better." I let my shoulders sag forward as I twisted my fingers together in my lap. "Three of you versus one saint? Just how strong are they?"

"It's more his age and experience that are problematic. He's had a lot of time to perfect his craft compared to myself and those closest to me."

The fact that the man who was threatening me and my family was in the process of being dealt with calmed my nerves ever so slightly. I knew it wasn't resolved yet, but it was a glimmer of hope, even if it meant the death of another. I was torn about how I should feel about that. It wasn't exactly a human life that would be ending, but the likes of the kind that was responsible for the deaths of Kade's parents.

"Three of you against an old man. And here I thought you were so strong," I teased, trying to find a way to lighten the mood.

Kade turned and his features darkened as his bangs fell into his face. Closing the short distance between us, the muscles in his arms flexed with every inch he moved. His heated gaze sent a wave of want through me, signaling my body to prime itself. I leaned back onto my forearms as he followed, hovering over me, his breath mixing with mine. I stilled in anticipation.

"I can assure you, I am very strong." His wicked smile returned and I grinned.

"So show me," I whispered into his ear as I grazed it with my teeth and offered a playful bite.

Before I could even let out a yelp, Kade had taken hold of both of my wrists and had them bound high above my head, held in place by one hand. His mouth was hot on mine, his tongue exploring as he ground his pelvis into me. Meeting his attack with equal enthusiasm, I writhed beneath him as I squirmed. I was eager to feel him, but without my hands, I had to settle for what my mouth and the rest of my body could do.

His free hand held my face firmly, securing me to him until I was out of breath. Once his hand left, I had to turn away, gasping for the air he had taken. His mouth moved toward my neck, seemingly unaffected by any lack of oxygen. His hand ripped open my blouse, startling me as the buttons popped. Lips planted harsh kisses to my exposed skin as his hand traveled down further. He only lifted his body high enough to fit his hand between us.

A tug at my hips indicated that my shorts were the next clothing item on his path of destruction. It gave him enough space to grant his hand entrance to my core and I was ready for his long fingers to dive in.

I welcomed him, grinding against his fingers as they curved into me, moving too slow.

Incredibly slow.

I wanted him to take me, and fast. I wanted him to fuck me so hard that I forgot about all of today's events and all of my worries. I wanted to be fucked senseless.

His thumb brushed across my clit ever so slowly and I let out a whimper. My body wanted and craved more. The frenzy that I felt when it came to Kade was out of this world, and nothing else could sate it until he entered me. I begged him to do so as his fingers lazily drew out of me and trailed a wet line up toward my navel.

I was going mad with want.

"Please," I begged again, now empty. I throbbed uncomfortably at the hollowness and I attempted to make contact with his lips but he backed away far enough that I couldn't reach.

"Stay still," he spoke gruffly, and released my wrists. They ached to some degree but that paled in comparison to what was going on with the rest of my body. I kept my arms up, watching him as he yanked my pants off of me, underwear and all, and he threw them across the room. He stood long enough to remove his clothes, and then crept back onto the bed, prowling toward me like he had before, his hooded eyes intent on my core.

My chest heaved at my torn shirt, my breasts threatening to spill from my bra. "You forgot something." I glanced down at it, waiting for him to rid me from the rest of my restrictions. I could part with this bra should he decide to demolish it as well, I wouldn't give it another thought.

He made it look so easy, snapping the cotton at its center, and my heavy breasts were released. He captured them with his hands and his mouth followed, teasing the peaks. My hands floated down and my fingers tangled into his hair but he quickly seized my wrists once more.

"Now, now." Kade flipped me over onto my stomach and tugged at my hips, raising them from the bed. He secured my wrists behind my back and pulled me high enough that my upper half was hovering above the mattress.

The head of his cock was now at my entrance and I was on high alert. I panted another plea, begging him to take me, praying to come undone.

He slammed into me and I cried out. As much as my body wanted to heave forward and rest upon the bed before me, I couldn't. I was restrained and under his mercy as he repeatedly beat his cock into my center. All my strength left my body as I continued to take it, pummel after pummel, thrust after thrust, I was going to come apart before we had even really begun.

The force in which he moved made the headboard beat against the wall. Each thud, a strike of exhilaration as he dove into me.

It happened so fast as the pleasure was too great. I wanted to muffle my screams into a pillow but I couldn't. I clenched my eyes closed as my body spasmed around him. He lifted me from my position and up against his chest, capturing my mouth once again as he slowed, finding his own release. He rocked into me, grunting into my mouth as he emptied himself.

His fingers found my clit once again and I moaned into his mouth as he made the circling motions that I had shown him a few nights ago. My body responded, ready for a second round as sweat began to form at the nape of my neck and I beamed in appreciation.

"Again."

CHAPTER 15

Violet

As I roused from a deep sleep, Kade was firmly attached to my backside with only a sheet between us.

I tried to remain still, unsure if he was awake or not. At one point he'd informed me he didn't require as much as I did but he could sleep nonetheless. I wondered if I would need as much as I did now if I went to Darthou.

Allowing myself to pass out after our rough and passionate lovemaking was a comfort that I loved to give in to. Last night had been a bit on the rougher side, but I reveled in it. When it came to Kade and our sexual relationship, that was something that I never wanted to lose.

As stupid or petty as it sounded, I felt like he had ruined sex for me with all other men. He had now set the standard so incredibly high that I was exactly that—high on him and the effect he had on me and my body.

And even though our relationship had admittedly had a weird start, it had grown exponentially within the short timeframe we had known each other. Kade had never once made me feel uncomfortable even when I admitted to the possibility of not accepting the tethering. He always took my feelings into account and tried to comfort me when I needed it most. My mind had been a war zone in the time since we had met, and even though his arrival was the start of it all, I couldn't seem to imagine a life without him now.

Although it frightened me that Kade seemed to make a point of making sure Damian and his existence came to an end, I couldn't help but fear for him in doing so. Sure, he wouldn't be alone, but I didn't want him to go after Damian if he was weakened by not completing the tethering ritual first.

I did wonder what kind of strength the ritual might bestow on my end, but that thought didn't really matter right now as it would be Kade's safety—and that of his sister and best friend—at stake. I looked forward to meeting the ones he spoke so fondly of. And to know that there were others like me in Darthou did provide me with a sense of peace.

It was with that thought that I had finally decided—if Kade really could make good on his word that no harm would come to my family and Damian would be dealt with for good, then I was ready. I was willing to accept the tethering and reroute the path of my life into one that would forever intertwine with his.

I didn't know what the future would hold but I guessed it would be no different than moving across the globe and settling down in China. He had a whole new world that I could explore, his own set of customs and traditions that I would take on as my own. I was prepared to leave my home to take my place in his. But for what little time I had left here, I had decided to leave him in the dark just a while longer. I would soak up the fleeting time I had left until we had to depart.

Until he couldn't possibly wait any longer for an answer.

"Sleep well?" Kade planted a kiss on my shoulder.

I turned to face him, analyzing.

"What?" His face morphed out of sleepy slumber to a look of confusion.

"How often do you sleep? Normally?" I poked at the center of his chest.

A small grin spread across his features as he realized I wasn't in a serious mood after all. "I can go days without it sometimes. Just depends on how much energy I exert. But with you, I would make it a regular routine."

"Would I still require sleep as I do now?"

"You would, to an extent. But your stamina would also increase greatly after tethering."

His use of the word *stamina* piqued my interest. I used my finger to tilt his chin so I could meet his lips and I kissed him tenderly.

I wondered what was going through his mind regarding the decision I had to make, as our time here was drawing to a close. How would he react when I finally revealed my answer? Would he whisk me away immediately without hesitation or a second thought?

"I love you," he declared softly, but clear as day, as we parted.

I blinked up into his eyes. It still amazed me how I couldn't even make out a reflection in them. Just black pools that never ceased to astonish me.

He hadn't expressed those words since our second night, confessing an onslaught of information as he revealed his love for me among many other things. But, even with my immense feelings for him, I couldn't bring myself to return those words just yet.

"I know." I half expected a reaction out of him about the fact that I couldn't say it back, but his expression remained as it was—earnest in its meaning, features soft.

I kissed him once more and while I knew it wasn't the same as reciprocating those words, it was all I could think to do. I could very easily believe I would say it someday, but as of now, I just wasn't ready. It was too soon, and it would be unfair to the both of us if I were to say it too early without feeling that phrase with every fiber of my being. This very predicament made me all too aware of the seriousness of my decision.

My hand pressed firmly onto his bare chest, and when he tried to cover it with his, I winced, breaking us apart. Fingerlike bruising was beginning to surface along my wrist and my jaw loosened.

"Sorry, I—"

"What are you sorry for? It's my fault."

He leaned up in a brisk movement, pulling me with him by my shoulder. He held my hands out so we could examine the extent of the marks. Even by the dim lighting of my apartment, I could still see the darkened spots on them.

"I'm so sorry." His apology lanced through me as his hurt became evident. He wrapped his hands around my wrists, and I wanted to yank them back. Warmth radiated from his hold and the pain melted away rapidly. In fact, it was much quicker and less painful than the night he had healed my foot.

He released me and I examined my wrists, now fully healed and without a trace of injury. "Just so you know, I regret nothing."

"I should have been more careful." His focus was still plastered at the site, though nothing could be physically seen anymore.

"Hey." I cupped the side of his face. "I'm fine," I reassured him, and he turned to kiss my palm, gently securing my hand with his.

"Seems like you have some healer in you. First my foot, now this?"

I hadn't confirmed with him yet about healing me at my grandma's house yesterday. But I knew that touch well enough to know that he had done something about the fuzzy cloudiness that had invaded my head. Even so, it hadn't been enough to combat whatever mind games Damian had bestowed upon me.

"My mother had some healer tendencies that passed on to me. But it's not all it's cracked up to be."

While I enjoyed hearing him speak of his mother, I was puzzled by why he could brush off the healing gift so absentmindedly.

I stared at him, skeptical. "Really? How so?"

"I can only heal minor things for others. With our kind, it is a rare quality to possess. We have the ability to aid and speed healing in ourselves, but to project that onto another is not a trait that every demon possesses. Now when it comes to death-like encounters—I have no experience with that."

"Staffan's wife could step in if needed though, right?" I tried to recall her name but failed.

That earned a smile from Kade. I really was trying to cram in all of the info I could, but some of their names were hard to remember. I only hoped that if I could put faces to them, maybe that would help.

"Rafina, yes. She is quite the force."

"Have you ever thought about learning from her? Furthering your healing abilities?"

He nodded. "Occasionally I have pondered doing so. But on the bright side, I've got nothing but time." Kade stood from the bed and held his hand out toward me. "Anyway, what would you like to do today?"

I placed my hand in his and joined him, our naked frames brushing against each other. "That depends." I weaved our fingers together and held the back of his hand to my bare chest.

"On?" His arm wrapped around me, locking me in place.

"On how much time we have." I bit my bottom lip, unsure of how long we had until he needed an answer.

He kissed my forehead, then rested his chin atop my head of wild hair. "You could have said yes the moment we met, or at any time since."

I swallowed hard, unsure if we had until tomorrow morning or sooner. It was five nights, right? I assumed that dawn, or close to it, was as long as I had.

Damian's voice rang through my head and I bit down the bile that wanted to form in the back of my throat. He didn't shy away from stating that Kadriel would steal me away, just wait and see.

If I didn't give Kade an answer before he needed it, would he do such a thing?

Demons, or at least my demon, seemed to honor consent above all else. He wouldn't go back on his word. Kade had stressed time and time again that it was my choice.

So why was I letting Damian get under my skin so much? Was it the lingering effects of his mind games? I wanted to believe that it was, but to be honest, I wasn't one-hundred-percent sure. And although that percentage was small, it still ate away at my thoughts, troubling me.

"You have until midnight to decide."

Kade had vanished for a few minutes to collect some clothes while I dressed. There was no rush to our morning but my stomach had started growling and that had put a little pep in his step to get out the door.

I was concerned about leaving the apartment today, but he assured me that we would be fine. Instead of driving, we opted to walk to a nearby restaurant to grab a late breakfast. I wanted nothing more than a carb-loaded feast after our night's endeavors which had bled into this morning.

Sweet kisses and soft caresses kept leading us back into each other's arms, and at one point, I'd been worried that I might never get any food. Kade did nothing to stifle his amusement in the matter. The sounds emitted by my stomach provided enough mortification on my end to divert our path toward finding something to shut up the unwelcome rumblings.

The restaurant we had chosen was busy with their morning rush, but since it was just the two of us, we were seated in a corner promptly. Kade eyed the menu and settled on a southwestern omelet, while I ordered their specialty tri-stack pancakes with strawberries, bananas, and whipped topping. And to boot, sides of bacon and sausage so I could get some protein in me.

The volume of the old-farm-kitchen-styled restaurant was loud enough to let us fade into the background among all the other individuals that were visiting. Daylight filtered in through the lacy blue curtains and the wallpaper was adorned with cows and chickens, creating a pattern along the borders of the ceiling.

"After we eat, what's next?" Kade leaned forward, elbows on the table as he scanned the crowd before returning his baby-blue eyes to me.

I shrugged, unsure. It was a day of lasts for me, but at the same time it didn't feel like it. I clung to the knowledge that I would get to come back and visit, so it didn't really feel like goodbye. Just a "see you soon."

"Is there anything you would like to do? We hit the carnival, but is there anything else you would like to see while you're here and not on…duty?" I chose my words wisely due to our surroundings.

"How do you do that?" he questioned, amused.

I raised a brow as I copied his elbowed stance on the table that separated us. "Do what, exactly?"

He beamed that hearty smile of his and shook his head, hair bouncing at the movement. "This could be your last day here and you ask me what I want to do?"

"I can still visit." I squared my shoulders. "Besides, up until now I've been free to shop and eat when I want. Go to the park for walks or binge-watch shows whenever I please. I don't have anything pressing that I have to do or get done."

My thoughts strayed momentarily to the small family get-together yesterday. The decent-sized group of relatives gathered around the table laughing and talking about anything under the sun—that was the memory I wanted to hold on to. That's what I wanted to leave with, knowing that I could come back to that. Be it a year from now or so, I would impatiently await that day.

"You never cease to amaze me." I could feel his leg beneath the table brush against my calf, and I blushed. How could he have this effect on me in a boisterous and crowded room? "Does that mean you might be leaning toward a yes?"

I twisted my mouth to the side. I hadn't meant to put my cards down so soon, so I reached for my drink as I pondered my answer.

He seemed entertained by my reluctance to respond and a small laugh escaped. I seriously doubted that he loved the sound of my laugh more than I loved the sound of his.

"I will anxiously await with bated breath." I could tell by his reply that he already knew my answer, but he wanted me to verbalize it. That, he would have to wait for.

A desire to change the subject came over me and I wanted to have a little fun with him. Keeping my mind off of our wait for food didn't hurt either.

"Remember how you said that you probably know me better than anyone else? You know, your stalker attributes I have tried not to get too hung up on."

Kade cocked his head to the side, focused on where this was going. "Okay, I'll bite."

"Prove it." I smirked. "Favorite season?"

"Fall, when the humidity dies down and you can snuggle up in a hoodie and blanket."

"Pet peeve?"

"People who chew gum with their mouth open."

"Favorite food?"

"Anything with buffalo sauce. Wraps, sandwiches, or even just plain buffalo wings with a side of ranch."

"Favorite treat?"

"The cookie bites that you get at the movie theater. You can never find them anywhere else so you have to get them every time you go."

I studied Kade. He didn't skip a beat when he met each question with a direct reply. This should have been creepy, but I had to admit I was getting a kick out of it.

"Favorite color?"

"Trick question." He leaned back in his seat. "Depends on the day and your mood. You used to joke that it was rainbow because that way you wouldn't have to pick just one."

"Favorite movie?"

"Another trick question. You have too many. You would probably be better off asking which one you never want to see again. What title would you burn all of the copies and take it down from streaming platforms if you could?"

My nose turned up just thinking about it—a certain horror flick with a doctor of sorts and an experimental procedure with numerous patients that made my stomach turn.

"Nope, not discussing it. Moving on."

The sheer joy on Kade's face as he nailed each question, and in detail, was a charm that he wore too well.

"How about you? Do you have a favorite food? Sweet or savory? What's something you crave?" These were all questions that I wouldn't mind him answering himself. By his own admittance, his favorite color was yellow. He had offered that information when he'd brought me flowers for date night.

"Hmmm…" He contemplated for a moment before he leaned in close, wearing a naughty expression that spoke in heated volumes. I began to lean forward as well, mirroring his body's motion. "Cotton candy was certainly a treat…and you."

My jaw fell open and my eyes widened in shock. But before I could scold him, a waiter returned, a tray of our food in hand.

Our meals had come in the nick of time and we both devoured them. I kept telling myself that I deserved this delectable pancake special because of the calories I undoubtedly burned when Kade and I were rolling around the sheets. If we kept at it every night, I might just make that my new workout regimen. After all, Kade did say that my stamina would increase, so I couldn't think of a better way to stay in shape.

Speaking of that, I was curious about Kade and his workouts. He had mentioned training, but what all did that include? He wasn't too bulky so I didn't think weights played that big of a part, but I could be wrong. He still had a definition that required some sort of work on his end.

I refused to believe he was just blessed with the body he had, or that he simply altered his appearance to the state he was in. Even if he shifted into this form, how would that affect his ability to fight and his agility to play basketball? There was no way it could just be a facade.

Our server cleared the table of our empty plates and Kade left a generous amount of cash for our meals and tip. We left hand in hand, weaving our way out of the restaurant. The hustle and bustle from churchgoers was evident in the attire that the guests flooding in were now wearing.

When we were finally greeted outside by the warm air, I breathed in deep as if the crowded atmosphere we'd just emerged from was almost suffocating.

"Is it cold where you're from?" We began to walk at a leisurely pace down the sidewalk in the opposite direction from which we came. "Like, would I need to pack all my long-sleeve shirts and jackets?" He was always so cold when he returned from Darthou and he had never offered any explanation, but then I had never asked until now.

"Actually, what would I need to bring?" I spouted off another question. Good grief, I hadn't actually thought about packing, what to do with my car and my things at work. I was perturbed that I was just now realizing this, and now I was running out of time.

"Honestly, compared to here and right now, yes. It is

colder. Once tethered you will acclimate to an extent, but as far as clothes go, you can bring whatever you want. But know that those can be taken care of for you there as well."

Slanting my eyes at him, I pushed further. "I could get a whole new wardrobe there if I want?" That aspect alone was intriguing. What kind of fashions did they have? What was everyone's day-to-day attire? Would I fit in with my clothes or would I need to conform so I didn't stand out?

"There are others who would be more than happy to assist you with your wardrobe."

"What about my apartment, my car and my job? I can't just vanish, people would freak. My family wouldn't understand."

The realities of my decision were starting to weigh heavily on me. I knew that we were in a time crunch, but the number of things that needed to be taken care of were overwhelming and I could feel my pulse quicken. These were the questions I should have asked long before now, before decision time.

Instead, I'd been so caught up in Kade, infatuated by his body and world, longing to get to know him in the short time that we had, that I had pushed this off to the last minute. Mix that in with our dealings with Brett, fending off inquisitive family members, and the saint problem; I was in a daze as to how I could have possibly made this all work any other way.

Kade stopped and faced me, it was soft and warm with affection. "Although it's rare, you are not the first to cross over and accept the tethering. We have a team in place that would take care of these matters for you. They would take into account your wishes for how you want things done, from what story to tell your family about your absence, to taking care of your belongings. You don't have to cut out all communication as you can still call or text. Just know that things will move pretty quickly once you accept, but I will be with you every step of the way."

I nodded in understanding. It was peculiar that everything was going to be taken care of on my behalf, considering I had been under Kade's watchful eyes for so long. There was a secret-service-like team to take care of situations like mine, and others to assist me with my wardrobe? There were plenty of opportunities if I wanted a job? Just how large was Darthou? How big was his community that I was soon to be a part of? Could I even call this demon world of his a community?

Letting that knowledge settle and coming to terms with the soon-to-be aftermath of my decision, I headed in the direction of the park that I frequented quite often for walks. It was lush in greenery with various strategic landscaping. As a kid, I used to refer to it as Central Park after seeing that massive place on my television screen.

It boasted giant trees and bushes that were trimmed to a pristine perfection. A large metal archway welcomed us and I could feel my nerves retreating. Cars weren't allowed in here, so it was peaceful for the most part. You could forget you were even in the city because once inside, all the carefully crafted foliage proved useful in blocking out the noise of the surrounding streets.

I wasn't sure what world awaited me in Darthou, but I hoped I could find a place of solace and ease such as this. I would dearly miss the serenity that it brought, the families at play and the regulars who would frequent the park with their dogs, or the random happenings that would take place here. There were occasional pop-up artists or musicians who would find their way in and display their talents for anyone willing to look or listen.

In my opinion, it was the most beautiful part of the city. For a Sunday morning, its activity was pretty scarce, and I welcomed the silence and tranquility within its confines.

We walked hand in hand and alone in our thoughts until I led us off the main path and onto a flagstone walkway. The grass among the stones was manicured in matching height and was a welcome and satisfying sight as we crossed them.

Throughout my time spent here I had seen numerous caretakers of the grounds, and had even gotten the chance to know some of them by name—some volunteers, others employed by the city. I could tell who had a green thumb and cherished their work, versus those who were just in it for the paycheck. Yet somehow, the two sides came together enough to make this place a vision and the upkeep never faltered.

This particular trail I chose spiraled off into a more secluded area that housed a tunnel overtaken by a blend of purple and white flowers. Its covering provided a welcome shade and a sweet aroma that filled my nostrils. If I could bottle that up and take it with me, I would. I slowed our wandering stride, taking in its beauty.

Eventually, our route led us to a giant female sculpture that was positioned as the centerpiece of a fountain. The Odelia Fountain, to be exact. She was clad in a cloth that draped around her figure, hugging her curves as water flowed out in six different directions around her.

Over the years, I had heard various explanations and myths regarding the statue, but that was just it—I knew nothing concrete except the placard that stated the fountain's name. It only furthered the allure of her and captivated me all the more.

Considering the state I was in right now with a demon by my side, I guess you could say that I had a slight fascination with the unknown.

There were two wrought iron benches on opposite sides, intricate in their designs that set them apart from the seating throughout the rest of the park. I tugged at Kade to follow me toward one of them, noticing that he was admiring the statue just as I was. I decided to let us both bask in the subtle charm that it had to offer.

"Beautiful, isn't it?" I beamed before snuggling into him. It was warm out, but not even that could keep me from desiring closeness with him.

"It is." Our hands clasped together as we sat there, the sounds of the water filling our ears.

In a park that I knew all too well, I had examined every nook and cranny of this fountain, committing it to memory. I had visited this spot in particular countless times, and it was still my favorite feature. Even after intense walks, or my lame attempts at running, I would take the time to stop here and rest before heading back to my apartment. The very same one that I had scrimped and saved for because of its nearness to this location.

The sun wasn't slowing in its ascent above the tree line, and its rays of light and heat came through. I should have opted for a tank top and shorts, but I'd wanted to look halfway decent going out to breakfast with Kade. I could feel my denim capris and my scoop neck tee cling to me with the rising humidity. Before long, my hair would begin to puff up and frizz out if it hadn't already as I didn't put any product on it earlier. I scooped my hair to one side of my shoulders and settled against Kade's side once more.

I was leaving tonight.

Was I crazy for wanting this? Was I delusional for accepting this demon of a man beside me and this unknown existence that awaited?

The very notion of my mental acceptance of it was thrilling, while also completely nerve-racking and mind-boggling. Even if there were people in place to help with my transition to this new life, I still had the urge to wrap things up here as best I could.

My grandma wasn't going to just take someone else's word on my whereabouts, and just how on earth were they going to take care of my car? Kade hadn't been in a vehicle until our courting, but were there other demons who had and could drive?

Then there was the matter of my clothes. They weren't going to pack themselves. Better yet, there were some personal items I would rather not leave behind for others to find and collect.

Come to think of it, what was I supposed to wear for the tethering? Kade and I would meet up with Staffan right away to complete the ritual, so should I dress formally for that? It seemed like their version of a wedding, so I probably needed to wear something on the nicer side, but nothing that might get ruined if I were to get blood on it. Just how deep did my palm need to be cut for this? Would Kade heal me after all was said and done?

The following day would include a celebration, which was even more concerning. It presented itself to be the equivalent to a reception that would follow a wedding in my world.

Being introduced to everyone as Kade's bride, so to speak, without having met anybody first? I might not have the stress of meeting his parents, as they were no longer around, but what if his sister hated me? What about his aunt, uncle and best friend?

I didn't know a single person in Darthou and I was going to have to dive headfirst into his world in the hopes that they would accept me. One thing was for sure though, I was going to be glued to Kade's side no matter what. Being thrust into a social situation with countless unknown faces was a worry I didn't want to contemplate right now, but it could very well be the reality of tomorrow.

I fumbled with my necklace, rolling the cylinder between my fingers. How could this small stone have been powerful enough to restore my memories? I had heard of crystals and how some people would wear them in their bra or place them in their pockets. I hadn't really given them much thought before now, unsure if it was all a hoax or what.

Maybe there was actually some truth to them after all.

"Whatever you decide, never let that leave your sight." Kade's tone was slightly demanding yet hushed, causing me to sit up. "If you decide not to wear it, at least put it in your pocket. It will help protect you."

I glanced down at it before letting it rest upon my chest again. "But you're going to deal with Damian."

"I am. I will see to it, I promise. But should you stay, and another saint finds you, you'll need it." His face fell bleak as he returned his focus toward Odelia. "As we've witnessed, their mind games are not to be taken lightly."

I could feel the blood drain from my face. I didn't know why that hadn't occurred to me before. Damian could very well have a network of saints just as Kade did with demons. Would another saint really try to swoop in and take over if Damian's mission failed? A terrible knot began to form in my stomach and the calm that I had experienced earlier was slipping away at a lightning speed.

Kade reached into his pockets and retrieved a mirror that was similar in size to my compact but with no lid, and it was encompassed by what looked to be black obsidian. The perimeter looked like my necklace, only its surface was worn and a bit rough. He hunched his shoulders to cast a shadow over it and the glass fogged over, but I couldn't make out anything else.

He abruptly stood a few seconds later and deposited the mirror back in his pocket.

"We have to go." He spoke adamantly, his eyes flashing dark as he carefully scanned the area around us.

"Is everything okay?" My heart began beating erratically as I stood with him. "Kade." I urged him to look at me as I tugged on his arm.

"We need to get back to your apartment, now."

Without another word, I led him through a shortcut out of the park, cutting through some bushes that I knew we were technically trespassing through, but I didn't care.

The effects of adrenaline kicked in as we moved swiftly through the busy streets and down the sidewalks in the direction of my apartment building. Kade could have easily left me in the dust with his strides, but he followed me by my side until we made it back. My chest heaved as we stepped into the lobby and followed others into the elevator. I tried to suppress my pants in the confined space and I was annoyed that I couldn't speak to Kade until we were behind closed doors.

The ding of the elevator chimed at my floor and we bolted from it and down the hall. I didn't have the slightest care of what the other tenants thought of our hasty exit.

Something was wrong. Something was happening and I didn't like the edge it had put Kade on. He wore the same look on his face as yesterday when we were on our way back to the apartment after my encounter with Damian.

Just how severe was this? Was it him again? Damian?

All signs pointed to yes. I couldn't think of it being anything else but that right now.

I fumbled with my key to unlock the door, my hands

trembling. I backed in and opened the door for Kade to enter, tossing my keys onto the table just to turn and lock the door behind us.

My apartment was almost too cool compared to the outside; the air hitting my dampened clothes sent an unwelcome chill through me. It didn't help that Kade was now conversing with my standing mirror and his words did nothing to soothe my worries.

"Are you sure?"

"And the council approved it already?"

"I agree, it sounds too convenient."

I was drowning in my thoughts, wishing I could hear the other end of the conversation. I crossed my arms but began to bite at the tip of my thumb, waiting for Kade to finish so I could be brought up to speed on whatever was transpiring.

"Ten minutes."

With the mention of time, the mirror's blurred surface dissipated and Kade turned on his heel to come meet me. "We've got a location on Damian." His brows were pinched, creating a mark in between them.

I blinked up at him, releasing my thumb, also wary about the timing of this. "What did you mean by 'too convenient'?"

Kade held his breath momentarily. I could see that the wheels in his head were spinning, and he was guarding me from whatever was going through his mind, but I didn't have the patience for it.

"Kade, answer me," I demanded. "Is this a trap?"

What were the odds that they found Damian on my last day with Kade? Were the demons just really good at their jobs, or were they walking into a trap? I feared for Kade and those who would be accompanying him. I knew he wanted to put a stop to Damian, but what if he couldn't?

"We can't be for certain, but I owe it to you to find out."

It felt as if Kade was going to war for me and I didn't know how to process that information. "But…"

I was at a loss for words and fearing for his very existence. I had just come to the conclusion that I wanted to spend the rest of my life with him, and now I might lose him before our time together even had a chance to begin?

"I won't be alone," he tried to assure me, but I shook my head in denial.

"Come here." I tried to resist his reach, but failed. He drew me into a strained hold and I kept trying to push him away. When he finally released me to look up at him, tears were beginning to sting my eyes.

"I don't want to lose you," I admitted through my jagged breaths.

"You won't." He spoke firmly but I had trouble seeing how he could believe that. There was no guarantee of the outcome.

"You don't know that." I didn't know the extent of his strength or powers, but the fact that they might need three demons for one saint still echoed in my head and did nothing for my nerves. They planned on questioning him before ending his life, but if Damian had done so well protecting his identify before now, why would he put himself out there to be found on my final day?

The Damian situation needed to be dealt with, I was well aware. Kade had said sooner rather than later, but I'd had no idea just how soon it could transpire.

I should have been relieved about the fact that it could be taken care of before I left the only hometown I had ever known, but I couldn't help the worst-case scenario images that kept barreling through my head. I didn't know if I could deal with the loss of Kade should things not go according to his plan.

And what of the others? Elias and Kade's sister? What if something happened to them because of me? They didn't even know me!

"Please, Violet. I have to go. You're just going to have to trust me." I could sense the urgency that his voice still carried and I knew his ten minutes was ticking away.

I threw my arms around him and kissed him roughly, scared for his life and the others who would follow him into this battle that I would not be witness to. Tears began to fall, flowing down my cheeks as I tried to squash any last thought about getting him to stay.

I knew he had to do this, but it didn't make it hurt any less.

I choked back a sob as I stepped away. All I could think about was if this was going to be the last time I saw him. I couldn't bring myself to look at the positives should this mission prove to be successful—and I tried to, I really did. This felt all wrong and I couldn't explain away the pit in my stomach that told me something bad was going to happen.

"Keep your door locked and whatever you do, don't leave. I'll come back to you." He cupped the side of my face and stroked my cheek with his thumb.

"I won't leave. I promise." I nodded my head as I held the small stone of my necklace in my hand so tight that I was concerned it might break.

I squeezed my eyes tight, unable to calm the waves of emotions overtaking me.

"I love you," he whispered as he placed a kiss on my forehead. And with the quick vanishing of his lips, I knew he was already gone.

CHAPTER 16

Violet

I hated this.

I loathed this position I was placed in. I felt like I was going mad within the walls of my apartment, overwhelmed with doubt.

The more time passed, the more I spiraled out of control. In the short time that I had known Kade, I now couldn't imagine my life without him. I would never be the same because of him. I didn't fully understand how I could have fallen so hard, so fast, but I had and there was no denying it.

He could have been one hell of a rebound, but I didn't want that, I wanted more. More of him, of us, and the chance at this new life even after all of the revelations that Kade had brought to light.

I needed the opportunity to start over now that I knew my life at my job was a lie, a coverup, some scheme concocted by

Damian. I didn't want any ties to him or that place. I probably didn't even deserve the job there to begin with.

And that was without even starting on my past relationships or involvements. I had never been fully satisfied until now. I'd never truly felt wanted or needed, desired even, until Kade. It wasn't like he was presenting this picture-perfect future, but it was a fresh start with a promise to stay connected to my family. My visits with them might not exactly be ideal, maybe it was selfish even, but it was time I started to think about what I needed out of my life.

I had attempted to start packing my duffle bag with a few essential garments and outfits that I didn't want to part with. As much as I tried to remain positive, my head wouldn't let me focus on any one task for too long and I was bouncing between tasks like the ball in a pinball machine.

I retrieved my childhood blanket from the couch and wrapped it around my forearms, gripping its material in an attempt to settle down, but it was futile. I couldn't seem to get my mind on anything else besides *three demons against one saint.*

Did they fight with weapons, magic, or their minds? Were they here in my city or in another plane of existence like Darthou?

I was still in the dark about so much, I didn't even know how Kade expected to put an end to Damian once and for all. Did demons and saints die like us humans? How did you even kill them?

Obviously, it was possible to slay demons since Kade's parents had been lost at the hands of a saint. That thought triggered another and I trembled at the image my mind conjured up. Did both of Kade's parents die by the hands of a single saint? Was that a part of the equation that told him he needed the three-to-one ratio for this encounter? Would two more demons really turn the tables enough to make this mission triumphant?

Not only did Kade want to kill Damian, but he sought information. How long would an interrogation like that last and what if it went past our midnight deadline for my decision?

Kade's full-time job was watching, and I knew that he had been in my world before to carry out punishment when needed, but I didn't think I would ever be strong enough to accept this as normal for him. If he pulled through this, we were going to have a serious conversation about it. I knew he was doing this for me and to protect my family no matter my decision. However, it didn't make the pill any easier to swallow. As much as I didn't care for his job as a watcher, I would certainly prefer it over seeker. Did they even still call it that if they were going after a saint instead of a human?

And how many demon lives were lost at the hands of saints? Or vice versa? I knew nothing of their battles and scores. This wasn't exactly covered in textbooks that I was raised reading in school.

I was betting on a man who I had never even seen fight. Sure, Kade had landed a swift punch to Brett's abdomen and practically dragged him down to the lobby, but that was probably just child's play compared to what he was dealing with right now.

Kade hadn't even been gone that long, but it was enough time to drive me almost to the point of insanity. What if I never saw him again? What if the next face I met was Damian's smug, two-faced, lying, son of a—

A series of three knocks on my door caused my head to spin in its direction. My heart leapt into my throat as I froze, unsure of who would be paying me a visit.

I glanced at my phone to find no missed messages or calls,

and I silenced it, afraid that if it went off for whatever reason it might give my presence away. I waited, hoping I might hear someone leave. But then, I had been so lost in thought that I'd never heard anyone approach in the first place.

The silence that followed held on to me in an uneasy state.

Three more knocks and a familiar voice could be heard through the door.

"Violet, it's Ms. Vanders, are you home?" There was a sense of worry in her voice that I couldn't put my finger on. Perhaps she was just checking in since the whole ordeal on Friday night. I had meant to go and apologize for the late-night interruption and thank her for her quick aid in calling the police. The instant guilt I harbored for not having got around to it until now was strong, but Kade's warning stalled me. I really shouldn't answer the door.

I tiptoed silently toward my duffle bag and placed my blanket inside before her voice carried through the apartment again.

"I just wanted to make sure that you were alright. I saw that man earlier and I wanted to check in." Never once had Ms. Vanders been anything other than polite, with me and the other tenants I had seen her interact with.

While her concern was touching, when she mentioned a man, my thoughts went immediately to Brett and I panicked. Had he really been here? And did she mean earlier as in today? Could he have visited when Kade and I were out this morning?

Padding over to the door, I looked through the peephole and saw my middle-aged cat lady neighbor with arms at her sides, eyes cast down and still, waiting for a response.

Going against my better judgment, I unlocked the deadbolt and knob, leaving the chain in its place so I could peer out.

Before I could get a word in, a blow knocked me backwards and I plummeted onto the floor, my elbow taking a hit that stole my breath. In the doorway stood Brett, eyes aglow with a fury I had never seen before. Dark circles encompassed his eyes and he looked as if he hadn't slept in days, still wearing the same clothes from the last time he was here.

Ms. Vanders' look of sheer horror was prominent on her, her small frame cowered as she revealed she was being held at gunpoint. Her reading glasses were at the tip of her nose and ready to fall from her face at the smallest movement. I tripped over my own feet trying to stand, too afraid to turn my back on him. I withheld a gasp when I tried to put weight on my left arm and teetered in another direction to come up.

"She has nothing to do with this, Brett. Let her go." My voice cracked as my heart rate went through the roof.

Brett sneered. "Gladly. Thank you for your help, Ms. Vanders." He brought the handle of the gun down on her head, sending her thin body crumpling to the ground with a thud.

I shrieked as she went down and made impact with the floor, unsure if she was dead or unconscious. Brett stepped over her, crossing the threshold and into my home. I needed to search for something to defend myself, but nothing came to mind to help me in my defense against a gun.

The realization hit me—if Elias was off helping Kade fight, was there anybody left to watch me or Brett right now? Was I truly alone and defenseless? My hope of a swift rescue was fleeting as Brett closed the door behind him, trapping me inside.

Brett laid his eyes on my duffle bag, and just when I didn't think his crazed expression couldn't get any worse, it did. He bared his teeth, almost eliminating the lines of his lips, and his stare hardened as he scanned the rest of my apartment. My stomach dropped as I laid eyes on the focal point in the kitchen. The unusual yellow flowers that Kade had brought Friday night drew unnecessary attention without even trying, a brightness in the darkened corner.

"Packing bags, flowers, and fucking gifts?" His voice rose, almost unrecognizable. I grasped my necklace as his eyes landed on it. Was there anything that wouldn't further fuel his rage?

"Can we just talk about this?" My voice betrayed me as it broke. I was unable to suppress the hysterics that were rising to the surface.

"Talk? That's all you ever want to do. Talk!" He pointed the gun at me and I held my hands up in surrender. I had nothing to grab and nothing to hide behind but my hands. I made the attempt to steadily shift toward the opposite side of the bed as he began to approach me. He was like a lion getting ready to pounce.

"Because you don't listen." I told him, shaking "But look at you. How is this going to help? Think about this, think about what you're doing! Please!" I trembled before him, unsure of how I could possibly get out of this without some sort of otherworldly miracle.

Just days ago, he was asking my grandma for permission to marry me, and now he was a madman striking women down and breaking into my apartment with a gun. I didn't understand this flip of a switch that he was capable of.

Perhaps I'd never really known him just the same as I never really knew Damian.

He lowered the gun momentarily and I thought that I might have broken through to him. His head lowered slightly and I was grateful that his hateful eyes were not upon me for a second.

I couldn't make it to the kitchen or the bathroom, those were too far away. If the front door hadn't been shut then maybe I could have escaped if I tumbled into him. But even so, I failed to see any resolution that didn't end with the firing of a gun should I attempt anything.

He'd taken Ms. Vanders down with such ease, I couldn't say that he wouldn't do the same for me. And if Damian or some saint was pulling some mind-game shit on him, how would I get through to the Brett I once knew?

There was no way in hell I could get this black obsidian close enough to him in the hopes that it might help. Even with Kade's admission, Brett had…*tendencies* as he had called them. Actions that I should have inquired further about before now, that hadn't gone unnoticed by demons. He now required an assigned watcher. So surely there had to be someone doing exactly that right now. Kade had to come, and soon.

I just needed to buy us some time.

"We…" he seethed with a voice that sank all of my hopes for a swift rescue. "We have nothing because of you."

Brett's arms tensed, veins protruding in his arm to the point that I thought they might burst. By the time I dragged my gaze back up to his face, he lifted his gun and fired.

Two deafening shots rang in my ears and I flinched at the ear-splitting effects.

My steps faltered at the impact and I studied Brett's face as it morphed. There was almost a glee of victory in the way his lips reappeared and turned up.

Confused, I looked down at my blue shirt as blood began to seep from it. I stumbled back, losing my balance as I didn't seem to be able to support the upper half of my body anymore.

I'd unknowingly backed into my mirror. The impact sent me down with it in a shattering crash. Once still, I glanced at my hand, wet with a crimson liquid.

I couldn't accept the reality that it was mine and that it was coming from my body.

There was so much. Too much of it.

Footsteps retreated and I blinked up at the ceiling in shock. I strained my voice to call out for Kade but I struggled to breathe and my eyes widened at the realization. My mouth began to fill with a metallic taste and I sputtered, trying to expel the contents, but my chest only offered a searing pain when I tried to cough it out.

This was how I was going to die. Not my failed attempt at suicide in high school by prescription drugs and alcohol. Not the accident that claimed the lives of my parents and brother, leaving me an orphan as a child.

Perhaps if I were out of the picture, the rest of my family would be safe. Surviving death two times was the reason I had a target on my back in the first place when it came to Damian. If I were no longer around, there wouldn't be any need for someone to come after my family to get to me.

But dammit, my family. I was glued to the image of us around the table yesterday, the laughter, joy, and liveliness around the kitchen table. I didn't want that to be the last time I saw them.

My thoughts strayed back over the years—all of the disappointments and my troubles seemed so foolish now. Highlights of family events, getting my diplomas, my first paycheck, and my car purchase flitted through my memory and brought me back to the few lingering memories I had of my departed family.

Was I cursed or something? Why was this happening to me? *I don't want to die! I don't want to be alone!*

I grimaced as I coughed and clutched my chest in agony,

pain ricocheting through my entirety to the point that I thought I might pass out. I wanted to breathe in deep in a desperate attempt for air. Spots began to dot my vision, distorting my view as I lay among the broken glass. I was beyond scared and shaken to the core at how quickly things had spiraled out of control.

It couldn't end this way, I refused to accept that.

"Violet!"

Kade was by my side, examining me frantically. Another being was in my periphery but I couldn't make out who it was, just platinum blond hair that left my sight just as quick as it had appeared.

I could feel the pressure of his hands against my wounds, but no warmth came from them. It registered that he was trying to heal me but I knew by his own admission that his healing abilities were minimal.

By now my extremities were beginning to grow cold and a numbness was beginning to creep in. I was becoming so tired that my eyes were growing heavy. I tried to fight it, but after every blink, my lids were slower to reopen.

"Dammit, Violet." Kade's anger and frustration was evident but I was so happy that he was alive and well—it was his life I'd been fearing for.

"I'm...sorry." It was all I could manage to rasp.

I wished that I could tell him that I was going to say yes, that I was going to accept him and all that he was and the tethering. I wanted to take that leap of faith with him and explore his world and everything that came with it—the life we could have had, that we could have made together.

Perhaps if I hadn't drawn out my acceptance, I could have been in the comforts of his world right now, and this never would have happened. I wouldn't have been shot. I wouldn't be on the cusp of imminent death. I knew it was coming, there was no denying that now.

"No, no, no!"

Kade's face was grief-stricken, displaying a misery that I longed to kiss away and soothe. I wanted to tell him that everything would be fine and I hated that I had caused him so much anguish. I loathed myself for not listening to him and his simple ask of me.

I only hoped that in time he would forgive me and move on. He would eventually find someone else—*tether* to someone else.

My vision began to grow dim, the sides closing in on me, narrowing my line of sight. Tears streamed from Kade's eyes and my body wouldn't respond to the need to reach out and comfort him. My limbs felt heavy like lead and my energy, depleted. I was exhausted from trying to breathe, failing to focus, and attempting to utter words that wouldn't come. My head rolled to the side and I faded into a darkness that welcomed me.

CHAPTER 17

Kade

"**D**ammit!" I beat my fists on the wall, expecting it to break down into a pile of rubble.

"Kadriel, I'm sorry. But you know you have to debrief—"

"I don't care!" I cut off Iselu without remorse. She was only doing her job. That, I was well aware of. Hell, I had done a few debriefings with her over the years. It was not optional. No matter the case or mission, this was the first stop upon returning to Darthou.

My fist hit the wall again and the crack in my hand gave way to a pain that I healed almost instantly. My chest heaved with my rising temper that was ready to go through the roof.

How could I have been so brainless? I never should have left Violet!

Not on my last day with her. I never should have taken the bait and led Aleena and Elias into a trap. By the time we'd realized it—from the smirk on Damian's face—battle had ensued. He had planned the whole goddamn thing.

An abandoned boxing factory had been his chosen location, about twenty miles out from Violet's. We should have done our due diligence before our arrival but I was adamant to end him once and for all. A threat to Violet was a threat to her family, and to me. Her worry would never cease until he was dealt with, and once I proved he was no longer a problem, the idea of Violet accepting my tethering proposal didn't seem that far-fetched.

Violet had no soft spot for Damian anymore as he had betrayed her to the point that she could never trust him again. I should have been relieved in that knowledge, but I wouldn't be until he ceased to exist.

Having to sit on the sidelines all this time had me at the ready to finish him off and I couldn't stand to wait another day. If Elias had found him, I had to make sure it was the last we saw of him. I wanted to break him down like the scum he was and gut him beyond recognition. But as we should have expected, finding him was too good to be true.

The saints he'd brought with him were lying in wait. They had fighting experience and muscle for sure, but they were nothing more than a distraction. He was using them to toy with us and they were perfect pawns in his game. The bastard stood by and watched as we each took them on. A sinister glee plastered on that face he had chosen to keep to for his appearance today. He had a confidence that dove under my skin and festered but I only used it to power my attack. If he had decided to join in on the action, we would have been outnumbered.

After I severed the head of my attacker, I surveyed the area. Elias was locked in a clashing sword fight with his assailant and

Aleena was whipping around hers, blood spraying as her claw-like weapons ripped his bulky frame to shreds.

Approaching the small flight of stairs Damian had perched himself on, I began to climb them. I was repulsed by his cocky attitude even though we were taking them head-on and winning. He might have been older in years and experience, but he had picked a lousy bunch to join him in a battle that he apparently had no plans to participate in. Which further begged the question—how far up the ladder was Damian, that he had this many saints at his beck and call? Saints usually worked alone and led their own lives. I had never known them to collaborate like this.

A glimmer of movement reflected in his eyes and before I could react, I could sense Aleena materialize behind me. Spinning around, I witnessed her accept a blow from another saint who had appeared out of nowhere. Miraculously, she still somehow managed to split his neck open to the bone before she went down.

As his body took a tumble down the steps, I caught Aleena as she collapsed. Elias was already on his way over to join us as her shrieks filled the dust-ridden air, her side sliced open and gaping. Elias had acted as a buffer between Damian and ourselves as I worked to close her wound, but it wasn't enough. Her gash was too great and I had grinded my teeth to the point that they might break in an attempt to try and heal her.

"Tsk, tsk, tsk. Time is not on your side, Kadriel," Damian had gloated, and my head spun. More saints were emerging from the shadows, malicious intent dripping from each and every one of them. There were too many. We were unprepared and growingly outnumbered.

Damian met me with a menacing glare before he'd uttered a few departing words that had haunted me from the instant they left him. "You've got a choice to make. Tick, tock."

Adjusting my hold on my sister and placing a hand on best friend, I got us the hell out of there, transporting us back to Darthou.

I'd failed at another attempt to heal her but Elias scooped her up, insisting on taking Aleena to Rafina. I, on the other hand, had been dragged into this debriefing before I could depart.

Iselu, who was the youngest of the bunch in charge of these meetings, had the power to hold me here until she was finished with me. Damian's words echoed in my head on repeat, terrorizing me, and I exploded.

"You don't understand, this was a trap. It was all a trap! I need to check on Violet! If you won't let me go then please, please just check with Eleander and make sure that she's okay!"

She stilled, tablet in hand. Her eyes fixated on me in a contemplative state, curls unmoving as she retrieved her pocket mirror and summoned Elias's father. "Is Violet alright?"

"Is Kadriel back yet? It's serious." My eyes shot open at the alarm evident in his voice. He was not one to get riled up, and it only drove me into more madness.

I was ready to launch myself at Iselu if she didn't grant me permission to leave. The annoyance that she had this ability to control the enchantments in this room had never bothered me until now. She had only allowed Elias to leave due to Aleena's battle wounds, but there was another debriefer who followed after them.

She returned her gaze to mine. "We'll pick this up later. Go to him."

Overcome with the release she granted, I left and sought Eleander at his apartment.

"What is it?" I was met with an older version of Elias who

looked like he hadn't slept in weeks even though I had just seen him two nights ago. Although we could manage without it for a while, it did start to take its toll if we didn't give our bodies the rest they required. Even we demons were susceptible to stress, lack of sleep and its effects. It was obvious that he had been pushing the envelope. I felt at fault because he and Elias had been taking over my workload and then some while I'd been away the past few days. But then again, I was never met with any resistance.

"Brett's gone, she needs you now. Go!" The unease and alarm in his words had me transporting into her apartment without looking ahead to see what I was walking into. I arrived at the foot of her bed, door wide open and no one in sight. But it was the smell of blood and the sight of her mirror that had met its end that had me skidding to the floor and to her side.

"Violet!" I cried out as I began assessing her wounds. Two bullet holes were prominent and the blood pooling out of them as she tried to catch her breath was not a good sign. Her mouth moved but no sound came; her body was shutting down.

Through gritted teeth, I made my best effort to summon all of my strength as I placed my hands on the sites of impact and applied pressure. I forced everything I had to try and seal off the wounds around the bullets and heal her enough to buy some time. If I could only clear her lungs so that she could breathe easier. It was apparent that she wasn't getting enough oxygen. But the bullets had already done too much damage.

Nothing healed and nothing slowed.

Fucking trap, it was a fucking trap!

"Hang in there, please," I begged as her gaze became unfocused, glazing over to the point that she was losing consciousness. "Dammit. Violet!"

"I'm...sorry."

My head dropped at her apology. I wasn't ready to say goodbye. We were so close to starting our life together. Six years of watching and waiting to have it come crashing down in disaster.

"Kadriel, we have to go. Now." Elias placed his hand on my shoulder and I jerked it off.

Violet was slipping away and I couldn't do anything, I was incompetent against the severity of her wounds. The bullets were lodged in their places and her lungs were filling with blood at an alarming rate.

Her mouth moved once more, but not a sound escaped.

"I can't leave her, she's dying." I willed everything I had into her, trying to reel in my rising panic as tears escaped and rolled down my face. My palms heated once more in another attempt and I could sense my energies depleting but I only pushed harder. If I left now, she would die before the paramedics arrived. The sirens in the distance were closing in and her time was as limited as mine was here.

Perhaps if I took her to Darthou, Rafina might be able to help.

No, she *had* to help. She had hundreds of years of studying and practice. I knew her expertise was more focused on demons, but she kept tabs on the human world and all their breakthroughs and advancements in medicine and technology.

Taking Violet was her best chance at survival. Her heart would stop beating before anyone else stepped through her doorway.

Gently lifting her from the ground, I tried not to focus on the amount of blood she had already lost. I eyed her duffle bag on the bed and ordered Elias to retrieve it. He obliged without hesitation and we vanished nanoseconds apart, appearing in the infirmary.

Elias called for Rafina and she appeared quicker than I had anticipated. I should have been relieved at her impeccable response time but nothing would calm me until Violet was stable. I was firm in my belief that Aleena would be fine although her recovery would be anything but pleasant. As much as I hated to tear Rafina away from her, it had to be done. I would ask for forgiveness later.

"Two gunshot wounds to the chest and abdomen. Her lungs are taking on blood. I tried to slow it down but I can't get it to stop." I placed Violet on an immaculate slab of marble as Rafina tied her long blond hair back and out of the way.

"What is the meaning of this?" Staffan entered from my right, his voice a boom that irritated me to no end.

Rafina continued her assessment of Violet as I held her hand. It was limp in my grasp and her pulse was weak, almost impossible to detect. It was faint, but it was still there.

"Has she even accepted the tethering?" Staffan's voice rose once more and I wanted to send him flying across the room in the hopes of cracking his skull. Now was not the time to be on my bad side, not when I was faced with the very real possibility of losing my soon-to-be tethered mate.

Everything leading up to my departure from her apartment earlier told me that Violet had been ready to accept, and the bag that Elias had retrieved was proof enough for me, but I couldn't admit that she hadn't actually spoken the words aloud yet. If I did, I would be signing off on her death. They wouldn't even think twice.

Gone were the years when demons took humans on their own terms and this had led to a decrease in their population here in Darthou. Trickery had been used when demons didn't get their way in certain cases. Luring them here with high hopes and empty promises. Those relationships had rarely ended well.

That was probably strike one of our bad reptation. The saints didn't care about our nonexistent reasoning all those years ago just as they didn't concern themselves with our improvements since then. Striving for consent now at every turn was no use against their hatred for us.

Their meddling and mind games also did nothing to help our view of them in return.

In this new era, we made it a point to get consent no matter what. Over the years, it had been an uphill battle that I continued to fight against those who were stuck in the past or wanted to ban any and all possible tethers to humans.

My family had been at the forefront of this change for some time now. My dad and my uncle especially, trying nonstop to lead us into this new direction. Consent was at the core from the very beginning when it came to having children, so why wouldn't we extend the same courtesy with human tetherings and those transitioning to become a demon?

"She has agreed." I nodded and produced a blade from its holster under my forearm, one I hadn't used in my earlier battle.

Rafina nodded in my direction. "It's the only chance we have. She's fading fast."

I sliced my blood-soaked hand from corner to corner before doing the same to Violet's palm. She didn't even wince as the blade cut through her tainted skin.

"This is outrageous, the girl can't even speak for herself." Staffan's words pissed me off as I took her hand in mine.

"So you would rather she die before you can get confirmation of her consent?"

His eyes bore into mine, challenging me, but I wasn't

going to back down. He was wasting time and I was having none of it. We had been toe to toe before but I wasn't going to let his black-and-white principles intervene with my chance of saving Violet.

"Produce the tie or I will summon another," I commanded.

My uncle had technically been next in line for Staffan's position, but at the time his wife Sarah had been pregnant and he'd turned it down. It was a decision that he'd later regretted, although he would never admit it to his other half.

I held Violet's hand in mine as I raised it over her body, allowing space for Staffan to bind us. He began his chant, tying our souls together as he began to wrap the cord from our elbows toward our hands.

I had never been in an audience for a tethering ritual, but I'd heard enough to know what it involved. When Staffan finished his words, I eagerly awaited the rope's disappearance.

It should have dissolved into our skin, linking us forever. When it didn't, I looked to Rafina whose hand lay upon Violet's neck, checking for a pulse.

A pulse that I couldn't detect anymore.

It had been almost undetectable at the start of the ritual. I hadn't realized that I'd already felt its last beat.

"I'm sorry, Kadriel. It's too late." Rafina's voice was soft enough that she sounded as if she were in an entirely different room. She removed her hand and took a step back, lowering her head. The room fell eerily quiet and I wanted to release the agony that was rising in my throat, but I kept it bottled up inside, fearful of what would erupt from me if I surrendered to it.

"No." My eyes fell to Violet's face and her lifeless body before me. I couldn't accept this. This couldn't be the end. Our journey together was just beginning, I knew it.

"What about Obsidian Falls?"

It was my last resort. The black waters that formed our obsidian stones were a mystical force of their own, capable of turning humans into demons.

I hadn't discussed it with Violet, nor had I even told her how the change occurred. I'd only warned her away from it because it was dangerous.

I'd known her curiosity would eventually lead her down the road of discovering what it entailed, but that was when I'd thought we had time.

"Don't be absurd." Staffan huffed as if the idea were ludicrous.

"Show some compassion." Rafina spoke to him but kept her gaze cast down. She had a bedside manner that escaped Staffan. How the two of them had ever decided to come to an agreement on their union, I would never understand. I was sure he saw power in her and he wanted it for himself. But for her, I could never determine what she saw in him.

I shook my head, not willing to accept defeat and give up. Violet had survived death twice in her short life and I wasn't ready to let a third take her. It wasn't an option.

Slipping the cord from our arms, I scooped up her body and vanished without another word, arriving at Obsidian Falls.

The cave-like atmosphere boasted massive obsidian rocks, jagged in every direction imaginable, that closed in around me. They grew in abundance here and we used them for our weapons as well as decorative pieces. These were the very rocks that I had fashioned Violet's necklace from years ago.

I kissed Violet's forehead, her face pale white and lifeless as I waded into the black water-like substance of the small lake. The air was cold enough here that I could see my breath, but the other side harbored a fiery and hellish terrain that held never-ending flames and a volcanic atmosphere—an inferno that helped create the stones we cherished, but also claimed the lives of those who no longer deserved to live.

There were two sides to Obsidian Falls. One could be a place of transformation and rebirth, a location we held in high esteem—and just behind it lay a site of the worst nightmares, an end that none would never want to meet with.

What I was aiming to do had never been done before and I would face consequences for my actions no matter the outcome.

While this could be a place of transformation, it could also be the very thing that ended life. Obsidian Falls was the most sacred ground that we demons cared for, and doing what I intended would draw a backlash that I chose to ignore.

I would be followed momentarily and apprehended, but I had to try. I would never forgive myself if I didn't exhaust any option I thought I might have.

"Fight, Violet. Fight like you never have before." I refused to believe she was gone, and I spoke as if she could still hear me. Her heartbeat might have ceased, but I pleaded to her soul in the hopes it had lingered thereafter.

I was waist-deep in the frigid water when I heard voices from behind me. Members of the guard, no doubt, ready to take me in and prepared for a fight should it come to that.

Not even a soon-to-be king was above the law, and I knew Staffan was going to have a field day with this.

Lowering her body into the waters, I held her down, her features disappearing rapidly as she dipped below the darkened water. I wanted her to spring to life and fight back as the liquid consumed her, but she only sank deeper.

The waters sloshed around as two guards came in to

retrieve me, but I wouldn't let them lay a single hand on her. They were no match for me; I had trained with all the members of the guard so I knew their moves like the back of my hand.

I sent Tamian, who was double my age and considerably larger in size, soaring in one direction, and the other disappeared before I could do the same to him. I had a suspicion that it was Senfur, one of the newest members, but he hadn't given me the chance to lay my eyes upon him before retreating.

While I was grateful to not have to deal with him, it still begged the question as to why he'd left without engaging. The only thing that came to mind was that he'd been called off almost as quickly as he was called in. To not carry out orders as given was to have the title of guard striped away. Given that he had just joined the ranks not long ago, I didn't think he was stupid enough to disobey.

Elias appeared at the water's edge, remorse written all over his face, and I almost lost it. Why was everyone so willing to accept the fact that Violet was gone? Why was I the only one fighting for her?

She was to be queen!

I shook my head, exhausted by the turn of events that this day had brought forth, and turned away from my best friend.

First Damian's distraction, then my sisters' injury in the ambush, and now this? Everywhere I turned there seemed to be failure. I couldn't protect my sister or the woman I loved, and now here I was, a devastating mess who felt as if I would be better off dead.

How could I possibly lead Darthou after this? How could I ever move forward?

A life without Violet would be no life at all. At least, it wasn't one that I wanted.

I hated myself for the dramatics but it was all true. I didn't desire this life without her by my side. She was my motivation, the cause of my drive, and my reason to stay on my path to lead. She was my everything and I didn't know how to exist without her.

My hands ran through my hair, exasperated. I heaved as I searched the area where I had released her, desperate for any indication that she might survive, a sign, anything. The cascading water ahead caused a ringing in my ears that only added to the heaviness that resided within me. I had no idea how long I could wait or how long a transition like this could take.

I was praying for a fucking miracle.

I resisted the urge to dive after her. I had to wait. I had to give it time no matter how hard it was to do so. I had to find faith that she would pull through this, just as I had hoped that someday she would release me so that I might come to court her. I'd had patience in the years leading up to finally meeting her four nights ago, I couldn't stand to lose it now.

"Kadriel," Rafina's voice came from behind me, gentle as she entered the water. Her hands were free of Violet's blood as she came into view and I closed my eyes.

There had been so much blood. Too much blood. How was her body capable of producing so much?

"Staffan has called the council and your uncle is here to escort you."

I shook my head at her prompt. *Sure, send in your tethered mate and my uncle when the guards failed miserably to carry out your orders.* Senfur hadn't even made an effort to make a move on me.

The timing couldn't have been worse. I couldn't deal with the council right now. If I was to be anywhere else but here, I would be exacting revenge on Brett. Snuffing him out of existence.

I wanted him to suffer just like he had made Violet suffer. To beg and plead for an absolution that would never come.

Once I was done with him, I would move on to Damian. The very saint who had his fingerprints on this entire affair. I'd been so dead set on ending him and providing a relief to Violet that I had rushed into things. It had been too good to be true, and now there were those suffering because of the decisions I had made. The choices I'd pursued.

But that wouldn't happen a second time. I would assemble my own army to take him and everyone he had under his thumb down. Even if it meant not getting the answers I sought, I would fucking kill the bastard.

"Kadriel, please. You must go," Rafina pleaded.

The longer I waited, the more time Staffan would have to spin the narrative to his liking. I couldn't stand the man, and my disgust for him only grew. He seemed so adamant to put up roadblock after roadblock in not only my path to securing Violet, but my rise to reign. He knew that when I rose to power, his grasp on it would lessen and he would lose his majority hold over the council.

"I will stay with her."

I knew she meant well, but the soul-crushing heartache I was experiencing was unlike anything I had ever endured before. I didn't even want to breathe without knowing what would become of my actions in bringing Violet here. The soreness in my chest was as if it had been pried open by the jaws of life, laid open and bare.

"Kadriel," my uncle's voice came from behind me and it took every ounce of strength to not collapse in his presence.

I had looked up to his and Sarah's relationship for so long

and I had been so close to having it for myself. They and my parents were the reason I believed in love. I owed everything to Uncle Zan and Aunt Sarah, as they were the reason I'd become the man I was today after losing my parents. The lengths they had gone to in order to keep my sister and I under their wing while still managing their own lives and family was something that I could never repay.

"Would Aunt Sarah be willing to wait with her until I return?"

If there was a chance Violet awoke, no doubt a friendly human face such as Sarah's would bring a slight comfort. If her transition proved successful, she might need help adjusting and I couldn't think of anyone better. Rafina meant well, but I would rather there be both demon and human in attendance if I couldn't be here myself.

I shifted slightly to see Uncle Zan nodding before he spoke to Elias, no doubt asking him to retrieve Sarah since he was tasked with bringing me to the very council board that he sat upon. Elias left without another glance and I began to retreat from the black waters.

"Would you like to change first?" he asked when I met him shoulder to shoulder.

"Do I really need to be babysat for that?"

I couldn't bother to look at my appearance. Even though I was in my protections of head-to-toe black garments, I knew the combination of blood, the scent of death, and the waters of Obsidian Falls were rolling off of me in mixed droves. It was a potent concoction that I didn't intend to hide from the council.

Maybe allowing them the sight of me in this manner would give them a glimpse of the shit show that today had turned out to be—a day that could have been filled with more than one victory and the happiness that was to follow after securing my other half.

Images of Violet's devastated body, broken and bleeding, flashed through my head unannounced. I wanted to plunge back into the waters after her.

I cringed as I shrugged Zan's hand off of my shoulder. He could have meant it as a comfort, but I could barely hold myself together.

"You've caused quite the stir, so I think you know the answer. For both your head and mine, let's just get this done quickly." And with another touch to my shoulder, we vanished.

EPILOGUE

Violet

My lungs burned. I wanted to scream but no sound escaped.

Blood. I choked on the taste. It wouldn't stop. *How do I make it stop?*

Pain lanced through my hand and I wanted to jerk away but I was frozen in an unmoving state. Trapped within the confines of my mind and blinded by darkness.

Voices. Different ones saying things I couldn't understand and coming from various directions. I wanted my head to turn in each and every way but I couldn't. My body wouldn't listen to me, why couldn't I move?

The choking won't relent, how am I supposed to breathe?

Weightless. It's as if I'm floating.

Is this what dying feels like?

Screams. *Who is that?* It didn't sound like my voice. In fact,

I didn't recognize it at all. The shriek was piercing in its increasing volume and it continued closer until it came to an abrupt stop. Yet, my vocal cords burned as if the sound had originated from me.

Then everything went calm.

I could breathe now and I relaxed, overcome with sleep. All other sounds faded away except that of my heartbeat—it carried on.

Whispers.

I could hear them but I didn't recognize the voices.

My eyes fluttered open and I was met with a high cathedral-like ceiling. Its architecture was beautiful, unlike anything I had ever seen in person. I couldn't make out any windows as I let my eyes roll from side to side to take in my surroundings.

I didn't know if it was day or night and the only light there was came from iron fixtures that hung from the ceiling.

I wiggled my toes and fingers, then moved on to try and check my limbs.

My lungs filled with an expansion of air and it was no longer painful. I was grateful to be able to breathe on my own, uninterrupted. I welcomed it as I took in another deep breath, relishing this small triumph.

Was I dead?

Brett's demented face flashed before me and I began to relive every moment of that encounter, and at full force. My hands shot up in a frantic manner hunting for bullet wounds, expecting to find bandages, but I was only wearing a luxurious robe that felt silky beneath my touch. I raised my fingers to my face to find a black substance stained upon my fair skin among the remnants of dried blood.

"Violet?"

An unknown voice from my side caused me to rise quickly to a seated position. A woman with shoulder-length auburn hair sat in a chair beside me with a look of disbelief. Was she one of the whispers I had heard?

When I glanced down, I found that I was clad in nothing but a black robe that stopped about mid-thigh, but what was more concerning was that every inch of my skin was covered in the same black substance. I rubbed my fingers together, examining it, but I couldn't figure out what it was. I felt gross and in desperate need of a shower, but I continued to examine my environment.

I was on a solid slab that was either granite or marble, narrower than the size of a twin bed, and there were almost a dozen others just like it in this room. There were a few shelves on the far wall that housed bottles and enough supplies to make me think I was in some sort of hospital.

While there were no curtains anywhere that would allow any privacy, there was a brown wicker divider in one corner that wasn't extended all the way. Although this place wasn't stark white and sterile-looking like the hospitals back home, it wasn't exactly inviting either.

It was unusually quiet—like, pin-drop silence. Every move I made felt like I was being too loud, from the shifting of my position to the rubbing of my robe against me. The lack of windows and natural light did nothing to reassure me either.

"Where am I?" I asked as I swung my legs around and off the side of the slab. I had a feeling I knew the answer, but I wanted confirmation of it. Turning my attention toward the woman, I continued when she took too long. "*Who* are you?"

A timid smile crossed her features, revealing a dimple on the left side of her mouth. The woman stood and met me in height as I pushed off of the table. Her hazel eyes clued me in that she was human. I had a small inkling that I knew who she was, but only because Kade had spoken so fondly of her and his uncle.

I noted how her clothing wasn't really all that different from what I would wear in the fall or wintertime. She wore what looked to be dark pants and a gray turtleneck, comfy and casual. If her style of dress was any indicator, my clothes might not stick out here as much as I feared they might.

"I'm Sarah. Kadriel's aunt." She beamed and I almost thought I could see her eyes becoming glassy, but she recovered and cleared her throat. "I'm so happy you're with us."

"Rafina!" she called off over her shoulder before returning her attention to me as she muttered under her breath, "I can't believe it worked."

A combination of shock and awe fell over her face as she scanned me over. I eyed her curiously as I turned my attention to my right at the sounds of approaching footsteps.

A gorgeous blonde with hair that swung behind her and past her bottom gracefully swept into the room as if she were floating. Her dark eyes were just like Kade's and I knew immediately I was in Darthou. Which meant I couldn't be dead, and although I would have bet I was on my way out, he'd saved me after all. I had to be living to cross over, so Kade must have found me in the nick of time. The realization washed over me and put me at ease.

But now, I just wanted to find him.

"Where's Kade?" I asked as I glanced about the room once more, as if I could have missed anything in this minimalistic space. Surely, he wasn't too far. I had little doubt that he wouldn't leave me on my own for long. I needed my demon whatever he was to fill me in, since my present company wasn't exactly forthcoming with any information. "And what's with all of this icky stuff all over me?"

Rafina drew closer and I grew grim. Her beauty was astonishing but it paled in comparison to the unexpected ferocity that came to settle in my stomach, urging me to go to war against her.

Screams erupted in my head and I began crouching down in torment.

"Ah! What is that sound?"

It brought me to my knees, smacking the hardened ground below, and I wanted nothing more than for it to stop. I covered my ears and looked up at the ladies who exchanged a glance as if nothing was happening.

"Don't you hear that?" I hollered, pain-stricken to the point that I thought my ears might bleed.

Their mouths were moving but I couldn't make out what they were saying. The bloodcurdling chorus of screams was too great. They both exchanged looks that I couldn't decipher.

Rafina left, and with her, the screams faded until they came to a halt altogether. I stood and used the slab to steady myself, meeting Sarah at her level once again.

"Could you seriously not hear that?" I panted, unable to comprehend the fact that neither of them had been able to hear the sound that overtook me. I shook my hands out, trying to shake away the effects.

"What exactly did you hear?" Sarah asked.

"Screams," I spilled, annoyed that I was alone in this. "Screams so loud that I thought my eardrums were going to burst." I rubbed at my ears in the wake of the assault.

She took a step forward and held a hand up to hush me, glancing around as if someone might be close, but we were the only ones present.

"Speak of this to no one." Her voice was laced with an urgency, a demand that caught me off guard. I would have backed away had I not been pinned against the slab.

"What? Why not? And where's Kade?"

I sidestepped around her, now focused on searching for a way out. I passed by slab after slab as I searched for a door. I had to find Kade. He would be able to explain this. Why wasn't he here?

I began to jump to worst-case scenarios, wondering if he was hurt from his encounter with Damian, or worse. But I couldn't accept that, he had to have been the one to rescue me, who else would have?

"Kadriel will be here as soon as he can, I know it," she pleaded as she followed after me.

I only ignored her. I wouldn't calm down until we were together again.

Not finding an exit in the opposite direction from where Rafina had entered and left, I had no other choice than to see what was around the corner where she'd come from. Just to add to the perplexity of this place, instead of discovering a door, I was instead met with a floor-to-ceiling mirror, the largest I had ever seen in my entire life. But it was the image that reflected back that stopped me dead in my tracks.

Sure, I was covered in the inky black mess from head to toe, and not only did it mar my skin but my hair was a matted mess from it as well. What I hadn't expected to find was a set of black demon eyes upon my face, staring right back at me.

ABOUT THE AUTHOR

Krystal Kae lives in the corn-filled Midwest with her husband, children, and pets. Her love of reading and writing started back in high school, but it was over a decade later when she decided to put her overactive imagination to work again and began filling blank pages.

Fascinated by all things paranormal, fantasy, and romantic-you can find these topics the center of her writing universe.

When she's not working her full-time office job or buried in a story, she loves to create memories with loved ones, travel, and take long walks in cemeteries.

Get the latest updates at **KrystalKae.com** and follow @krystalkaewrites